FAIRYTALE DRAGONS

A Dragon Soul Press Anthology

Edited by
J.E. FELDMAN

Editing & Formatting by Dragon Soul Press
Cover Art by Lily Dormishev Art

CONTENTS

LYDIA ANNE STEVENS

NATHAN SLEMP

For those who crave an incredible story to wash away their daily troubles.

New adventures are only a page away.

R.L. DAVENNOR

Raelynn Davennor has been creating and discovering fantastical worlds for as long as she can remember—often getting scolded for reading while her teachers were talking. She holds a minor in creative writing and a Masters Degree in music. Though formally trained as an oboist, Raelynn began writing and composing after graduate school, utilizing her creations in her fictional worlds. She's made appearances with artists such as The Who, Weird Al, and Hugh Jackman, and performed on many of the largest stages in the United States. Her inspiration takes no mercy on her despite her busy schedule.

After years of existing only in her head and feverishly scrawled in countless notebooks, her debut dark fantasy novel, *Bloodlust*, publishes in 2020.

Even when completing the most mundane of tasks, Raelynn is often hopelessly lost in her own head, flying across the sea on the back of a dragon or humming a tune she can't wait to scribble down. In her little remaining free time, she enjoys pampering her small menagerie of pets and pretending she isn't an adult.

DRAGON LAKE

R.L. Davennor

*M*en are foolish, predictable creatures.

This one was no different.

I peered out from the tree concealing me and waited, scanning the moonlit forest for the prince that believed he chased a helpless, innocent maiden.

I was neither.

The dragon within me writhed as she always did at night, clawing and scraping at my insides even harder now that my target was near. He'd fallen behind and wouldn't be able to make out details through the mist.

He wouldn't be able to tell the dragon was me.

I gathered my dress in my fists. Silver embroidery trailed up the sleeves and the garment wasn't cumbersome—a rare find. The minute I shifted, it would be ruined like all the others. If I took it off while still in one piece, I could retrieve it later...and surely I deserved such a luxury on my final mission. Once this was done, I'd be free of the dragon forever.

Bunching the skirt, I threw it over my head and pulled. And *pulled*. How many layers did this damn thing have? It'd felt light while I was running, but perhaps that was just excitement flooding through my veins. The dragon thrashed against my ribcage, making my task no easier.

And now my arms were stuck. I gritted my teeth and swore, yanking despite the discomfort. I couldn't see, and the prince's voice was getting louder. Closer.

My petty desire was proving to be a fatal mistake.

The fabric gave way at long last. My shoulders popped free, and my arms soon followed. As the dress floated to the ground and the prince's silhouette became visible through the mist, my dragon came alive.

The act of shifting wasn't as painful as it was cathartic. Talons were first to sprout, bursting through the ends of my fingers and toes with such violence that splatters of crimson flecked the ground. Though the still-human part of me wanted to scream, I bit my tongue. The same moment hair retreated into my scalp, wings burst from my spine, and this time I couldn't stifle the guttural shriek that tore from my throat. Bones twisted, popped and snapped, and through my blurring vision, the world shrank until even the tallest oaks became little more than twigs. The pain subsided, and my sight went from hazy to razor-focused. I pinpointed the prince chasing after me. I heard his elevated heart rate clear as a war drum. I smelled his exhilaration turned to fear the moment he glimpsed me.

I yearned next to taste his blood.

He staggered backward, and a draconian laugh quaked the ground beneath our feet. The beast took over when he started to run. Snarling, I stepped forward to crush a handful of trees. Trunks and other carnage fell in his path, and he screamed before darting to find an exit.

There was one thing I loathed about this body; it was cumbersome. I could fight and kill in each of my forms, but the beast better concealed my identity, and when the dragon took over, things like emotion never got in the way. The dragon yearned for blood; nothing more, and nothing less. The human in me, no matter how much I tried to shut her out, *felt* things...so I needed to make this quick.

The sooner this ended, the better for all involved. Once I finished him, I could go home for good. Ten princes, ten kills, and I would never be tormented by the dragon again. That was the deal Rothbart and I had made...well, most of it. There was still the matter of my master's other demands, but the dragon shoved those thoughts aside.

I had a prince to devour.

He spotted the exit. The *one* exit among the trees I'd felled. *Dammit.* I smashed a log, splintering wood everywhere, but gods was he fast. Debris clouded the air, but he sprinted on, all traces of clumsiness gone as he gained ground faster than any prince I'd fought before.

I turned to the side, aware of where he stood. I could crush him, but that was no fun; the dragon preferred bones snapping and crunching beneath her teeth. Utilizing the momentum from my behemoth body, I swung my tail in a continuing arc, taking with it nearly all the trees covering the hillside and starting an avalanche of rolling trunks. The only place left to run was straight into my clutches.

But he surprised me yet again.

With nimble grace I wish I possessed, the prince faced the danger head-on. He leaped and dodged, and by some miracle made it to an outcropping of rock seconds before he'd have been crushed by a wayward boulder. He wedged himself beneath the stone, using the shield that protected him from the relentless waves of debris.

Clever as it was, it certainly wouldn't protect him from *me*.

I lowered my maw to the ground, waiting for the avalanche to subside before timing my strike. Our eyes met, and for reasons the dragon didn't understand, my heart skipped a beat. He was pleading.

He was afraid.

I wanted to scream. Didn't he know I was too? Didn't he know I was doing this to set myself free from one torment only to be immediately enslaved by another?

He was a prince. He'd never known torment a day in his life—save for what I was about to do.

I bared my teeth. His hand shot to the pommel of his sword, enraging the dragon and bringing our conjoined minds to a state in which I had little control. The rubble slowed, and though I preferred to wait before lashing out, the blade changed things. I shot forward, teeth grazing stone and earth in their search for flesh and widened my maw just enough to fit him inside.

I'd misjudged. A feral screech tore from my throat when my snout scraped the jagged surface of his shelter, and as I recoiled, blood rained down around us. The outcropping's narrow opening *had* been enough to keep me out, and my overconfidence now meant I was wounded.

The dragon's rage built to dangerous levels. My eyes narrowed into slits and my claws dug into the earth. The prince drew his sword in preparation for my strike, but when our eyes met, his gaze trailed over the blood coating my snout.

I growled. It would be *his* soon.

The prince began waving his arms like a madman. With his sword still in his hand, the blade clanged against the rock shielding him from me, and even my human half was confused. Was this a challenge? A threat? The desperation of a man who knew he was about to die?

A sword answered my question.

With another deafening shriek, I turned away from the prince and towards the forest. A company of men stood at the ready, weapons poised to strike while crests bearing the prince's colors flapped in the breeze. Turning my head back towards where he'd been trapped, I saw nothing but a wall of rock.

He'd escaped.

Their mission accomplished, a few of the men took off while the rest stood firm, banging their swords against their shields and yelling unintelligible nonsense. Cowards and fools respectively. If they thought they'd saved their beloved prince, they were sorely mistaken.

I'd kill them all.

I lunged forward. One man crunched beneath my foot while I snatched another in my jaws, his armor doing less than nothing to protect him. Before I spat him out, I went for another, relishing the sensation of bones snapping as much as I relished their screams.

I made quick work of the fools who thought they could face me, knowing the cowards who fled already had a head start. Wings beating to help propel me forward, I stomped through the trees, eyes darting in every direction to scan for movement.

There.

A straggler screamed in vain for the companions all too eager to leave him behind. As I'd done with the others, I snatched him in my claws—but this time, I didn't crush him. My taste for blood had been sated for the moment, and with a handful of victims remaining, I could have some fun.

I lifted him to my face, wanting him to feel my breath. I wanted him to see the blood of his companions staining my teeth as I bared them.

Most of all, I wanted him to scream.

He thrashed within my claws serving as a cage, suspended too high to jump. I pierced a claw into each of his feet, ignoring his howls of agony.

When he met my gaze, I tore him in half.

Blood oozed down my legs as I tossed the pieces to the dirt, already on the hunt for those that remained. My speed wasn't impressive, but my size meant each stride spanned a hundred yards. It wasn't long before another straggler fell behind; badly limping, he soon collapsed altogether. I pinpointed his location, intending to crush him as I continued my chase.

But the prince turned around.

He sprinted for his fallen man, reaching the straggler before I did, but there was no time to escape. Their only choice was to face death as one.

Instead, the prince faced *me*.

Siegfried.

Shock rippled through me at the remembrance of his name, and I skidded to a halt. Trees quivered, and even the men stilled as they watched what I would do to their prince.

Raising his sword, Siegfried screamed words the human part of me understood. "It's me you want, yes?" Without waiting for me to respond, he headed toward the lake. He may not have explained himself to his men, but his message to me was clear.

Don't harm them.

I growled. What right did *he* have to tell *me* what I should and shouldn't do? I could crush them all—especially with the way they stared at me now as if their prince's supposed sacrifice rendered them immune. I should slaughter them out of spite.

No. What little was left of my humanity forced its way to

the forefront of my mind. *He's the last one—the last prince. After this, no more.*

No more.

I started after him.

Siegfried kept his breakneck pace. The closer we drew to the lake, the wetter the ground became, and the harder it was for me to slog through. I beat my wings to no avail, screeching into the color-changing sky that reminded me I didn't have much time. As soon as the sun began to rise, the dragon would leave me, and my hunt would start over. Every fiber of my being demanded Siegfried's blood, and not because I'd been ordered to end him. It was because he'd made a fool of me *and* my master. If Rothbart knew I spared those men, he'd chain me in the dungeon for at least a week —most likely more. *Best make sure he* doesn't *find out*, the human in me chastised, but keeping *anything* from the sorcerer was much easier said than done.

Cliffs lined the lake's eastern shores, offering Siegfried nowhere left to run. He gripped his sword tighter the more my shape shrouded him in shadow. *Shadow?* The sun peeked over the horizon, evaporating any traces of darkness.

I had only minutes.

Wary and afraid, he stared at me like a caged animal. If only he knew just how much I could relate.

"Did you kill her, too?"

I narrowed my gaze.

"You did, didn't you?" Siegfried's shoulders relaxed the longer he studied me. It was nearly as puzzling as the way he'd leaped to the defense of the men meant to be doing that for him. "She was just a *girl.*"

He had no idea he was talking about me.

"We knew you'd come for me. We didn't know when, but

knew it would be eventually." Siegfried tossed his sword at my feet. "You sure as hell took your time."

Sunrise drew closer with every word he spoke, but I couldn't bring myself to do what needed to be done.

"I also knew I stood no chance of killing you."

I rumbled; it was true. Perhaps as a human, but never as a dragon.

"You understand every word I'm saying, don't you?"

He did it again—held me captive with his eyes. Unlike the rest of him, they were light.

Siegfried reached to unfasten his cloak. "Then understand this. I may not be able to kill you...but I *can* ensure you're not what kills me."

He jumped.

A strangled cry tore from my throat. I stumbled, belly striking stone while my neck dangled over the edge of the cliff. The lake sparkled below, reminding me it was too high a height for a human to survive the landing.

But not a dragon.

I dove after him.

The first rays of dawn licked at my scales like fire, melting them where it touched. Human skin began to surface and my limbs started to flail, no longer recognizing my mind as the entity in control. I kept my eyes on Siegfried, beating my wings before they were sucked back into my body. Ignoring the pain that shot up my arm, I reached for him. We clasped hands—*human* hands—and though mine were slick with blood, I refused to let him go.

Somewhere between forms, I pulled him against my chest, fighting against the curse harder than ever before. My wingbeats grew further apart, and with Siegfried's added weight, we were falling much too fast.

Even for the dragon.

I struck the lake first and hardest. Blinded by the pain, Siegfried slipped from my grasp and into the depths below. I couldn't even scream.

I could only surrender.

I OPENED MY EYES EXPECTING DARKNESS, BUT INSTEAD, I saw *him*.

Siegfried floated lifelessly in the lake. Eyes closed, his arms were spread wide in surrender, and nothing but peace was written all over his face. A chill that had nothing to do with the cold shot down my spine. My body screamed for the surface, but I swam toward him instead.

He didn't react when I looped an arm beneath his. The water made his weight easier to handle, but not by much. Each desperate kick not only burned energy I didn't have to spare, it sent aches of pain pulsing from my ribs to my toes. I kept my gaze trained upward but seeing what I yearned for only taunted me.

When at last I sucked in a breath, I couldn't get enough. A final pull ensured Siegfried's head was above water, but all I could do was heave and sputter while my mind cleared its haze. Little by little, my memories flooded back, confirming my deepest fears.

I'd put *his* safety over my own—and he wasn't even breathing.

I transitioned from treading water to swimming like a madwoman, wondering why the fuck I even cared. I needed him dead, and he'd seen to that himself. Yanking the body was a chore, but a justifiable one; Rothbart never minded proof of my kills. I dug my heels into the muck, muttering obscenities under my breath the entire way to the shore.

Siegfried looked far worse than he had underwater. His pale skin appeared even paler, devoid of the color that gave him life, and when I brushed my hand against his cheek, it came back icy.

It was done. I was free.

But only of the dragon.

For five long years she'd plagued me. Driven from my own kingdom with no explanation as to why or how I'd been cursed, I turned to the one man capable of helping me. Though he'd accepted me with open arms, Rothbart had a condition of his own. The magic enslaving me was old, dark, and complex, and he'd only reverse the spell if I agreed to marry him.

But first, I had to kill for him. Princes were competition, especially for someone with no viable claim to any throne. Was it vile? Were there plenty of other men who would make kinder kings? Yes—but none of those men could help me.

Save for one.

Like every curse, mine could be broken by simpler means than acquiring the aid of a sorcerer. Killing men was far easier than finding one willing to love me and *only* me. Who could love a monster—let alone a monster who'd slaughtered so many? It was like a ridiculous storybook.

But this was real life. And fucking stupid.

He coughed, and I started so badly I swore it woke the dragon.

He was *alive*?

No. Oh, no. This couldn't be happening. To kill him now, I'd have to get my hands dirty. There were plenty of options —choking, drowning, skull-bashing—but none of them clean. It had to be done. Rothbart was my only hope of reversing the curse.

Unless I could break it.

I laughed aloud and couldn't stop. I'd sooner get Odile to compliment me.

Siegfried stirred, and I bit back a scream. Rolling on his stomach, water spewed from his throat and made hideous noises that made me want to vomit right alongside him. The torrent seemed endless; perhaps I could still get away. I pictured where I could place my feet, shifted my weight, and took the first step...

He lifted his head and looked at me.

Fucking idiot. Now I *had* to kill him.

"You're naked."

I'd forgotten that I was with my dress somewhere in the forest. Crossing an arm over my chest, I seriously contemplated the skull-bashing, but his gaze hadn't wandered.

"Who are you?"

I shook my head, blindly fishing for a stone.

"I mean you no harm. I swear it." Holding my gaze, he shuffled within reach.

I knocked him in the temple with the rock—hard enough to bruise, but not enough to kill. He slumped to the side, and rather than allowing him to tumble back into the lake, I took him in my arms.

Making *me* the fucking idiot.

With his head cradled in the crook of my elbow, I studied him yet again. He had sharp, angled features, but they weren't harsh. Full lips, a strong jaw, and firm hands, yet smooth skin wherever I touched him.

Touched?

I recoiled—only for my palm to come away crimson.

Siegfried was bleeding. Retracing my caresses, it didn't take long to locate the injury's source: a jagged cut up his side. And what could be a more perfect bandage than a clean white dress?

I shook my head. Was I seriously considering *saving* him? Choking the life from him would be relatively painless, and once done, I'd be *free*.

But even when I'd believed Siegfried dead, I hadn't felt that way. An even heavier chain constricted my heart at the thought of being married to Rothbart. He'd never once taken my feelings into consideration, not even when I'd accepted the marriage as my fate and tried to get to know him. I didn't know why he wanted me and was certain the answer would disgust me. The man was selfishness personified.

What if Siegfried was the opposite? I'd never know if he bled out in front of me.

"Fuck."

We couldn't stay in the open, but I knew the perfect hiding place. It had shielded me from Rothbart on more occasions than I could count, and I even kept a few things stashed there. No clothes, but some food meant to keep, a blanket to ward off the chill, and most important, a blade.

The one thing I truly felt naked without.

I regretted knocking Siegfried unconscious about halfway to the cavern, but the injuries I'd sustained—a stab to my rear, and bruising from the fall—were slowing me down even more than his weight. I slung his arms around my neck and bore his weight on my back, but it could only work for so long. The strength granted to me by the dragon was waning fast. Sweat pooled at my brow and I gritted my teeth to keep from groaning, but eventually, we made it.

We collapsed against the stone in a tangled heap. Though daylight was wasting and Rothbart would surely be searching for me by now, I allowed myself to catch my breath, relishing the coolness of the cavern floor at my back. The only condition was that I keep my eyes open; if they closed, sleep would claim me.

After propping Siegfried against the wall and draping the blanket over his still-wet form, I snatched my dagger from its hiding place and set off into the forest.

The trek that would have taken an ordinary human ages was, for me, uneventful. My injuries had started to heal thanks to Rothbart's magic, I knew exactly how to pick my way through the destruction caused by my dragon, and wasn't slowed by the large indents carved into the earth. I located the dress by scent, donned it, and started back towards the cave.

As the entrance obscured to an untrained eye came back into view, a knot began forming in my gut. Part of me hoped Siegfried had awoken and left.

But a stronger part of me yearned to see him again.

My conflicting emotions were starting to make me want to rip my hair out, but I'd save that for the dress. I hadn't gotten a good look at Siegfried's wound, but judging from the blood coating my palm, it needed bandaging. Using one hand to pull back the curtain of foliage, I rested the other on my brow to help my eyes adjust to the darkness.

He was awake.

And he'd removed his shirt.

Our eyes met. Siegfried leaned against the cavern wall, crimson seeping through his fingers. It appeared I'd interrupted his search for supplies.

I gestured for him to sit, and thankfully, he obeyed.

I didn't approach right away. We needed a fire. Siegfried watched as I fed logs into the makeshift fireplace; nothing more than a natural indent in the cave wall I'd used for the purpose. As I prepared to strike flint, his voice startled me.

"You, ah…live here?"

He either didn't remember or hadn't been paying attention to my hair. Not many sported ashen locks in these parts.

I didn't answer even once the fire was a decent size. I crossed to the opposite wall, reaching behind a crevice for the pail that collected rainwater seeping through a hole in the ceiling.

"Do you speak common? Can you understand me?"

I shot a glare in his direction informing him that, unfortunately, I did.

"O-okay," he stammered. "We don't have to talk—"

"You seem to be doing plenty for both of us."

He drew an audible intake of breath, eyes widening.

"What? You asked."

"I…I suppose I did." Siegfried eyed me as I settled near him with the pail. "Are you a healer?"

"Yes," I lied. "Let's see it."

He twisted to give me access to his middle. The skin was beginning to swell, framing a long slice that spanned nearly the length of his ribcage. The moment my fingers grazed its outline, a groan escaped his lips, but I could tell the wound wasn't deep. He was lucky. A good wash and bandage, and his body would do the rest.

"It's not as bad as it looks—"

"Or feels, I'd imagine," Siegfried forced through gritted teeth.

"—but I'm sure it stings like a bitch."

His head whipped in my direction.

I tore a strip of fabric from the dress I'd worked so hard to preserve. "I told you I understand common. Even the colorful bits of it."

"I misjudged you."

You don't know the half of it.

Siegfried was silent until I began tracing the now-damp rag over his injury. He tensed where I touched him, but didn't shy away. "Who are you?"

There was no harm in telling him my name. It seemed only Rothbart knew it nowadays; at his court, I was simply referred to as The Dragon.

"Odette."

"Odette," he echoed. "Does that mean white in some language?"

He may not have noticed my hair before, but he certainly noticed it now. "I've no idea." *What a strange question.*

"My name—"

"I know who you are." I lifted my gaze to his. "Prince Siegfried of Kreston."

Color sprang to his cheeks. "Was it that obvious?"

"Yes."

"I hate that," he muttered almost too quietly for me to make out—but the dragon heard everything.

"Hate what?" I was finished wiping him up, but wanting to hear his response, kept the rag pressed to his skin.

He hesitated. "That I'm always *me*."

"What's that supposed to mean?" I tightened my grip around the bloody cloth once part of my unblemished dress.

"Haven't you ever wished you could just...disappear?"

"More than you know." The words came tumbling out before I could stop them, and rage boiled beneath my skin. He *didn't* know, and he certainly didn't know me.

"Is it your hair? It's beautiful, but does stand out."

I'd been so prepared for him to question my response that when he didn't, I snapped my mouth shut.

No one had ever *not* questioned me before.

"Something like that." Too far. I'd gone too far. My insides twisted into knots in rhythm with my fluttering heart, proving my body and mind were at war. My heart knew the pain of losing.

It wouldn't a second time.

"I'm sorry," he said, startling me. "I didn't realize that was a touchy—"

"Don't be."

I worked in silence after that, bandaging his side with more strips torn from my dress. It was monotonous work: a blessing for my hands, but a curse for my mind. *Don't look,* I chastised myself each time my fingers strayed a bit too far, and each time my touch lingered too long. I refused to allow my eyes to meet his face, so they ravaged his body instead, drudging with them memories I'd worked hard to bury. *Stop it. You know better.* Heat crept to my cheeks as I secured the final knots. Nearly before I was done, Siegfried stood, all but ripping himself from my grasp.

"Thank you for your hospitality, but it's time I was on my way."

Siegfried shot out a hand to steady himself as I raised an eyebrow, unconvinced. "And where exactly would you go? Do you even know where you are?"

"It's daylight. I'm sure I could figure it out."

"You truly don't remember anything, do you?"

Siegfried scoffed. "It's...*fuzzy*, but of course I remember. I was walking in the palace gardens when I saw the most beautiful—"

He snapped his mouth shut; eyes wide as he stared at me. "Y-you—"

"*I* saved your life." I pursed my lips and tensed, preparing for a fight. "The dragon was sent to kill you—"

"No *fucking* shit!"

I held my breath, mentally picturing where I'd placed my dagger.

Siegfried's expression softened. "Odette, I didn't mean to frighten you—"

"*You* should be frightened of *me*." I dove to the other side of the cavern, curling my fingers around my blade's hilt and holding it aloft. My eyes burned, and silently, I challenged him to come closer. *Just give me an excuse.*

I might complete this mission yet.

He could have walked away. He could have turned tail and *ran*—any intelligent man would have. Instead, he stared at me. Studying me.

"Don't pity me," I spat, trying to ignore my shaking arms.

"Who did this to you? The dragon?"

"You could say that."

Siegfried's eyes narrowed. "You work for him?"

"Her," I corrected.

"And you went against her orders—orders you've taken before. You saved *me* over all the others she's killed. Why?"

He pressed too hard and too fast. I refused to lower my knife as I held his gaze, unable to force the answer from my unwilling throat.

"How many princes have there been before me? I know of Fredrik, Stefan, Philip—"

"Stop it—"

"Why me?" he demanded. "Why the last?"

'I thought you could love me' couldn't be uttered, so I settled for the next best thing. "You're different," I blurted out. "It's because you were different."

"Different?"

"Are you always going to repeat everything I say?" I lowered my weapon but did nothing else to indicate an invitation. "Your men. You'd have sacrificed yourself for them."

"And that was *different?*"

"None of the others did it. They all died like cowards, but not before trying in vain to save their own skins."

Siegfried shook his head. "That's a ruler's job—never ask your people to do anything you wouldn't do yourself."

I laughed darkly. "Sounds like you'd have actually made a decent one. Too bad you'll never get that chance."

"What do you mean?"

"You can never return to Kreston. Not if you wish to live."

He scoffed. "I can't just abandon—"

"You can and you must," I snarled, closing the distance between us with a few practiced strides. Once we breathed the same air, I pressed the dagger to his unflinching throat. Our eyes met, and I was impressed by the fire I saw within. He was every bit as brave as he preached.

"You *can* refuse." I pressed until the tiniest bead of his blood coated my blade. "But if you do, I'll kill you here and now."

As I should have from the start.

Nothing prevented Siegfried from backing away. I hadn't shoved him against the wall. The man was unarmed. *Very* unarmed, as I was all too aware. My front pressed against his bare chest as it was the only way I could reach his neck, and it felt nicer than I wanted to admit.

Stop it.

Siegfried glared at me with enough venom to make it clear my growing desire was one-sided. He huffed in my face, gaze narrowing into slits. "You're bluffing."

Gods, even his *breath* smelled sweet. "I'd think twice

about questioning the woman holding a knife to your throat."

"You didn't kill me last night. You didn't leave me to drown. And you did the *opposite* of killing me not even five minutes ago."

I stood on the tips of my toes, twisting the knife at a careful angle. "You're right—I *don't* want to kill you. But that doesn't mean I'm not changing my mind with each word you speak."

He ripped his neck away and snatched my upper arms in the same fluid motion. Before I had a chance to lash out with the blade, Siegfried twisted me around so my back pressed to him, my own head barely reaching his chin. Locking his arms around me with one hand controlling the knife, he squeezed, assuring himself he had me.

He didn't, but I certainly didn't want him knowing that. Not yet.

"And I don't want to hurt you," he whispered in my ear. "But you're right—returning to Kreston is suicide. Which is why *you're* going to help me kill the dragon."

I laughed. And *laughed*.

Siegfried's grip loosened enough for me to breathe through my hysterics. My voice echoed off the cavern walls, the volume of it hurting my sensitive ears, but I couldn't bring myself to stop for a long while.

"What in God's name is so funny?"

I couldn't answer and struggled to draw a deep enough breath. The hold around me loosened, including the hand meant to control my knife.

"Are you alright—"

"Are you certain you didn't hit your head when you fell into that lake?" I glanced over my shoulder and whipped him in the face with a sheet of white hair. "How the *fuck* do you expect to kill a beast of such behemoth proportions? *You?* A man?"

"I don't," Siegfried growled. "Not without your help."

I ripped my arm from his grasp and jabbed my elbow into his nose, feeling cartilage crunch beneath bone. As he staggered back, I whirled around, once again gaining the upper hand. Blood seeped through Siegfried's fingers and poured from his nose, and as disappointing as it was to have marred such a beautiful face, I didn't feel the least bit sorry.

"*First* of all," I snarled, "do *not* fucking touch me. And second, I've *told* you your options. Disappear or die. And I'm beginning to care less and less if you choose the latter."

It was a while before he spoke.

"You fight well."

My jaw dropped to the floor. *You fight well.* No 'fuck you,' no 'I'll not be ordered around by a woman,' no mockery or sarcasm.

A compliment.

"You disobeyed orders. The dragon wants me dead. We both need the same thing."

I glared at him.

"*Survival.*"

"And you think *killing* the dragon is the answer?"

"I suppose you would still be loyal to the beast. *Fine.* But you cannot stop me." Siegfried turned on his heel, snatched his shirt from where he'd shed it, and started for the mouth of the cavern.

Rage swelled within me. "And where do you think you're going?"

"To find someone who *will* help me." He turned around so I could hear him, walking backwards toward the exit.

"You *fucking* idiot," I spat, but he didn't slow.

"You may be content to hide, Odette, but I'm not—*what in God's name are you doing?*"

Siegfried froze the moment he noticed me holding the dagger to my wrist, eyes wide with horror.

He didn't have to be afraid. Death didn't scare me—not nearly as much as living sometimes did.

Siegfried swallowed. "Odette, *please*—"

"If you kill the dragon...you kill *me.* If that is your choice, I'll save you the trouble."

And your life.

"You don't have to do this." He took a tentative step forward, but my response was to dig the blade in till it tasted blood. The sting was intoxicating.

"Yes. I do."

"Do you mean this literally? The dragon's life is linked to yours?"

To keep from saying too much, I nodded.

"I didn't know. Please, don't do this. We'll find another way."

"*We?*" I scoffed. "You were in this for yourself just a moment ago."

"That's not fair and you know it. If the dragon can't be killed, you must know *some* way to defeat it."

"There is no way."

"Odette—"

"Will you stop saying my name? I regret telling it to you."

"I don't regret knowing it."

A chill shot up my spine. "Why?" I whispered.

Siegfried gestured toward my arm. "Put down the knife and we'll talk."

Trembling and with monumental effort, I let the blade clatter to the floor. My knees gave out, but before I collapsed

Siegfried was at my side. He took me in his arms, and we sank to the floor as one, a tangled heap of limbs and blood.

"I can put you down if—"

"Stay," I ordered.

He did.

I waited for my heartbeat to settle before speaking, relishing the sensation of something so real surrounding me. I didn't enjoy being touched...but right now, it wasn't so bad.

"Love," I eventually uttered.

"Love?"

"To defeat the dragon, she has to be loved."

He was quiet for a while as I focused on steadying my breathing. At some point, he began running his fingers through my hair, and the act was so comforting, I had to fight to stay awake.

"You're certain this is the way?"

My eyes fluttered open. I shifted so I could look at his face, and before I knew what I was doing, trailed my fingers along the nose I'd bloodied. "You cannot kill a monster, so you must *love* her instead—her and no other. Whoever cursed her knows it is impossible, as well as laughable."

Siegfried winced, and I wasn't sure if it was due to my words or my touch.

"Let me clean you up—"

"No. You need to rest."

I made a feeble attempt to sit up, ignoring the rush of dizziness and nausea. "I'm fine."

"And I'm a unicorn. *Sit*, please, and stay put."

He propped me against the wall, and I watched as he fetched my rag and bucket. Once he'd wiped the blood from his face and yanked his shirt back over his head, he settled opposite me, eyeing me in a way that made me want to sock him in the mouth all over again.

"I said I'm *fine*—"

"You don't have to do this, you know. Not with me."

"Why are you still here?"

"Do you want me to go?"

My silence was enough to betray me.

"Then I'm yours, at least until you're feeling better, but I hope to be much longer than that."

Heat crept to my cheeks. "What do you mean?"

"I'm hoping you're willing to help set *both* of us free. If I'm to love this dragon, as you say...who better to teach me how?"

"Her, and no other," I reminded him. "No more chasing pretty girls at court, and no following through on whatever marriage was arranged for you. You're prepared for that?"

"Of course."

"Forever?"

"Far longer than forever."

I blinked. "You're a fool."

"Perhaps. But for the record...the only pretty girl I ever chased was you."

Dammit—he was too good at this. To keep from blushing yet again, I stole a glance at the encroaching shadows near the mouth of the cavern. It was barely midday, and Siegfried was right—I needed rest before nightfall, and Rothbart was sure to be on the prowl. I was in no condition to face him now, and especially not one to lie to him. I needed food, sleep, and a clear head.

I nodded towards the knife. "That's probably safer in your hands."

"I can't say I disagree."

"Just keep watch, will you?"

Siegfried frowned. "But the dragon only hunts at night."

"There exist monsters *far* worse than dragons."

I was too comfortable.

An arm draped lazily over my hips, fingers barely grazing stone. Steady breaths struck the nape of my neck, flooding me with warmth, and when I lifted my head, the glimmer of a knife flickered in Siegfried's opposite hand.

Keep watch, my ass.

I pushed his arm from me and then myself into a sitting position, fully prepared to give him a piece of my mind until I turned to look at him.

Siegfried's bunched-up cloak supported his head while the rest of him remained the perfect shape to fit my body, arms splayed to welcome me back if I wished. Dark, unruly locks framed closed eyes—hair I longed to twirl between my fingers—while pale skin reflected the light of the setting sun.

Curling my hand around his, I pulled the dagger from his grip.

And then I ran.

The dragon began suffocating me before I made it far from the cavern. She writhed against her internal cage, but I fought back. The sun still hung low in the sky, a palpable reminder of how little time I had left as a human, but fuck if I wasn't determined to milk every second that I could.

I stumbled through the forest with less grace than usual. My feet slid through the piles of leaves and debris, threatening to rip my legs out from under me, but I managed to grip the trees for support. Glancing through the gaps in the foliage, I gritted my teeth at the way the setting sun reflected on the surface of the lake. Brilliant reds and oranges and even some lush pink formed a breathtaking palette of wonder, colors mixing to form a natural watercolor portrait reflecting the sky.

To me, it looked like shit.

The first stabbing pain in my gut sent me doubling over. I groaned and clutched my chest, and it took effort for the sound not to turn to an animalistic snarl. Worry settled in my core. The dragon knew I disobeyed orders, and this was only the beginning of her punishment.

I made my way through the woods by instinct rather than conscious effort, unwillingly headed towards the opposite bank. There was a small inlet there; the one place where I could stand in the shallow waters as a dragon, and simply by touching me, Rothbart could return me to my human form. I tasted his scent in the air and knew he was close.

And I knew he'd require an explanation for my absence.

A *convincing* one.

When the dragon's second warning hit, I was more prepared, and gripping the dagger tighter helped to brace myself. I yearned to sink it into flesh if only to watch something other than myself bleed and in response, my arm lashed out of its own accord. The blade buried itself into a nearby tree, and though it was only sap that oozed from its wound, it was still oddly satisfying.

"*Odette!*"

I dropped into a crouch, breath hitching in my throat. The initial panic turned to rage, especially since the voice that called for me wasn't Rothbart.

It was Siegfried.

He tore through the forest resembling a drunken newborn moose. He flailed his arms wildly, more than once getting his sleeves caught on branches, and continued calling for me like an idiot.

A fucking idiot.

I yanked the knife from the tree, grimacing when my fingers became coated in sap from the blade. "Do you *actually* have a death wish?"

Siegfried didn't slow. "We were supposed to work *together*!"

"Plans change."

"Mine didn't," he called breathlessly, doubling over less than thirty yards out. "Please, don't do this—"

"We've had this conversation before. I listened then—but I cannot now."

"You *can*, you just won't," he hissed through gritted teeth.

I squared my shoulders before the dragon dug her claws into my gut. Sputtering as I fought to keep her contained, a thin line of blood trailed from my lips.

"You're right."

I hurled the dagger in his direction.

I didn't wait to see whether or not the blade found its mark before I sprinted deeper into the forest. I hadn't thrown to kill—only to shock Siegfried long enough to put ample distance between us. Once shifted it would be all over, and he couldn't bear witness to my transformation.

Not if he had any chance of remaining alive.

I didn't make it far before he called for me yet again, his voice fueling my strides. I shrieked when talons came bursting through my extremities. I yanked on my hair as it disappeared back into my scalp, digging instead into my flesh when wings ripped free of their cage. My dress constricted me for only a moment before the dragon's immense form tore it to pieces, shredding with it any lingering traces of my humanity.

When I lifted my head, I saw the world through the dragon's eyes.

At the sight of me, Siegfried halted in his tracks, stumbling backward until he fell on his ass. I lowered my neck and roared in his face.

He ran.

The pull to Rothbart was strong now that I'd assumed the dragon's form. Shapeshifters were drawn to other shapeshifters, evidenced by the way I was already headed towards our spot. I was happy to let the dragon take over; the sooner we left this cursed lake, the safer Siegfried would be.

It wasn't more than a dozen strides to the inlet. I skirted around the lakeshore, careful with where I placed my feet and tail, and tasting the air for signs of Rothbart. He was close, but I hadn't yet seen him. I snorted. Fucking bastard wanted to make me wait.

Such was his game. He wanted me to *need* him.

When I stepped into the water, I was cold. A longing to be back in the cavern burned within my chest—the fire, the warmth, *Siegfried*—but I swallowed the desire. There could be no more of that where I was going. I sat on my haunches, curled my tail around my feet, and waited.

Rothbart took his damn time. Even as darkness fell, a deeper one enveloped my psyche, digging in its roots until it became difficult to draw breath. I flicked my eyes in every direction, but there was only the breeze whispering to the trees.

Hello, my swan.

I flinched at his voice in my head.

You're not happy to see me?

I can't see you, I shot back.

You simply forget where to look.

Through a gap in the foliage emerged a solid black owl. Piercing amber eyes bored a hole through me as the creature landed on the bank, but it was already beginning to transform. Wings turned to arms and talons turned to feet without any of the blood or agony my dragon demanded, possessing an unearthly grace instead. Rothbart's human appearance was rather bird-like to begin with, given his hooked nose and sunken eyes, but his more unattractive features were concealed by the facial hair he kept gruff to hide it. He knelt until the shift was complete, lifting only his head once it was done and curling his lips into a sinister smile.

"I've missed you, Odette."

I couldn't say the same.

A fully clothed Rothbart stood, black cloak billowing around his hunched shoulders. His shifts never rendered him naked, which he said was yet another result of the curse I couldn't wait to be broken. I pranced, eager for him to touch me, but he shook his head.

"Not so fast, my swan. You must tell me why you did not return to me immediately. You know I don't like to be kept waiting."

I answered inside his head. *I got cold feet.*

"There's no need for that. We agreed to only wed once you were ready."

I would *never* be ready, and he knew it. I bit back the growl that formed in my throat, allowing silence to linger instead.

Rothbart clapped his hands. "Well, you're here now, and that's all that matters. Prince Siegfried was an easy target, I imagine?"

I nodded stiffly.

"*Details*, Odette. You know I like hearing the details."

We can discuss once I'm human.

Rothbart's head snapped up. "What did you say?"

I only meant that I've spent an additional day in the wilderness. I'm exhausted and famished, and eager to return to your fortress—

"*Our* fortress, my swan."

—so that I may rest. I bowed my head so low it nearly touched the surface of the water.

Rothbart clicked his tongue. "I do not doubt that you are exhausted, but you would not be had you returned to me when you were meant to."

He wanted me to fucking grovel. Fine, so long as we got out of this damned forest—and away from Siegfried—as quickly as possible. *I apologize, master. I was foolish and I see that now.*

"You're lucky to have such a forgiving master."

I stifled another growl. *Yes, I most certainly am.*

"In addition to being forgiving, I am also generous." He removed one of his gloves. "You need your rest more than you realize. At sunset tomorrow, we announce our engagement to the court."

I was so focused on him changing me back that I didn't register his words right away.

"I'll need you bright and beautiful," he continued, "but then again, you always are."

Before I could respond, he pressed his palm to my hide.

Water surged around me, entangling my limbs in glowing aquatic ribbons. There was no blood or pain as the world around me shrank. I continued sinking until I was a head shorter than Rothbart and regained my balance on two legs instead of four. When the waters settled, I raised my hands to my face, flexing my fingers to confirm the transformation.

Rothbart draped his cloak over my shoulders, but not before roving his eyes over my naked form. From behind, he trailed a hand down my arm.

"Better?" he whispered in my ear.

"Much," I forced, yanking the cloak so tightly it threatened to suffocate me. It didn't stop Rothbart from brushing hair from my shoulder, exposing my neck. *Don't you fucking dare*, I thought bitterly, but before he could press his lips to my skin, the snapping of a twig turned both our attentions to the forest.

Siegfried peered through the trees. And judging from the way his mouth hung agape, he'd seen everything.

Fucking idiot.

Rothbart reacted fast, but I reacted faster. Seizing the hand that had assaulted me on more occasions than I could count, I sank my teeth into flesh with no intention of letting go. As Rothbard howled and blood dripped down my chin, my eyes met Siegfried's, communicating only one thing.

Run.

Even when Rothbart began beating against my skull, I didn't release him. I clung to the obscenities that spewed from his lips, happy to wear each as a badge of honor.

"You lying, scheming *bitch*! Fucking *whore*, I'll see to it you're *never free again!*"

He ripped himself free, but not without tearing away a chunk of flesh in the process. I spat out the blood and muscle that filled my mouth, fighting to stay both conscious and on my feet.

I managed neither once the final blow found its mark.

More fucking water.

I couldn't escape it no matter how I thrashed or twisted. The icy torrent soaked me to the bone and didn't cease even when I begged. I continued screaming despite my mouth filling with the hellish liquid, and at a certain point, allowed it to make its way uninhibited down my throat.

Better to drown than be this fucking cold.

When breathing became difficult, the torrent ceased. I took a heaving breath and blinked in the darkness.

Rothbart sank to my level as I was unable to rise. My arms were extended to their full length, chains securing my wrists to each wall. My skull throbbed as if I'd been beaten, and the metallic taste of blood lingered in my mouth.

I lunged at Rothbart. "You *bastard*—"

"I'd save my strength if I were you."

"What did you do with him?" I demanded, ignoring the chattering of my teeth.

"You're not concerned with your current predicament? Interesting."

I yanked on the chains. "I've had worse—as have you. How's the hand?"

Rothbart pulled his bandaged palm closer to his chest as rage flickered in his eyes. "I underestimated how desperately you would cling to your humanity even after murdering so many."

"I'll ask again," I hissed through gritted teeth. "What have you done to Siegfried?"

"A *murderer*, Odette. That's what you are."

"For *fuck's* sake—"

"The bigger question is what you *didn't* do." Rothbart began to pace. "He was meant to be your last kill. Why throw it all away now?"

Because I fucking hate you. I bit my tongue on the off-chance Siegfried was still alive.

Rothbart halted and yanked my chin to face him. "Choose your next words carefully, my swan."

I fought the urge to tear myself from his grip. "He escaped and I didn't feel like tracking him down."

"*LIES!*" Rothbart slapped me across the face.

I slumped forward as stars danced in my vision.

"You will tell me why you spared him, or he dies here and now."

"He's alive?" I breathed, raising my gaze to Rothbart.

The cruel smirk that spread across his features answered both our questions. "My little swan, I do think you're in *love*."

"I am incapable of love."

"Are you, now?" Rothbart gripped a rope dangling from the ceiling. "Then surely *this* won't bother you."

Something came tumbling from above. It struck the ground with a dull thud, and only once I'd gotten a good look did I shriek.

A corpse clutched the dagger I'd hurled at Siegfried.

The body was charred beyond recognition, but the dagger was proof enough. A wave of nausea threatened to spill the nonexistent contents of my stomach while tears blurred my vision. I needed to draw breath, but a heavy weight settled atop my chest. I hardly noticed when Rothbart leaned in close. Even though my wrists had been rubbed raw by the chains, I thrashed, praying my dragon would emerge to shatter them.

Rothbart brushed the hair from my shoulder. "That looks an awful lot like love to me."

I turned to bite any part of him I could reach, but he wouldn't be caught off guard a second time. As Rothbart staggered back, he spat in my direction.

"A shame, really. His last words were a vow to love only you."

He'd have broken my curse.

If I couldn't speak before, I certainly couldn't now. Sobs threatened to drown and suffocate me all at once as I stared at what remained of Siegfried's body.

Rothbart tossed something at my feet. "I'll let you two catch up, but don't stay too long. The ball will go forward as planned—with one small adjustment. Can't have anyone seeing those bruises."

I glanced at what he'd thrown.

A mask.

With a snap of Rothbart's fingers, my chains came undone. I collapsed onto Siegfried's chest. The dungeon door bolted shut, leaving me alone with my rage and pain, but there was one small detail Rothbart had overlooked. My fingers curled around the dagger.

I picked myself off the floor, clutching the mask and knife.

I hoped my master was pleased with himself. I hoped that tonight, he'd be dressed in his finest garb, and stuffing his face with the finest food. I hoped Odile would be by his side to watch.

Because tonight, I would end him.

HE'D GIVEN ME A WHITE DRAGON MASK.

I traced a finger over what was meant to resemble scales, eyes flickering to where lights reflected from the chandelier. Illumination came from every direction now that the ball was in full swing, so despite my embellishment, I couldn't be certain which reflections came from me.

Rothbart hadn't spared a single expense. Surrounding me on all sides were magnificent gowns, elaborate masks, and indulgences of every sort. Couples danced and laughed without a care in the world. In the far corner, a group of musicians played a lively tune. Food, drink, and even sex awaited me if I wanted it, but I pushed it all aside, scanning the crowd for only one man.

I swear I was shedding feathers. Picking up the heavy skirt was little help, and only succeeded in getting down stuck between my fingers. If I had any say in the matter, I'd have worn something simpler and more discreet, but Rothbart had insisted.

I couldn't wait to sink the dagger strapped to my thigh into his cold, wicked heart.

He'd been avoiding me all night, and we hadn't spoken since the dungeon. Every time I got close, he'd make a swift escape, remaining close to his daughter's side. Odile eyed me from where she and her father stood in their own private box, high above my head and far out of reach—for now.

I'd figure out a way up there even if it killed me.

I was far from the only one in a mask. Rothbart's was decorated with owl feathers while Odile wore a dragon mask eerily similar to mine. It was identical in every way save for the color: black as midnight, matching both her gown and her father's cloak. Now that I'd gotten a good look at her, I realized even her hairstyle copied mine, but it came as no surprise. She'd always been the jealous type and mimicking appeared to be all the rage. Most of the other masks were fashioned after animals. Foxes, wolves, bears, and even mythical creatures waltzed the dance floor, their elaborate designs managing to conceal identities. Even the servants donned simple black and gold masks, which unlike the guests, obscured their entire faces.

I *would* need a drink to get me through this. At any moment, the music could stop, and Rothbart would announce our engagement.

And I'd want to fucking vomit.

I staggered to a table sporting glasses of wine and downed the first to come within reach. My fingers curled around the now-empty glass, nearly shattering it. No more fucking around.

It was time to kill a sorcerer.

When I glanced up at where he'd been, both Rothbart and Odile were gone. Panic replaced the determination that had been there only moments before, intensifying further when I spotted the pair at the top of the stairs. The musicians began to quiet, and all eyes turned to Odile as she began descending the elaborate staircase. From the way her gaze lit up beneath her mask, I could tell she devoured the attention the way a starving dog would a bone.

Rothbart spread his arms, and the chatter died down to silence. "Lords and ladies, and all of my esteemed guests, welcome to this night of celebration. We gather here to honor not one, but two unions, one of which will unfold right before your very eyes."

Two? I raised an eyebrow. Had Odile grown tired of fucking each of the guards in turn, and settled on a single man? I'd have sooner imagined the stars falling from the sky.

"I have news of my own, but my daughter's will come first. Who here wishes to ask for her hand?"

Surprised murmuring broke out among the crowd as Odile sank into a deep curtsy, eyes scanning the sea of faces hungrily. With the attention focused on her and whatever imbecile foolish enough to marry her, it was the perfect opportunity for me to get to Rothbart.

I pushed my way through the bodies, paying no mind to the irritated grunts and drunken curses spat in my direction. I never took my eyes from my target. Using one hand to propel myself forward, I slipped the other beneath the folds of my gown, reaching for the blade Siegfried had so graciously left me.

This is for you.

When I placed my foot upon the first stair, Rothbart clapped his hands and laughed. I froze, but he wasn't looking at me; turning, I followed his gaze.

Odile had managed to get herself a suitor.

He rose from one knee, dressed in an elaborate doublet and tight-fitting trousers. His shoulders were broad and strong, and he wore a mask adorned with raven feathers. My eyes traced the shape of his lips, and I could have sworn that I'd stared at those lips before.

I couldn't speak. I couldn't *breathe*.

Siegfried.

I was both certain it was him and certain I was hallucinating. He planted a kiss upon Odile's undeserving palm before leading her to the dance floor. Odile whispered in his ear and seeing her lips so close to his face sent a stab of physical pain piercing through my chest.

The dragon heard every word. "I knew you'd choose me."

But how?

My palms trembled as I watched them waltz to the center of the ballroom. Odile clung to him like a parasite, grinning as though she'd won the ultimate prize, and began dancing in a way that made me both envious and nauseous at the same time. They were *good*, and they looked good. Siegfried knew the steps well and maneuvered his partner through even the most complex twists and turns, and Odile danced with the grace of a swan...if swans were jealous, scheming whores.

"Beautiful, aren't they?"

Fingers locked around the elbow meant to snatch my knife. Rothbart's scent lingered over my shoulder, and before I could move, he snaked his free arm around my waist. He pulled me against him, and even through the layers of my dress, I could feel his arousal pressing into my backside.

"He looks better with her than he ever did with you, I'd wager."

"You lied to me." I yanked against his grip.

He squeezed me so hard tears sprang to my eyes. "I said nothing of the sort. *You* were the one to assume the sorry villager I burned at the stake was him."

"But the dagger—"

"The one strapped to your leg? He made the mistake of dropping it in the forest. I simply picked it up."

My vision began to blur, and I couldn't be sure if it was the tears or the sudden fatigue that had settled in my bones. Rothbart's grip was the only thing keeping me on my feet. "He... He wouldn't—"

"He thinks Odile is you."

And Siegfried did, judging from the look in his eyes. The way he'd looked at *me* a few short hours ago.

Rothbart's beard tickled my earlobe. "And it looks as though he's about to make a certain vow..."

"*No*," I whispered.

"...blissfully unaware he's breaking another in the process. He swore to love Odette, and dances with Odile."

As the music died, Siegfried and Odile turned to us hand in hand. With Rothbart holding me immobile, I could do nothing but watch as Siegfried knelt once again.

"My Lord Rothbart, I love your daughter more than anything else in this world. You would do me an incredible honor by granting me her hand."

That look in his eyes—he *knew* something was wrong, that something was off. I opened my mouth to scream Odile's name, but Rothbart spoke faster, digging his fingernails into my skin in the process.

"You honor *me*, Prince Siegfried. I grant you my daughter's hand on one condition: that you vow to love her, and her alone, for the rest of her days."

Don't do it, I tried to scream, but a groan escaped my lips instead when Rothbart's boot came slamming down on my foot.

"I swear it upon my life."

Odile cackled, and all I could see was red.

I was vaguely aware of Rothbart's fingers tangling in my hair to drag me down the staircase. I didn't protest when he ripped the mask from my face, nor when he tossed me at Siegfried's feet.

I only came to when he whispered my name.

He cupped my face in his hands. "Odette, I didn't know. It was all a sick fucking joke. *Please*, you must believe me—"

But soon, even his pleas faded away.

I curled into a ball and drowned the rest of the world out. Siegfried, Rothbart, Odile...none of it mattered. They'd broken me. They'd won. I yearned for the darkness to take me. I didn't want to live, and yet my body refused to die. Part of me clung to this world—the part that would live forever now that Siegfried had made it so.

It wasn't difficult to channel my despair into rage.

If they wanted a fight, I'd show them a fucking dragon.

I called to her like I'd never called before. I welcomed her power, her strength, and most importantly, her bloodlust. If I was going to die, I'd take everyone in this godforsaken castle with me.

Screaming filled my ears as the beast took hold of both body and mind. I'd taken on the dragon's complete form without shattering the roof, but the minute I stood to my full height, the stone crumpled as easily as paper. Enormous slabs of rock shattered on the dance floor, crushing dozens of guests, but plenty still remained for me to devour. Lowering my maw to the ground, I snapped my jaws, rewarded with blood. Swiping my claws and swishing my tail yielded even more victims, but it still wasn't enough.

As much fun as I was having, I couldn't move properly. My wings yearned to spread, and more than once, my scales scraped against a stubborn piece of architecture, drawing blood even as I spilled it.

"*Odette!*"

I knew that voice. Covered in dust and splattered with crimson, Siegfried had barely survived the carnage, but survive he had.

"It's me you want, yes?"

This was fucking poetic. Despite *everything*; despite the betrayal, and despite that he'd damned me to remain a dragon for all eternity, I still wanted him. I still wanted *only* him.

Siegfried sprinted down a hall I hadn't yet demolished, presumably hoping I'd chase after him.

I'd do no such thing.

Lifting my gaze to the sky, I used both my bloodstained talons and aching wings to pull myself from the wreckage. Once free, I left behind the crumbling fortress and set off towards the only place capable of bringing my heart any solace.

The lake.

Night air caressed my scales as gently as Siegfried once held me. The moment I reached the shore, I collapsed, barely clinging to consciousness. I didn't feel myself shift back into a human—but then again, I couldn't feel anything over the agony in my chest. My insides were on fire though my heart was barely beating. I clenched my now-human fist, wishing I'd kept my talons to slice my own throat and be done with it.

"*Odette!*"

Him again. Would his efforts never cease?

Siegfried wrapped his cloak around my naked form and took me in his arms. How he'd gotten here I had no idea, but a giant dragon wasn't exactly difficult to track.

"Leave me be."

"This is my fault," he whispered against me. "All my fault."

It was, but I didn't have the heart to tell him so. "You don't need to see this."

"And you don't have to die." He pulled away to stare into my eyes—a mistake on both our parts.

"I do," I whispered. "It's the curse."

That you were meant to break, not seal forever.

Siegfried gripped me tighter, tears streaming down his cheeks. "Why didn't you tell me you were the dragon?"

"Would you have believed me?"

"Stranger things have happened...such as a prince learning to love one."

I laughed, but it only succeeded in shooting pain up my side. As I spasmed, Siegfried held me tighter and steady.

"No laughing, then," he whispered.

"There's something else I'd like instead."

I fixated on that soft mouth I'd yearned to kiss since my first glimpse of it. I leaned in close—so close I felt his breaths on my cheek—and lingered there, my lips hovering in a silent question.

He answered by pressing his to mine.

Siegfried tasted of wine, blood, and sweat. We kissed long and deep, and it was impossible to discern whose tongue had slipped into whose mouth first. All I knew was that I wasn't ready when the kiss ended but pulled away when he slipped something within my grasp.

The dagger.

With my hands gripping the handle and his hands over mine, he pointed the blade toward his chest.

"Kill me."

I hesitated. Two separate urges warred within me; one that wished to see the knife plunge into his heart, and the other that wanted to toss the blade into the depths of the lake.

And the scariest part was that I had no idea which was stronger.

Ah, Odette. Indecisive as ever.

It couldn't be—but there he was. Perched high in a tree was a black owl.

Turning back to Siegfried, I peeled his fingers from the blade. "I've made my choice."

Have you, now? Rothbart cooed inside my head. *How will you do it—slit his throat? Stab his chest? Or better yet, the femoral artery. I've always* loved *watching someone bleed out.*

Neither, I thought only to myself.

He'd come here to witness a tragedy—not live one of his own. There would never be a more perfect opportunity.

I hurled the knife at Rothbart's breast.

An even worse pain constricted my chest when the dagger found its mark, twisting and yanking on my insides as if ripping them apart. Not an owl, but a human man tumbled from the tree, eyes wide with shock at what I'd done. I fought my way through my own agony just to watch the light leave his eyes.

"I've always *loved* watching someone bleed out."

And gods, was this satisfying.

Siegfried supported my back against his shoulder. "You're bleeding."

He was right. A deep crimson bled through the blue of Siegfried's cloak, mirroring what I'd done to Rothbart.

But I no longer felt any pain.

The sunrise reflected brilliant colors over the lake, featuring hues I swore I'd never seen before. Swans emerged from their nests with rows of cygnets trailing after them, and songbirds filled the air with music grander than a symphony. Nature was celebrating, as if she knew she'd never be plagued by the dragon again, and my heart swelled right along with her.

Siegfried wrapped his arms around me. Weaving his fingers through mine, he didn't move even when I began to grow stiff and cold, and nor when I didn't answer the whispers I could no longer hear. I tried to urge him to go, but he wouldn't listen either.

Men are foolish creatures.

But perhaps this one was different.

KAY HUMBLE

Kay Humble is a graduate of the University of Northumbria holding a joint BA Honours degree in English and History, largely because she couldn't decide between her two loves. She has since worked as a SEND teaching assistant in a secondary school in northern England where she now lives.

She grew up on a steady diet of *Redwall* and *The Animals of Farthing Wood* with her favorite genres now being history and fantasy, especially historical fantasies.

She loves traveling and has made it a life goal to visit all six Disneyland resorts. She is also the proud parent of one beloved cockapoo.

STEELSILK

Kay Humble

*I*t was a clear day when they came so the call went up while they were still a good distance away. It gave the townspeople plenty of time to find cover before their huge forms took shape.

Valeria was in the tailor's shop, as usual, when she heard the commotion. Her hands at the weave froze their nimble work. It had been a long time since the call had gone up. Over a month. Unless there had been a patrol while she was collecting silk in the mountains a few weeks ago, but she had heard nothing.

She left the weave, tucking her dark hair behind her ears and leaning close to the window to see. In the street women were tugging young children by the hand to hurry them home, older siblings running ahead. Doors slammed and locked. Curtains were pulled across windows. In only minutes, the town would become as silent as midnight.

Valeria turned the lock on the shop's heavy front door before passing through the back room where she stored bolts of material, threads, ribbons, buttons, and all manner of fabrics. She locked the back door with another glance outside.

It was rare that anyone would be bothered by the patrol so long as they stayed indoors and made little fuss. In a town like theirs, it was simply a matter of procedure. Still, everyone remembered brave Nathaniel Black standing up to the soldiers when the invasion was fresh and their presence still rankled. He had disappeared after that. Some said he was executed that same day. Others said he had been fed alive to one of the fierce creatures they rode. No one had risked trying the same thing just to find out.

Pulling the curtains across the shop's front windows, Valeria lit a small lamp to see by and returned to her weaving. Keeping her hands busy kept them from trembling. Besides, she was the only one in town, possibly in the whole country, who knew where to find and how to harvest the silk she had discovered being made by strange little creatures in the mountains. Her work was in high demand and she couldn't afford to waste any time. It would all be done in half an hour or so anyway. They never stuck around long.

The beat of huge, leathery wings sounded overhead and her fingers paused their work. She looked up and it was as if she could see them through the roof. Huge, dark bodies. Long necks and streaming tails. Wings stretched wide like giant bats. Fearsome claws and teeth. Each beat reverberated through the air sending a shudder down her spine.

Perhaps they were just flying over. That happened sometimes. They flew in low, but didn't land and everyone could go about their lives with relief.

Everything went quiet for a few moments and Valeria listened intently for the 'all clear' to sound.

Nothing came.

Somewhere in the town, there must be soldiers. Somewhere just outside the town would be their dragon steeds, waiting impatiently on their masters' return. She had never seen one of them up close and was more than happy to keep it that way. She didn't even want to see the soldiers. Since the invasion, their presence was nothing but a menace. A phantom threat hanging over everyone. The only way to cope with it was to pretend it wasn't there.

That was what Valeria did now. She simply tucked her hair behind her ears again and returned to weaving.

The tramp of heavy feet sounded in the street. Her hands kept working, but her head angled ever so slightly towards the door. A patrol. They would pass by soon.

The feet stopped and so did her breath for a moment. Had something caught their attention? Was someone outside?

A loud thumping at the door had her heart in her throat. She froze as silence returned, too scared to even move from the loom.

The sound repeated, this time accompanied by an order. "Open up."

What could they possibly want with her? She hadn't done anything, surely?

Somehow getting her legs beneath her, Valeria moved quickly and quietly into the storage room. If there was no one out back, she would run. She knew it was foolish, but they had no reason to know she would be in the shop. Esther's house was only a few streets away and she could probably make it that far. Her friend would let her in, she was certain.

She twitched the curtain aside and immediately knew it

was impossible. Two black clothed soldiers stood guard. There was no way out!

A banging came from the other room, the sound going straight to her knees and making them buckle. The soldiers had given up what passed for them as politeness and were already breaking down the door. She stumbled back just in time to see the wood splinter. A huge crack appeared and the door flew open, banging loudly against the wall. Valeria jumped, covering her mouth to hold back a scream.

Three tall, broad chested soldiers streamed in. Head to toe dressed completely in black. Even their faces were completely covered by dark masks giving them an intimidating and inhuman look.

"You know what we need," said the one in front. His voice was deep, coming up from the hollow cave of his chest. "I'll get the girl."

Valeria's heart plummeted through the floor. Her legs were weak with fear, but as soon as he took a step towards her, she turned to flee. Even knowing it was futile, she threw herself at the back door, fumbling with the lock. It had barely opened, a slash of light and air reaching her before the soldier was there. His hands were rough, jerking a scream out of her as she was pulled away from the door. One arm went around her waist, pinning her arms to her sides.

"Get off me!" she screamed, kicking and twisting and fighting his iron grip. "I haven't done anything. Leave me alone!"

If she was loud enough, would someone hear? Would anyone come to her rescue even if they did? She already knew the answer and yet she screamed anyway.

She could hear the soldiers in her shop, knocking things

over as they searched for something. She couldn't think what and, in that moment, didn't care too much to know.

"Get off me!" she demanded again. Her nails scratched at the soldier's leather riding gear wherever she could reach, but it was useless. There was no way she could break his grip. He was so much bigger and stronger than she was. In his arms she felt small, almost like a child, and Valeria was so unused to feeling like that it put her into even more of a panic. She was taller than most of the women in town and more than a few men. She had never felt so tiny or weak before.

"All ready, Captain," said one of the men. Their ransacking of her shop had been quick and efficient.

Valeria twisted painfully to try and see what they had, but before she could, a hand was across her mouth, silencing her protests and ragged breathing. Her body went suddenly stiff. If he wanted to, the captain could probably snap her neck.

"Good. Let's go."

She found herself being dragged backward a few stumbling steps before they turned. Her hands were pulled up roughly and bound at the wrists.

"Gag her too." Pressed back against the captain's chest, his voice vibrated through her skin. She barely had a chance to open her mouth before the gag was there, muffling any sound. Her head twisted to the side in defiance, grey eyes glaring at the faceless masks surrounding her until the captain jerked her in rough warning.

Outside the shop, Valeria tried to dig her heels into the ground to stop herself moving but the captain picked her up and threw her over his shoulder as if she were a child. Though his shoulders were wide, it still hurt her stomach to be left hanging there so carelessly.

She still protested as loudly as she was able, though to little affect. No one opened their doors or windows to come to her rescue. None of the soldiers even seemed to glance at her, though it would have been hard to tell from behind their dark masks. Certainly, the captain gave no indication he cared for the noise she was making.

They made quick progress, reaching the edge of town in minutes. Unceremoniously Valeria was dumped back on her feet with such force that she almost fell. A rough hand on her arm was all that kept her upright.

A hot huff of air hit her back and she turned quickly only to almost fall again.

She had never seen a dragon up close before and it was as terrifying as she would have imagined. Its huge, leathery head was only a meter from her with its sharp, gleaming teeth protruding from under its top lip. The creature's nostrils widened as it stretched forward slightly, no doubt smelling the fear she knew was coming off her in waves. It huffed again, its breath unnaturally hot.

Valeria couldn't move. All thoughts of fleeing fled themselves as she looked at the huge, black beast. If she ran, it would catch her in a moment and snap her in half between those fearsome jaws.

The dragon stared back at her. Its eyes were a dark brownish-red and they looked at her with a curiosity not completely void of hunger.

A jolt of panic swept through her body as she was pushed forward until she realized they were not moving closer to the beast's mouth and all those teeth but past it. The creature didn't turn its head, it was too well trained, but it did watch her from the corner of its eye.

Down the dragon's body she was dragged. The creature lay on the ground to allow its master easier access to the saddle strapped to its back. Its wings were tucked neatly, its clawed feet almost hidden beneath its huge mass. If Valeria had felt small next to the captain, she now felt positively tiny. She was a mouse standing next to a lion.

The captain let go of her now, vaulting smoothly up into the saddle. He reached down for her and before she knew what was happening, hands were on her from behind and lifting her, protesting, up to him. She felt the dragon's black leathery hide as she was heaved awkwardly up onto its back. It was almost a surprise to find it warm and alive. Some deep part of her had always had the sense that dragons were all but made of rock like the mountains they came from. Cold, hard creatures whose only intention was to destroy. Maybe that was why they obeyed their masters. Maybe they were hewn from the same impenetrable mountain rock. They certainly looked similar.

The captain pulled her roughly back against his chest with one arm firmly about her waist. He cracked the reins with his other hand and bellowed an order so loudly that Valeria couldn't stop herself flinching.

Suddenly, the great creature beneath them was rising up onto its feet. Its wings unfurled, seeming to stretch out forever. The body rolled as it took a few lumbering steps and then suddenly it was galloping. It looked like they were going to plough straight into the houses at the edge of town, smashing through brick and glass and bodies until nothing was left. She sucked in a tight breath, but then the great wings were flapped with a few heavy beats and they were rising off the ground.

Valeria shrank back against the steady body of the captain as they rose steeply upward. The wings pounded the air again and again until they were high enough to glide. Valeria's stomach rolled as the houses shrank away beneath them. She tried to look for her shop, for that one speck of familiarity, but from above everything looked the same and it was hard to tell.

Her eyes stung and tears clung to her lashes coldly. She tried to believe it was only because of the fierce wind whipping them.

Though she didn't want to, she clung with both hands to the arm at her waist. It at least made her feel like she wasn't about to slip out of the saddle and go plummeting down, down, down to the tiny toy houses below.

Closing her eyes tightly, she turned her face to the captain's arm and pressed it against the unforgiving leather.

They swooped high over the town and then the deep, green valley that lay at the foot of the mountains. In only minutes, the jagged peaks of the mountain range were looming over them. Occasionally the dragons would beat their great wings, but they were gliding for the most part, coasting easily on the air currents.

Valeria had almost adjusted to the feel of the great creature moving beneath her when they suddenly angled downwards. She gave a sharp yelp of alarm and scrabbled to get a better grip on the captain's arm. Downwards they dropped, the arm about her waist tightening, her skirts whipping about her legs. The wind felt cold and sharp enough to cut as they plummeted.

The faster they dropped, the more her heart was in her throat. Even with her eyes squeezed tightly shut, they were still watering and her ears stung as they were blasted by the wind.

Just as it felt they were surely going to plummet right into the unforgiving ground, the dragon pulled up. Its wings pulled in sharply and with just a few smooth steps, they came to a stop. Valeria continued trembling even though the dragon was now still.

She half slid and was half dragged from the saddle. Her knees buckled as soon as she touched solid ground and this time, the captain let her fall. Shaking on her hands and knees, Valeria tried to catch her breath. Apart from where her cheeks had been whipped red by the wind, her skin was now ashen. Her tangled hair fell down, shielding her face and skimming the dusty ground.

The soldiers were talking around her, but their voices sounded so far away, as if she were listening from under water.

How long she stayed in that position, she didn't know. It felt like minutes and hours all at the same time. She groaned softly as she was hoisted up by one arm, this time gentler than before. Perhaps that was because they knew she had nowhere to run. Nor did her legs have the ability to.

With her feet scraping the dusty ground, Valeria was pulled thankfully away from the dragons. As the cold mountain air started getting into her lungs, she managed to settle her breathing a little and lifted her head enough to take in some of her surroundings.

All around them were small brick buildings. She could see doors and windows hewn into the mountains themselves up ahead, making the most of whatever space they could find. It must have been a military base because the only people she could see were soldiers. Most weren't wearing their masks and more than a few curious eyes fell on her as she was dragged past. Valeria dropped her head again, not wanting anyone to see her.

They disappeared between the buildings, walking at a pace Valeria could have kept up with if her legs weren't still shaky from flying. The captain's hand at her elbow remained firm.

Past the bulk of the buildings, they came to a wide-open space. To their left, the mountains rose steeply, eventually falling away to the right, perhaps to a valley or maybe just in an ever-descending cliff. It was too far away for her to see. The rising mountainside was dotted with too many dark caves to count and in between, she could steps roughly carved into the rock. Scattered here and there were little doors and windows.

As they passed one of the caves, something small and shiny caught her eye. Just a little flash like sunlight on water, there for a second then gone. Valeria turned to try and catch it, but there was nothing. A snorting huff came from the depths of the cave and the sound of something large shifting. Before her eyes could adjust to the darkness, they were already past.

"Here."

It was the first thing the captain had said to her in so long that it almost made her jump.

They turned into the nearest cave and before her eyes could become accustomed to the light, something large was growling softly in front of them. Her feet planted in the ground. She wasn't sure if that was what made them stop or if the captain had been planning to anyway.

"Quiet, Austaras, it's only me."

The captain removed his mask, pulling it off his head in one smooth move. Valeria glanced up and through the darkness saw a square jaw and long dark hair but little else. The creature before them huffed softly. It almost sounded like a greeting.

Her stomach knotted as the captain reached out and the dragon eased its head forward to let him pat it on its wide, flat nose. Its nostrils twitched, taking in his scent. Then the great head swung towards her. Valeria took a step back. Something clinked in the darkness and the dragon stopped. Looking down she realized it was held in position by heavy chains about its feet and neck. At least that meant it couldn't get any closer. She had already been closer to any dragon than she ever thought possible and was not developing a taste for it.

"Your name is Valeria, yes?"

It sounded strange to hear her name coming from a soldier's lips. She somehow didn't want them to know her name but it was too late to deny it. She looked at him and nodded.

"Yes."

"Good. I've brought you here to heal Austaras."

He must have mistaken her for someone else. "Heal? I don't know the first thing about dragons! I can't--"

He pulled her by the arm again, leading her further into the darkness. One of the dragon's wings had been stretched out and pinned down tightly at the tip and again where a little claw like shape protruded from the top of its wing.

"Bring some light over here," called the captain and immediately a soldier hurried forward, hanging a lantern on a nearby hook. He continued about the cave lighting others as the captain continued speaking.

"You see the damage to his wing?"

Under the steady lamplight Valeria could indeed now see that the creature's wing was riddled with holes. Some were tiny but in the center was a large tear. If she lay down, it would probably be almost the same length as her. There was no way it could fly with its wing in that state.

"He was injured. Badly. Our enemy got lucky and hit

him. He tore himself open when we crash landed. It took a lot to get him back here."

Valeria looked up. The captain's voice was tight and he had turned his head to look at the dragon's face instead of its injured wing. This was his steed, clearly, and he had put a lot of effort into saving him.

"His other injuries have healed, but not this wing," he continued. "Obviously he cannot fly like this and without being able to fly..."

Without being able to fly, he was useless. She had known a dog once, when she was a child, who had broken its leg so badly, it had to be amputated. The dog survived, but it couldn't herd sheep any more so its owner just kept it as a pet. She saw them around town all the time. The old man and his three-legged dog. A dragon couldn't be kept as a pet though. If it couldn't work, they couldn't keep it around.

"I've been looking for a way to fix these wounds and give him a chance," said the captain, "and I think you will be able to help me."

Once again Valeria was lost.

"I think you have the wrong person," she said hesitantly. "I'm not a doctor or a--"

"You're a tailor, are you not?"

"Well, yes, but..."

"And you have developed a new type of fabric, haven't you? Lightweight and flexible, but as strong as steel. I believe you call it steelsilk."

Valeria gaped. How did he know? Had news of her fabric really travelled that far?

"I didn't really develop it. I just found it."

"But you can sew it over Austaras' wounds. If you do it

right, his wounds will be covered and he will still be able to fly."

He looked at her properly for the first time. His eyes were dark, shining in the lamplight. She could see the hope there, almost hidden by the thin line of his lips and the harsh angles of his face which were even starker in the semi-light.

"I don't know if I can stitch into its skin," she said. "The wings might be too fragile."

"Dragon wings are thick and strong," he insisted. "I'm sure you won't harm him." There was a warning in his tone. She wouldn't hurt him because if she did, she would be hurt all the worse. Valeria felt herself shrink a little.

"I – I don't have my equipment."

He turned and snapped his fingers. At once, two soldiers appeared, each carrying a bundle of fabric and tools. An ache went through her as she watched them deposit the materials into a basket. Her poor shop. What damage might they have caused when they ransacked it? Esther had a spare key. Would she think to lock up for her? Then again, hadn't they kicked down the front door? She wanted to have faith in the townspeople, but what if they saw the shop as abandoned and took whatever they liked from it? All her precious materials and creations. She had spent so many years building the shop and her reputation as the best tailor in town and now all that might be left of it was here on the floor of a cold and dusty cave.

"If you need anything else, my men will retrieve it for you."

She looked at the captain again. There was no room for argument. She could see it in his face. He wasn't a man used to being argued with.

"Follow me."

He turned and walked away with long strides that had her hurrying to keep up. They left the cave and the captive dragon, turning left at the entrance to where a narrow set of stairs had been carved from the stone. The captain moved up them confidently but Valeria was more cautious, bracing one hand on the cold stone wall as she went.

At the top, they came to a small ledge. A heavy wooden door and a small circular window were all that marked the abode hidden in the mountainside. The captain pushed the door open and stood aside.

Valeria crept forward. It was dark inside, like a miniature version of the cave below, and it took her eyes a moment to adjust.

The room was sparse to say the least. Against one wall stood a bed, piled high with blankets. On the other was a little black stove, a pipe rising from it and traveling along the wall until it escaped outside. A thick wooden chest sat closed beside it, probably full of kindling, and on the wall were two shelves filled with knives, spoons, cups, plates, pots and pans. A door on the far wall led to what she hoped was a vaguely civilized bathroom.

"You will remain in here unless you are in the cave with Austaras," said the captain, still waiting in the doorway. His huge frame blocked most of the light. "There will be a guard posted nearby if you require anything. I expect your work to be done in no longer than seven days."

"Seven days?" Valeria turned form her inspection of the room. The dragon's injuries were bad and she had no idea how long it would take to successfully stitch its wings with her steelsilk. Seven days wasn't a very long time at all.

"In seven days, there will be an important strike on an enemy base," he explained. "Austaras is expected to be able to join or he will be taken out of service."

"What does that mean?" she asked warily.

A muscle flickered in the captain's cheek. "He will be considered ineffective as a steed and turned out into the mountains."

"But with his wing injured, he won't be able to fly. How will he hunt?"

She didn't know why it bothered her enough to ask, but she thought once again of the three-legged dog. He hadn't been turned out just because he couldn't work anymore.

The captain paused a moment as if considering what to say before deciding on simply, "That is procedure."

Valeria opened her mouth again but he cut her off.

"You have seven days to mend his wings or he will be considered surplus to requirement. As will you."

A weight like a stone dropped in her stomach. What did he mean by that? What was going to happen to her if she couldn't complete this task?

Turning before she could ask, the captain left the little room carved into the mountain, calling back over his shoulder, "You will start work immediately."

BEING ALONE IN THE CAVE WITH THE DRAGON FELT DIFFERENT to being there with the captain. When she entered, the chained beast growled under its breath. Valeria paused before reminding herself it was held captive. Still she gave its large head and fearsome teeth a wide berth.

The dragon's tail swept the ground. It too was held by a chain, but it was allowed enough movement to show its displeasure as Valeria crouched by the wounded wing.

Reaching down, she delicately traced her fingers along the thick membrane. The skin was warm and surprisingly smooth. The rest of its hide looked so rough and scaly she had expected something similar of the wings. Her fingers skimmed closer to the big tear in the middle and the dragon flinched suddenly. A sharp growl came from it as it tried to turn its head, the sound almost lost under the rattle of the chains.

Valeria pulled back and her heart beat tightly. "Shh," she soothed, "it's alright. I won't hurt you."

She said it as much to calm herself as to calm the beast. She needed her hands to remain steady if she was to complete her task well enough for it to fly again. She also needed it to trust her enough to stay still or the job would be impossible.

Valeria straightened up, dusting off her dress. She retrieved a lamp from its hook on the wall and placed it beside the damaged wing, making sure to work as far from the dragon's head as possible, just in case. Then she went to inspect the materials from her ransacked shop.

Just as she was crouching down, she saw a little flicker of silver just like the one in the cave they had passed earlier. She turned just in time to see it disappear into a crack in the wall. The little creature was about half the size of her hand, running upright like a tiny human. There was a strange shimmer to its skin almost like the luminescent fungi she found growing in the caves where she harvested her steelsilk. But its hair was what she noticed most. Its hair, flowing down to its waist, was a silvery-white color that streamed out behind it as it disappeared from view.

Valeria paused. What was that strange little creature?

She moved the basket cautiously, worried that others might be hiding amongst the fabrics and tools inside. When she was satisfied there were no others, she unpacked the basket and took stock. It seemed she would have enough to cover the dragon's wounds so long as she made no mistakes. Of course, they had only brought the original undyed material meaning the patches would be a shimmery grey rather than matching the dragon's natural black but they probably cared more for functionality than aesthetics.

She set to work on one of the smallest tears first, measuring and cutting the material – a tricky procedure given its strength and flexibility – before attempting the first stitch. She tried to be gentle but the thickness of the dragon's wing membrane made it difficult.

The wing twitched and the creature growled at the sudden pain as the needle finally went through.

"Sorry," she said instinctively, though most likely the creature couldn't understand her. It growled again when she pushed the needle back the other way. This time, it sounded more like a warning. Valeria kept half an eye on the large wedge-like head as she worked, but the dragon made no other movement. It simply huffed under its breath and twitched its wing occasionally, tolerating whatever pain she was causing.

When she had finished and was satisfied with the job, Valeria sat back and flexed her fingers. They were feeling stiff already. Sewing through dragon skin was nothing like any fabric she had worked on before.

With a soft sigh, she looked across the many wounds in the dragon's wing. Seven days didn't feel like very much time at all.

FOOD WAS BROUGHT TWICE A DAY BY A SILENT AND ALWAYS masked guard. Valeria couldn't tell if it was the same one each time or not. They were all equally anonymous behind their masks. The captain showed up early afternoon on the first day to find her hard at work. She didn't dare pause as he entered. He was the only one to remove his mask around her.

Austaras snorted a welcome when he entered and offered a little grumble, as if he were complaining about her workmanship. She glanced up at the gold eye that rolled her way. Already the creature had become more familiar to her and so long as it remained chained her fear remained manageable.

The captain patted the creature's nose and let it nuzzle his leg. Valeria's stomach knotted at how close that huge mouth was to the captain. Even with the chains, there was nothing to stop it snatching his legs out from under him. There was certainly nothing she would have been able to do to stop it nor would she have tried.

And yet it didn't. It made no move to harm its master even though it could have easily overpowered him. She watched curiously from behind the curtain of her hair as she stitched. It had always seemed to the people of her town that the dragon riders must be so fearsome a people that they had managed to bend even dragons to their will and yet now, she wasn't so sure. Watching the captain pet his steed's head and murmur low into his ear a question occurred to her: had the dragons been forced to bend or had they done so by choice?

Austaras snorted softly again and nudged its master's legs. For just a moment the captain leaned his head forward and rested it against the great beast's. They stayed like that only for a few seconds, but it was enough to make Valeria turn back to her work. The moment seemed like something that wasn't her business.

"How does the work go?"

He fingers twitched just as she was about to insert the needle once more through the tough skin. "Well."

"And is he behaving himself?"

She looked up, surprised to find a wry smile on the captain's lips. He looked back at the dragon, but Austaras was only watching her. There was a look in his golden eyes that seemed to say he understood what was being asked about him and that he was worried what the answer may be. Valeria shook her head slightly to clear the thought.

"He has been excellent," she said and only realized she wasn't lying as the words left her mouth. She must have been causing the dragon at least some discomfort and yet he accepted the procedure for hour on end, until her fingers were too stiff and cold to work anymore. The whole day he lay with his body chained down and his wing stretched out. She hadn't realized until then how uncomfortable he must be.

The captain smiled again and patted the dragon's neck. "Good boy," he said softly. "I'll take you for a walk to stretch your legs later."

Finishing the patch she had been working on most of the day, Valeria reached without looking towards her basket of materials. It was only at the last second that she realized something among the fabric was moving. Valeria recoiled with a sharp scream that had Austaras clinking his chains as he tried to turn.

She had expected a mouse, or worse a rat, but it was one of the tiny, silver haired creatures she had seen the day before. At the sound of her scream it leapt from the basket, a scrap of red fabric billowing behind it like a banner.

It disappeared into a crack in the wall just as a sharply thrown stone from the captain clattered behind it. The little creature made a sharp sound not unlike a mouse.

Valeria clapped her hands over her mouth and looked up at the captain. All the softness he had shown while tending his dragon had disappeared, once again replaced by tension and harsh edges.

"Elves," he explained. "These caves are riddled with them. Make sure to guard your materials. They'll steal anything they can get their thieving little hands on."

Valeria only stared at him. The elf had only taken a small scrap of forgotten fabric. It would have been useless on Austaras' wing.

The captain turned on his heel and marched out, patting his dragon's nose as he passed. Austaras whined softly as his master left, but Valeria wasn't sure she felt quite as sad at his departure.

Valeria didn't heed his warning, whether out of disagreement or defiance, she couldn't say. She kept her basket of materials close and carried it up the precipitous steps to her room every night for safekeeping, but while she was working, she allowed herself to become distracted. If the elves happened to take one or two small items, what was the harm? After all, it was only the steelsilk she needed, not the scraps of other materials that had been scooped up by mistake in the soldiers' hurry to find what they were looking for.

Every now and then, she became aware of a little chittering sound or the flash of silver that signified an elf was somewhere nearby. She tried to surreptitiously watch them, but they mostly stayed out of sight.

After a few days without being able to wash properly, her hair had become unpleasant and she had taken to tying it back with a strip of material. She hadn't needed the full length of the strip and so had trimmed it down, leaving the remainder hanging tantalizingly from the edge of the basket. She continued about her work, finally feeling like she was seeing some progress on the wing, though she was still avoiding the large tear in the middle. It was quite some time before a little movement at the corner of her eye caught her attention.

From a crack in the wall scuttled a little elf. Its hair fluttered out behind it as it ran, disappearing behind the basket. She saw the material dangling from the basket jerk and then whip out of sight. With an excited chitter, the elf scampered back, the dark material bundled in its arms. Valeria was still watching, barely moving, as a second elf appeared in the crack at the wall. This one looked different to the first. Its long hair was the same color and its skin had the same strange shimmery quality, but this one was dressed in a little red tunic.

"Oh," Valeria gasped softly as she recognized the red fabric that had been stolen when the captain had been in the cave. And the little creature wasn't simply wrapped in the material. No. It had somehow cut and stitched itself a perfect little shirt.

"Oh," she said again, this time with more understanding. The elves weren't stealing for fun or out of curiosity. They were making clothes!

She remained staring at the hole in the wall long after the two elves had disappeared until Austaras snorted and turned his mighty head to see why she had stopped working.

"Sorry," she said, feeling silly to be responding to the creature as if he understood. Then again, if the elves were intelligent enough to make their own clothes, maybe the dragon was intelligent enough to understand her more than she realized. And if that were true, perhaps she should be a little nicer to him, just in case.

AS THE DAYS WORE ON, THE CAPTAIN BEGAN VISITING MORE often. Every afternoon, when Valeria took her meal up in her room, he would free Austaras from his chains and take him out into the big open space in front of the caves. There, with only a loosely held chain at his neck, he would walk the dragon. Valeria would sit on her bed while she ate, watching through the little window.

There seemed to be no pattern to how they walked. At first, it would begin as a circle, tracking the edge of the space, but whenever the dragon's interest seemed to be caught by a sight or sound or smell, the captain would let him wander off track.

At the far side, where the ground dropped away, Austaras would stop sometimes and look out. His snout would go up to breathe in the mountain air and the scents riding on it and then he would try to stretch out his wings. The right – the uninjured one – would unfurl itself easily and thud against the wind, but the left he kept almost still. Valeria could see the steelsilk stretched across his wounds. She could also still see the large tear through the center that she hadn't yet touched. Until that was fixed, he had no chance of flying and seemed reluctant to do anything more than furl and unfurl his wing cautiously.

When the captain walked the dragon back to his cave, Valeria would wait a little while, wanting to be sure he was secured before she returned. Usually she waited until the captain had left before she picked up her basket and headed down the steps.

But sometimes he didn't leave. And on those days, she would reluctantly carry her equipment back to the cave, ducking her head as she passed him and kneeling back at the creature's great wing.

"Is he being difficult?" the captain asked one day, startling her as she was preparing the fabric.

"No, he's being very good."

"Hmm," he said tightly. "Then why is progress so slow?"

A wash of heat burned down her neck at his words. "I... I'm going as fast as I can. I don't want to make mistakes."

She didn't dare look up. She had been able to tell as soon as she entered the cave that the captain was tense. Certainly it must look bad that the worst of the injuries still hadn't been touched but he didn't understand how painstaking the process was. All of his wounds had to be covered, the fabric stretched tight and stitched securely. If anything came loose or there was a single gap, she didn't know what the consequences would be. She had never had to sew dragon wings before.

"You have two days to be finished," the captain growled. "He must be able to fly in two days. Do you think you can do that?"

The way he asked made her jaw clench tightly. He wasn't talking to a child or an idiot so he didn't need to make it sound like he was.

"Yes," she replied stiffly.

"Make sure you do. And I told you not to let those little thieves near your fabric!"

His foot swung out with such speed and force that Valeria threw her hands up to cover her head and screamed, expecting him to make contact. A stone whistled past her head and struck with a thud, causing a sharp squeal from its victim. Her head shot back up, realizing too late the kick hadn't been intended for her but for an elf. Her heart thudded in her chest as the little creature leapt back to its feet, abandoning its stolen bobbin of thread, and fled to safety.

She was still staring, mouth open, as the captain turned and stomped out of the cave. She listened to the sound of his receding footsteps without moving. Slowly and after some time she turned to check that he had definitely gone. Even Austaras seemed cowed by what had just happened. The huge creature laid his head flat on the ground and looked up at her unhappily.

Valeria rose slowly to her feet. She scooped the bobbin up from where it had fallen and, glancing once over her shoulder, went to the hole in the wall where the little elf had disappeared. Crouching down she placed the bobbin in the hole, pushing it a little way in.

"I'm sorry he hurt you," she said softly. She wasn't sure the little creatures could understand her, but it made her feel better to say it. "I hope you're alright. You can take the thread. I don't need it, but please don't take anything else while I'm working. I promise I'll leave you what I don't need."

She stayed there a moment longer before slowly rising. There was no sign from the hole that any creature was listening. Good to her word, when the sun began to set that night and she gathered up her belongings to leave, Valeria left a few pieces of fabric and even some scraps of steelsilk by the hole alongside the thread. Whether it was an act of compassion or defiance, she didn't know, but either way she was pleased to see the next morning that her gifts had disappeared.

THE REST OF THAT DAY, VALERIA WORKED WITHOUT SIGHT OR sound of the elves. No more disappeared from her basket and she was able to finish covering all but the largest tear in Austaras' wing. She sat back with a sigh as she looked at the long gash.

Her back and neck were stiff from hunching over and her fingers ached. Her legs were sore from spending so much time sitting on the cold cave floor. She tried to massage some feeling back into her shoulder muscles, but nothing seemed to help. Sympathetically she looked across at the patient dragon, understanding a little more how he must feel.

At some point that afternoon, she had started to feel cold. The mountains were hardly a warm place to be and she relied heavily on the heat from the stove to keep her warm at night in her little room but still it seemed as if the temperature had dropped rather sharply.

The sun crept down toward the horizon as she cut the large swathe of fabric needed to cover the last wound. She rubbed her eyes more than once while doing so. A pressure was building up behind them that the fading light didn't help.

"Alright," she said softly to the dragon, "this is the last one."

Austaras glanced at her lazily.

Valeria patted the now familiar leathery wing and began her work. She would never get it done tonight, but if she could at least get it started...

Austaras flinched as the needle went through the first time, making her pause. It had been a while since he had reacted to her ministrations. Cautiously she pierced back up through the skin and he grunted, wing twitching sharply.

"Sorry," she said tiredly. "I'm being as gentle as I can."

Again and again she pierced the skin around the wound, the dragon whimpering and grunting and jerking his wing with increasing frustration. The stitches were messy. Not her best work at all. She didn't even trust them to hold, meaning she would have to go back over them in the morning.

Valeria sat back with a heavy sigh. The cave was lit only by the lanterns on the wall now, the sun having sunk beyond the ridge. She looked out, her vision blurring, and had to close her eyes as the world tilted beneath her.

A shudder went down her spine as she regained her balance. She had been working too long and now she wasn't even working well. It was time to stop for the night. She would feel better in the morning after a good night's sleep.

When she tried to rise, Valeria found that her legs had stiffened to stone and she had to grit her teeth to fight past the sudden pain without making a sound. Feeling years older than when she first sat down, she slowly eased herself up. Her muscles wouldn't seem to fully unknot themselves.

Already she had prepared her little gift of thread and fabric for the elves and took it from the basket. She braced a hand against the wall as she leant down and dropped the offerings by the hole. She probably should have taken the basket back to her room, but it suddenly seemed like it would be so very heavy and besides the elves hadn't stolen anything all day. Valeria put her faith in them to take what she had left and nothing else and headed back to her room. Austaras offered a little growl as she left and she smiled at him weakly over her shoulder, silently promising tomorrow would be the last day he had to put up with her.

Once in her room, she immediately lit the stove, piling it

high with kindling and wrapping herself in a blanket. The room was small enough that it usually warmed quickly, but as she lay down to sleep she found herself unable to stop shivering.

Darkness crept in as she drifted in and out of a fragmented sleep. She could feel all the muscles in her legs, her arms, her back, her neck tensing and clenching as she shuddered. It felt at times like her very bones were shivering. Some part of her, the distant part that was still awake, realized that it was not the air around her that was cold but her. The cold was coming from inside her. She wrapped herself tighter in the many blankets, too exhausted to do anything else.

It was sometime during the night that the fever started. As suddenly as she had begun shivering, she started to sweat. It felt like the stove had overflowed and filled the room with flames. Heat was everywhere, leaking out from under her skin and soaking the bed with her sweat. She kicked back the blankets in her sleep and tugged feebly at her clothing. The heat was too much. Everything was too much.

Her breath came in shallow gasps, drying her lips as it passed through them. She licked them but it only made it worse. Her hair lay matted to her forehead as wave after wave of heat washed over her. Vaguely she was aware of weak sunlight leaking through the window. She had slept, on and off, all night but felt less rested than when she begun.

That was when the shivers began again, pushing away the fire under her skin with ice water that left her trembling and piling the blankets back over herself. Crawling from the bed with great effort and a needle-like pain assaulting her muscles Valeria stoked the fire until it was glowing with warmth. The heat skimmed over her skin but couldn't seem to penetrate it. Inside she was still frozen.

She should be down in the cave working. Austaras' wing still wasn't fixed and she only had one day to finish it. If she didn't, he wouldn't stand a chance at flying and if he couldn't fly they would abandon him to the wild where he couldn't hunt or protect himself. Her thoughts unraveled like the messy stitches she had completed the night before would as soon as he flapped his great wing. He wouldn't even be able to take off.

And what would happen to her then?

Would she be abandoned in the mountains as well? She would have failed the captain. Failed Austaras. Maybe they would feed her to him as punishment. One last meal before he had to fend for himself. Maybe they would just kill her outright as punishment.

A wave of nausea rushed over her, knocking her sideways. A sound like rushing water filled her ears and her vision shrank to a pinprick. It was all she could do to lower herself to the solid stone floor as pressure built up under her skin. For a moment it felt like she would simply combust, explode into flames and burn herself out from the inside.

And then it was gone.

Slowly her vision returned to normal and the heat subsided, replaced once again by a frantic shivering. Valeria crept back to her bed and the nest of blankets. She couldn't work like this. Her hands were shaking too badly to even hold a needle let alone stitch with it. If she just rested a little longer maybe she could gain enough strength to work that afternoon. She would work into the night if she had to.

Bundling herself into a cocoon of blankets, Valeria closed her eyes and fell into another fitful sleep.

She dreamt, off and on, of soaring on Austaras' back. The wind was whipping her hair and chilling her to the bone as they soared up and up and just as they reached the peak of the mountains she would look sideways and see the great holes in his wing as her steelsilk tore free and then they were tumbling and tumbling toward the ground. She would always wake before they crashed, coated in sweat that made the blankets cold against her skin. Before they had dried, she would be shivering again and before she could force herself up to work, she would be asleep and falling back into the same broken dreams.

The sun rose and set over the mountains without her knowing. Two meals were brought to her, as always, by the guards and both were removed untouched. She didn't hear them either time. Night time enveloped the mountains again – the last night before Austaras would be tested. And Valeria remained unaware of it all.

The sickness had claimed her so entirely that she no longer woke. She didn't know whether it was light or dark, day or night. She was unaware of the dragon down in the cave, waiting. She was unaware of the little flashes of silver white that darted about her room in the darkness. She was unaware of everything but the fire and ice fighting inside her until they finally wore each other out and she was able to sleep. It was a heavy, exhausted sleep but a one without dreams that carried her all the way through to dawn.

THE FIRST LIGHT OF THE DAY WAS BARELY REACHING BETWEEN the mountains when Valeria emerged from her room. She was still wrapped in a blanket and winced slightly as the pale light pressed her eyes. Her legs felt like water and it was slow going down the stairs to the cave.

Austaras lifted his head slightly and snorted. She gave him a weak smile in return.

She had no idea when the captain would show up to take the dragon but maybe they would get lucky and she could finish in time. She had to at least try. If she looked almost done, he might allow her a little longer.

Her basket was where she had left it and the steelsilk still lay across the tear in the dragon's wing. Carefully she lowered herself and picked up a needle. She was fumbling to thread it when her hands suddenly stilled. She blinked a few times in the weak light and rubbed her eyes. Where a day earlier she had left the material in position but barely stitched she now saw that it was attached to the wing as neatly and firmly as anything else she had done. Valeria reached out, skimming her fingers wonderingly over the smooth fabric and tracing the line where it met the dragon's flesh. The stitches were tiny, but perfectly neat. She couldn't have done a better job herself.

Valeria looked up questioningly. The gifts she had left at the hole in the wall were gone but there was no sign of the elves. Whether they were watching her inspect their handiwork from some secret spot or not, she didn't know.

"Thank you," she said softly, just in case one of them was listening. Exhausted and overwhelmed with gratitude, she felt a sob bubble up in her chest, tears blurring her vision. It was at that moment she was interrupted by the stomp of heavy boots. Quickly drying her eyes on the back of her sleeve she turned to find the captain marching towards her.

"Is he ready?" he asked brusquely.

"Yes." Valeria stood and somehow managed not to sway. "He's ready."

Without another word, the captain set about unlocking the chains that held the dragon in position. Austaras snorted and nudged him with his head as he passed. The captain didn't respond, his jaw clenched tight and his hands moving quickly on the chains. For the first time, Valeria didn't vacate the cave as the dragon was released. She simply stood back and watched as he stretched his wing in and out experimentally and followed his master out of the cave.

Valeria clambered unsteadily back up the stairs as they crossed over to the ridge, taking a seat on the top one. She pulled the blanket tighter about herself.

Austaras stood patiently as he was saddled. Two other dragons took off, launching themselves from the ridge and flapping up into the sky. They were there in case anything went wrong. The thought made her empty stomach role painfully.

Clutching at the blanket with gently trembling fingers she watched as the captain climbed into the saddle and made his final preparations. She saw him snap the reins and then Austaras was lumbering toward the edge of the ridge. He picked up speed quickly, his wings beating. The left was a little slower than the other, but it seemed to be moving alright. Valeria held her breath as he reached the edge and leant forward as he launched himself off.

For a second, the dragon dropped and her heart went with him. He disappeared almost out of sight and then suddenly he was climbing. His wings were beating in time and he was rising up, up. Valeria released a breath. The dragon climbed and dropped and twisted on the breeze. Even from a distance she could see the joy in the way he moved, finally free of his chains and able to soar again.

A high-pitched chattering came from below and she

looked down to see a cluster of tiny, white haired elves watching with her from the cave mouth. Some were wearing little tunics, others pants and shirts. A few even had little hats on their heads. She saw reds and blues and even the same shimmery grey that caught the light on the dragon's wings. They were all dressed a little differently, but every one of them was dressed in tiny, elf-sized clothes made from the fabric she had given them.

It was only a few moments before one caught her smiling down at them and froze.

"Thank you," she said, sure they could understand her this time. The elf who was looking at her squeaked and darted back out of sight, the others following in a sudden flash of silver and white. Valeria laughed softly.

She turned back to Austaras with a relieved smile, watching as the early morning light shimmered against his wing.

ASHLEY L. HUNT

Ashley L. Hunt is from Pawtucket Rhode Island, but currently lives in Florida. Even when she was very small, she would make up great adventures for her collection of dolls and stuffed toys. She loves tarot, astrology, and of course dragons. Her favorite animal is the sloth, but she can't have one as a pet, and that makes her sad. Instead she has two cats and two dogs. Aside from writing and reading, Ashley loves to swim, so it's a good thing she lives in a place as bright and sunny as Florida. Currently, she's working on fairytale rewrites with vampires.

Ashley L. Hunt has been published in nine anthologies, including *Forgotten Places*, *Devil's Armory*, *Barbarian Crowns*, *For The Love of Leelah*, *JEApers Creepers*, *13 Bites Vol. III*, *13 Bites Vol. V*, *Caluche Chronicles*, and *Plan 559 From Outer Space Mk. II*.

CINDER AND ASH

Ashley L. Hunt

*T*he tower clock in the distance tolled eleven, mocking Cindra as she raced through the woods. Sloane, ever patient, was waiting in the cave, trapped between two realms. Cindra nearly turned her ankle on a loose stone, reminding her to re-stuff her worn old shoes with straw when she got home. Rising from the cliff, black against the starry night, the distant waterfall glowed white. Cindra reached the familiar part of the river that was easiest to cross, with calmer water and evenly spaced rocks. With practiced ease, she hopped across from rock to rock, barely wetting the tips of her shoes. From this distance, the roar of the waterfall was deafening. Cindra pushed on, feeling her way on the smooth rock face, she followed the familiar path. Time was short; if she didn't make it to the secret place by midnight the portal would close forever.

In just a few steps, Cindra reached the mouth of the cave. Trembling fingers pulled the stolen pendant from her neck and pressed it to the right crevice in the wet and cold stone, revealing a swirling blue portal. With a sigh of relief,

Cindra stepped through. Sloane lifted her scaly red snout and huffed a large plume of smoke from her nose.

"You shouldn't have come in this weather. You'll likely get caught in the rain," Sloane admonished, lighting a nearby lantern with her breath. Cindra pulled off her shoes and wiped as much soot from her feet as she could.

"I wanted to come earlier, but Thessaly was in a mood and Winnie was piling on. The twins are good at finding work for me, and Madame Bourguignon treats them like glass." Even after thirteen years, Cindra couldn't bring herself to call her stepmother 'Mom'. "Thessie decided she wanted a bath; I had to fetch water from the spring and heat it." She removed her worn, tattered, and long grey cloak and carefully hung it on a branch growing through a crack in the cave wall. Cindra moved closer to the rocks to sit, and caught her reflection on an old suit of armor.

Wide grey eyes stared back from either side of a long narrow nose, perched atop her light-pink generous lips. A gentle forehead sloped down into wide chipmunk cheeks and the small button chin, giving her a youthful look. Floating around her head almost like a halo, was thick ginger-blonde hair. Her small ears were tucked close to her round head.

Sloane smiled, as only a dragon can. "You look remarkably like your mother."

Sloane blinked her crimson eyes slowly. "You need to get out of there, Cin. Take your mother's inheritance and go."

Cindra shook her head. "Not without you. Madame Bourguignon has the amulet. Once I turn eighteen, she has to hand it over. Then we can both go."

"Leave me. It's not worth the way you are treated. We have been over this before."

"Stop being so noble. My answer won't change." Cindra

sat on a boulder close to Sloane's head and shuffled her feet along the coal dusted floor. She had done it so many times over the years, a set of grooves fit her feet to perfection. "I have news... of a sort," she added, pulling a carefully folded envelope from her sleeve. "Madame Bourguignon tried to hide it from me, but I heard her talking to the postman. He said my name."

"Is it from your father?" Sloane let out a long plume of smoke as Cindra opened the envelope.

"It's from the magistrate. 'Dear Ms. Marchand, in lieu of your inquiry--'" Cindra frowned and turned the paper over in her hands. "I didn't make an inquiry"

Sloane arched her long red neck. "Maybe your stepmother did and pretended to be you. It's despicable enough, but why?"

Cindra shrugged and continued reading. "My father has been declared lost at sea for seven years. They will legally declare him dead in a month!" Cindra jumped to her feet.

"No!" Sloane roared. "That's too soon. Your inheritance will go to your stepmother!"

"How do we stop her?" Cindra paced the floor nervously. "We can't expect my father to come home. Even if he did, it wouldn't change my plans." Cindra steeled herself for the wave of guilt she always felt about her father. A daughter should love her father more than she did. Even before he was lost at sea, her father had existed as a ghost in her life. It was only a coincidence he was home when her mother died.

"Was my father--" Cindra stopped, afraid of the answer. "When I was born?"

Sloane laughed with a soft roar. "He refused to leave your mother's side for a month. Drove her absolutely mad. She could be fierce, but she was so gentle with you."

Cindra smiled. "I remember her, somewhat. I remember coming to visit you with her. But not in this cave."

"She used the amulet to open the great chasm beyond, but it's in with your inheritance."

The mention of the inheritance jolted Cindra's attention back to the letter in her hand. She smoothed down the once white apron in her lap.

"What can we do about the magistrate? Madame Bourguignon read this letter; she won't rescind her claim unless we use the law to push the day back."

"Can you write to the Magistrate and change the day?" Sloane thumped her scaly tail in agitation.

Cindra wiped her hands nervously along her once splendid dress. "No, I don't think so. The Magistrate doesn't make the rules. I would have to get an audience with—"

"The king," Sloane finished and looked out through the waterfall beyond the cavern. Beyond that, the sleeping town, the clock tower, and the great palace were lit with chandeliers from within. Intricate chandeliers that would hold great candles burning throughout the night. Outside, it would be bright under the full moon between the heavy clouds.

Cindra felt her heart sink at the thought, "How will I ever get a meeting with the king?"

"Don't worry about that now. Figure out what you want to say first. Work out the rest as we go." Sloane nuzzled her red nose to Cindra's cheek.

"You had better get back home. It's almost midnight, and there is no point in both of us being stuck here," Sloane warned.

Cindra pulled her shoes back on. One good rain and they would be destroyed. She quickly adjusted the lantern that would light her way home.

"Madame Bourguignon likes her breakfast precisely at sunrise," she slipped on her once green cloak and tucked back her thick hair. The only sign that the cloak had once been grand was the matted ermine trim. Although mostly ornamental, the cloak was still functionally warm, as long as it was kept dry.

Cindra was halfway home when the sky opened up and she quickly made her way to an outcropping of stone. It was more of a hollowed-out rock than an actual cave, but it was big enough to keep the rain out and the fire going. Cindra collected the nearby brush and soon had a cheery little blaze going. She sat warming herself for a few minutes before realizing someone was standing close by.

"Please don't be alarmed," a man's voice called. "I was hunting and got lost."

"Come sit by the fire. It's past midnight."

"I have been lost for a very long time. I don't know where the rest of my party is now."

"Looking for you, no doubt." Cindra sat up straighter. The handsome stranger wore the clothes of a nobleman. He was unquestionably the son of a lord or a duke. The cave was too dark for Cindra to get a clear look at his face. "I apologize for my disheveled appearance, fair maiden."

"Lost in the woods for many hours, it's not a surprise." Cindra dipped her head politely.

The stranger laughed suddenly. "My father has always said the low class has no manners; you have proven him wrong in five seconds."

The stranger's flippant tone made Cindra's temper flare for a moment. "What makes you think I am lowborn?"

"No highborn woman would know how to make a fire. I meant no offense, good woman." The nobleman tilted his fine hat in deference.

Cindra decided that was an apology. "I am hardly the exception to the rule. Many of us are polite. I have met highborn who could work on their manners," she added, thinking of Thessaly. "But you have shown to be different from my expectations."

"I shall take that as a compliment, good woman. What are you doing out in the woods so late?"

Cindra bit her lip. Although the nobleman seemed polite, she didn't trust anyone with the secret of Sloane's location. She squared her shoulders and shook her head.

"I'm sorry, perhaps it's not my place to ask such things."

"It's nothing, thank you for your concern," Cindra replied. "I had something important to tend to, but I got caught in the rain. Once it lets up, I can lead you to the edge of the woods. I trust you can find your way home from there?"

"Indeed. Were it not so late, I would take you to meet my father. He would reward you greatly for assisting me."

Cindra dipped her head, aware of just how tattered her cloak looked, even in the dim light of the fire. "You are most kind, sir."

The noble laughed again. "It is your kindness, my lady, that has kept us both safe. I am in your debt."

Cindra felt the paper in her sleeve and shook her head. "The only thing I require would be too much to ask, even of you. There are things even money can't buy."

The nobleman nodded thoughtfully. "I have met a great many who think they would be happy with more money, but I have never found that to be true. Many see my name and rank as a step toward a bigger goal, and I often find myself wondering if my friends are truly people who care or who only want what they can get from me. The only exception..." the noble man laughed and shook his head.

"Tell me."

"It's silly."

"I won't laugh. Promise."

The nobleman looked down. "My father's stable hand. He is only a year older than me. The only thing he cared much about was tending to the horses. All he asked is that I respect his expertise."

Cindra placed more wood on the fire and waited for the stranger to continue.

"We don't talk much now. I have my responsibilities and he has his."

"That's a shame. Perhaps there is a way to make time?" Cindra thought about Sloane, always in the small cave waiting.

The tall man shook his head. "It would be worth trying, but I wonder that he would care so much to see me when he has the time."

Cindra looked out as the fire crackled. "The rain has stopped. I need to get home."

The nobleman wrapped his cloak over Cindra. She felt warmer immediately. She quickly fashioned a torch and handed the lantern she carried to the young lord.

"Tell me something of yourself, fair maid?" the stranger asked in a friendly manner.

Cindra shrugged. "Not much to tell. My mother was— a woman of sunlight. I remember her always laughing. She taught me manners and joy." She smiled at the memories. "She called me sunflower. And Father called me hummingbird."

"Called... they no longer do?" The nobleman stopped. "Sorry, not my place."

Cindra pushed back her hair and nodded. "Mother died when I was small. Around five, actually. My father is a merchant and wasn't around much. I live with my stepmother and her daughters. Twins a little older than me...."

"So, a new mother and some sisters. At least you had someone to play with."

Cindra wrinkled her nose. "I'm not fond of Thessaly's games. Winsome has trouble thinking for herself." Cindra stepped over a large fallen log. The nobleman held a hand out to help her across. "She goes along with Thessie."

"Then it's Thessie's games or nothing?" the nobleman asked. "Sounds fun."

Cindra hid a grimace. "Something like that. My stepmother, she keeps things going because she has custody of me. At least, until I have my inheritance." Cindra stopped, unwilling to dump all her problems on this kind man. At the final line of trees, a group of men stood with lanterns as the pair emerged. In the sudden light, Cindra realized just how tattered she looked beside the gentle stranger.

"Your Highness. We were worried. The kingdom has barely slept." The waiting crowd bowed to the nobleman. Cindra's breath hitched as she recognized the emblem on the prince's chest.

"I was thrown from my horse and got lost, but a fair maid helped me," he smiled and placed his arm gently on Cindra's shoulder. "We must see her home."

"No, Your Grace... I thank you, but... my family is—They don't need to know I'm out. They would worry." She knew it was a stretch, but she wasn't ready to explain everything. Cindra bowed as best she could and removed the deep purple cloak that the Prince had handed her earlier.

"Forgive my liberties, your grace. I meant no disrespect."

The prince smiled and bowed more elegantly. He pressed the cloak back to Cindra. "All is well, and my offer still stands. You know now that anything you ask is within my power to grant you."

Cindra hesitated. The letter in her sleeve pushed against her arm uncomfortably. If she said the words, she could have the meeting with the king set up tomorrow. She could ask to be emancipated right away. She could ask a decade's continuance on her father and it would not be denied. Just as she opened her mouth to speak, she saw it. A small glimmer in the prince's brown eyes flickering by the lantern light. Vulnerable, fleeting, a little bit fearful. His words in the shelter washed over her.

"No. I thank Your Majesty, but I will ask nothing of you." Her heart sank at her own words, but the warm, grateful smile the prince gave in return told Cindra she had made the right choice.

The prince mounted the spare horse brought forward, and nodded to Cindra. "Until next time, fair maid." He smiled as most of the company rode off. One man stayed behind, and Cindra could see the emblem of the high chancellor on his chest.

"You're more maid than fair," he sneered. "I don't know what games you're playing, or who put you up to it, but stop at once. Prince Raphael may be charmed, but I'm not so foolish."

Cindra bowed meekly. "Sir, I don't want--"

"Do not talk back to me, *peasant*." The high chancellor threw a dozen gold coins at Cindra and rode off. With nothing else to do, she collected the money and went home. Cindra climbed over the small garden wall and entered through the kitchen in the back of the house, locking the door behind her. A long horn sounded in the distance, and Cindra froze as voices were heard from the parlor.

"Did you hear that? The prince has been found." Thessaly said in an excited voice. "The kingdom can rest!"

"Cindra will be happy to know," Winsome clapped her hands in joy. "Shall we tell her?"

"No, stupid. She's too lazy to get out of bed and sit with us, then she won't care." Cindra bit her sleeve. Thessaly would never climb all the way up to Cindra's room. Winsome snorted and muttered about Cindra being lazy.

Madame Bourguignon's voice swept through like poison velvet.

"Girls, enough. It's time for bed now. I shall deal with Cindra in the morning."

A chill ran down her spine as she contemplated what her stepmother might mean by that. A beating, or whipping, or worse. Madame Bourguignon's favorite punishment seemed to be giving Cindra extra work.

Overcome with sudden exhaustion, Cindra crept into a warm little corner of the pantry and slept the few hours to daybreak. The sun was barely peeking over the horizon when Cindra woke again, preparing her stepmother's breakfast. Madame Bourguignon always had the same thing, which made it easy for Cindra to remember. Two soft-boiled eggs, fresh cut bread drizzled in butter, clotted cream with berries and whatever cold meat was on hand (usually mutton) would fill the plate. To drink, a warm cup of chocolate and some hot tea. Madame Bourguignon was very particular about her tea. Cindra was careful to measure out the exact amount. As a child, she had been proud to make her stepmother's breakfast just as she liked it. From there, it grew. "Cindra, you are so much better at sweeping the floor than poor Thessaly. Perhaps you should take it over. Cindra, Winnie was supposed to do the dusting, but you know how things are too hard for her. It's laundry day and I just don't feel well... Winnie needs her own room. She would feel better if she had yours and you took the guest room... oh Cindra, guests are coming. You don't mind only for a few nights? Winnie wants to cook her own breakfast, but she will burn the house down. You don't mind, do you?" On and on until Cindra alone had all the chores. She tried to argue at ten, at fourteen, and at sixteen, that the others could help, but Madame Bourguignon had such control by then. And her father's final words had been weaponized against her.

"I know this is a lot for an eight-year-old, but I know my Hummingbird will keep things going. Do as your stepmother says and take care of things around here for me."

"I will, I promise." Cindra agreed with all the enthusiasm and trust a naive child had, just as she promised her mother to be kind and patient.

Cindra was pulled from her reverie by the whistling teapot. She jumped to her feet and measured out three even tea leaves. Winsome and Thessaly would take their breakfast later, so Cindra left the bread warming in the oven. She collected the food and placed it on the tray before rushing to Madame Bourguignon's room just as the sun was truly rising.

"Cindra, my dear. Did you sleep well?" Madame Bourguignon asked in a silky voice Cindra learned long ago not to trust.

"Well, Madame Bourguignon, but not long. I fretted all night about the prince when Thessie told me the news." Cindra knew her stepmother would not call out her lie without proof. "I didn't think you would want me to sit with you. My tears were quite loud."

"How considerate of you. Well, you may save your tears

for now. The prince is safe. He returned home just after three."

Cindra twisted her apron, feeling the gold in her hidden pockets. "That is indeed good news. I shall have a spring in my step with all I do today."

"Good. You may actually do your chores on time today." Madame Bourguignon turned to the tray in her lap and tapped the first egg, Cindra's cue to open the drapes. "I want you to polish the silver again. And don't be so lazy about it, like last time."

Cindra bit the inside of her cheek. She could never prove it, but she was sure Thessaly convinced Winsome to lick the spoons after they had been polished.

"And the drapes of course. Take them all down and wash them thoroughly. And Winnie could use some help with the spinning wheel. And don't forget to mop. Also, the mending and the dusting and the sweeping. I trust you haven't made too much of a mess of the kitchen?" She smiled and sipped her tea calmly.

"I shall have the washing up done within the hour," Cindra promised. Thessie and Winnie she knew wouldn't be awake until almost ten. Winnie would spin for hours before Thessie pulled her around town for shopping trips and gossip. Cindra wouldn't see them again until supper.

"And another thing." Cindra's stomach tightened. Her punishment was coming, she could see it in her stepmother's brown sharp eyes. "I want quail eggs with dinner. Fetch them."

Cindra's heart sank. Quail eggs would take hours to procure. Madame Bourguignon pulled out a small purse and counted out four silver pieces.

"Madame Bourguignon, I would need at least 2 gold for

even one decent egg--" Cindra stopped talking as the sting of a sharp slap pressed her cheek.

"Cindra! What would your father say to know you refused me so rudely? Begging for money after I have fed and clothed you all these years? After I have kept a roof over your head? You ungrateful child!"

Cindra rubbed her cheek to rid it of the angry red mark. "Yes, stepmother. I'll have the eggs." She bowed slightly and walked out.

The market place was bustling and buzzing with an excited crowd of shoppers. The gossip flew from stall to stall about the prince being lost and saved by a mysterious woman. Cindra's favorite rumors were an elderly wise woman who lived in the caves, and a tree sprite who took pity on the prince and led him out. The prince himself was keeping silent about the whole thing, so speculation ran rampant. Cindra kept her head down and moved to the poulterers as fast as she could. She pulled the gold from the high chancellor and bought two eggs. That's when a new rumor sent her spinning. The 'Strange Savior' had let slip two names: Tessa and Winifred. Cindra felt her face flush. How could she be so foolish? Sure, the tales had spun the names wildly away from the twins' actual names, but it was only a matter of time....

"Don't worry," a somewhat familiar voice said in Cindra's ear, making her jump. "The gossip will die down in no time."

She looked up at the smiling Prince. "Your Grace, I didn't--forgive me..."

"Calm down, milady, I didn't mean to startle you." The prince smiled politely and steadied her basket.

"I didn't think you would be here in the market," Cindra replied.

The prince smiled. "Most commonly, I don't, but my

father is planning a ball. As it's in my honor, I decided I should have a say in the food served."

"A ball sounds like fun," Cindra smiled pleasantly.

"Would you like to come?" It seemed repaying her had become a game for him.

Cindra blushed. "I couldn't ask that of you, sir. It is a gracious offer, but of all the ladies in the kingdom, I should not be the one you invite."

"Perhaps I shall have to invite every maiden in the kingdom just to ensure you come as well."

Cindra laughed. "Indeed. Because offering fresh oranges is too much work. I best get home. I have... much to do." Cindra collected her groceries and bowed one last time. She hurried home and rushed through her chores. Winsome was more than happy to spend hours at a time at the spinning wheel, so Cindra knew she didn't really need help. The rest of her chores were easy, but tedious.

By seven, she was almost finished when there was a loud knock at the door. From the sitting room, Madame Bourguignon called. "Cindra, the door. Do not leave them waiting, child."

Thessaly looked up from her card game and snickered. "Hurry up, we don't want to wait all night," she sang out as Winnie gave a short laugh.

"We don't have all night," she echoed.

Cindra opened the door to a pair of men in castle livery. One bowed low and handed her a gold envelope embossed with a red wax seal of the royal crest.

Cindra's heart leaped to her throat. Had she been found out? Was Sloane discovered? Would she have to explain to her stepmother why she was out in the woods at two in the morning?

With heavy footsteps, Cindra entered the sitting room. "It's a letter... from the king."

Madame Bourguignon yanked it away and glared at Cindra as though she had tried to hide the letter.

"'By order of the king, upon the request of the prince...'"

The next sentence threw the room into pandemonium. Cindra's head was still swimming an hour later when she was finally able to make it to the cave.

"It's not funny!" Cindra insisted as Sloane positively roared with laughter.

"It's kind of funny. Read it again." Sloane suppressed another round of laughter as Cindra settled into her usual seat. She pulled the royal proclamation from the hidden pocket in her dress and read aloud.

"'By order of the king, upon the request of the prince, His Majesty King Alexander, high lord of the land. We hereby request the attendance of every eligible maiden in the kingdom to the royal ball in honor of His Majesty Prince Raphael.'" Cindra waved the paper at her dragon friend. "He's toying with me."

"You gave him a challenge. He rose to the occasion." Sloane shifted a large pile of gold aside and uncovered a sizable trunk. "Open this and you'll find what you need."

Cindra obeyed and unlatched the trunk to find a collection of elegant gowns and assorted jewelry.

"They're beautiful, but Madame Bourguignon would never allow me to go."

"It's not her choice. The king commanded all maidens, that includes you. Besides, you're the one the prince wants to see. Find a way." Cindra held up a long green gown. "This is the best chance you have to see the king. Don't throw this opportunity away. "

Cindra squared her shoulders. "How selfish of me!"

Sloane pushed aside another pile and retrieved a dozen pairs of shoes. "It's not selfish to refuse using a person as a pawn or a stepping stone."

Cindra held up a blue velvet gown. "I would look like I'm wearing a tent in these. The ball is in two days. I can't hem them in before that."

"Leave it to me," Sloane assured her. "I'll have them snug as if they were tailored to you."

"What about shoes?"

Sloane examined a fur-lined shoe that was half a size too small. "I'll have it sorted. You just need to think of what to say to the king."

Cindra looked at the portal entrance, locking Sloane within. "Perhaps I should just ask for my inheritance to be passed to me now."

Sloane eyed Cindra and nodded. "Now get back. I'll have everything ready tomorrow. And don't let Madame Bourguignon find out you're going. She can't interfere if she doesn't know."

The house was still buzzing when Cindra returned late that night. The twins had removed every frock from the wardrobes. Winsome had wrapped herself in yards of lace and silk, and was positively drowning in shawls. Thessaly was running about with every brooch and necklace she could find. Her hair was in a sloppy bouffant that was already beginning to collapse. Winnie's thin hair was a tangle of messy curls. The girl had tried to braid it herself, but she'd always had trouble with dexterity.

Cindra gently pulled the brush from her and quickly unknotted her stepsister's hair. Thessaly sloshed over in a bright orange dress covered in small beads.

"I want to wear pink!" Winnie exclaimed suddenly. Thessie giggled and tossed a shawl on Cindra's neck. "Isn't this so exciting? We're going to a ball and I'm going to dance with the prince."

"I'm going to dance with the prince too. Dance in a pink dress." Winnie repeated.

Cindra braided her hair patently. "You would look like a princess in pink, Winnie."

Thessie huffed out a breath. "It's just too bad you can't go, Cindergirl, but the prince already has a maid."

"You're not going Cinder? It will be fun," Winnie said thoughtlessly.

Thessie pounced before Cindra could respond. "Of course not, stupid. She doesn't have anything to wear and she's such a mess. Look at her hair!"

Cindra fixed Winnie's thin brown hair into a simple, elegant braided bun and shook her head. "I can fix my hair and if Thessie would lend me a dress...."

"I'm not lending you a thing, you filthy serving girl!" Thessie waved a hand wearing too many bangles and gathered her yards of skirts before stomping off. Winnie, whose mountain of fabric looked like a shapeless pile of laundry, turned to Cindra. "You can't borrow any of my dresses, either."

Cindra shrugged. "It was just a thought." She placed the brush back on the table. "I'll just have to stay here and perhaps you can tell me about it after."

Winnie stood, shuffling out from her heap of dresses and walked up to her room. Cindra cleaned up the clothes, dreaming about the dress she and Sloane had chosen for her. They had planned for Cindra to pick up the dress and jewelry the night before, that way she could smuggle them to her room and iron the gown before going to the ball. After talking to the king, Cindra could return and unlock the portal before midnight.

Sloane grinned widely as Cindra tried on the dress. It was a light purple satin with small flowers bedecked on the waist hugging corset. The wide skirt floated to the floor like soft clouds. The sleeves were sheer lace and dropped from her shoulders to the elbows. Cindra gave it an experimental spin.

"You look amazing, but we need some shoes for you."

"Winnie wears a smaller size than Thessie. I can probably sneak a pair of her shoes. She won't know unless I get coal dust on them..."

"Coal dust. I have an idea." Sloane gathered the loose coal that covered the floor and indicated the place where Cindra often buried her feet in the soft dirt floor. "Stand there and hold your skirts high."

Perplexed Cindra did as she was asked. Sloane piled the thick coal dust over Cindra's feet before helping her step out.

"Stand back," she warned before blowing fire over the foot impressions. Cindra watched as two solid objects formed from the superheated coal. Cindra picked up one of the objects and carefully brushed off the remaining dust to find a diamond shoe.

"How beautiful!" Cindra exclaimed and pulled them on. "They fit perfectly!"

"Of course, they are molded to your feet." Sloane replied. "Now, get home before you are missed."

Cindra spent the next day helping the twins prepare for the ball. Fixing Tessie's hair and helping Winsome into her gown. The shocking bright pink made Cindra's eyes swim. Thessie's orange dress was so bulky she could barely move. Thessie didn't miss a single opportunity to mock Cindra for not going, but she held her temper in place. Finally, the pair were bundled into the coach Madame hired to take the trio to the ball. Cindra quickly changed into her own gown, pulling the cloak the prince had given her over her shoulders. She ran to the old gilded coach that had belonged to her mother. It was out by the pumpkin patch, but the wheels were still in good shape. Though it had been years, Cindra remembered what her father had taught her about hitching a coach and driving.

The ball was in full swing by the time she arrived, with many couples whirling along to a lively tune.

Several pairs of eyes turned as Cindra descended the steps to the main ballroom. She caught sight of Winnie, in her bright pink ball gown standing nervously in the corner. Thessaly was trying to get some noblemen to talk to her. Several people pointed in Cindra's direction and she realized how silly she looked still wearing her cloak. The prince met her at the bottom of the stairs.

"You made it," he smiled and kissed her hand.

"You made me," Cindra teased and curtsied. "But I would be hard-pressed to turn down such an offer."

"May I?" The prince helped her remove the cloak and handed it off to a nearby attendee. Several gasps nearby reminded Cindra that her gown was not the simple ragged dress she wore most days. At the last minute, Sloane had sprinkled small flecks of diamond and gold dust all over the dress, making it look like a starry sky.

"Care to dance, my lady?" The prince smiled charmingly and took Cindra's hands. She allowed herself to be led to the dance floor.

"I have to confess, there is another reason I came tonight," Cindra admitted.

"Have you thought of a way for me to repay your kindness?"

"You don't owe me anything for that, but I do need to

have a word with your father." Cindra bit her lip. She didn't want the prince to feel used, but she had to help Sloane.

"Shall we go now?" The prince's smile was less enthusiastic and Cindra hesitated.

"I believe we are in the middle of a dance," she winked.

"Then perhaps at dinner? But you would have to sit by me."

"I would be honored," Cindra smiled. She caught a glance of Madame Bourguignon's scrutinizing gaze, but left it alone for the time being. If she could get the king to listen, Cindra would be free by morning. She felt an odd sense of tenderness at the thought of losing Winsome.

"Are you alright? You're suddenly pale." The prince frowned and led Cindra to a chair. He looked at a nearby table and fetched a silver bowl. "I nearly forgot. Look."

Cindra peered inside to see the bowl was filled with oranges. Each one was stamped with the royal seal. "You mentioned them in the market the other day."

"And you procured them. How thoughtful." Cindra plucked one of the sweet round fruits from the bowl and examined it. She looked back at the prince as a soft bell rang somewhere in the palace. The prince helped Cindra back to her feet and the crowd gathered around the long table set with silver platters. The king sat at the head with a plate of gold. Thessaly tried to sit with a group of dukes, but a servant shooed her back to Madame Bourguignon and Winsome as the company waited for the king to take his seat. The prince directed Cindra to sit on the king's left side across from the queen, who smiled warmly at the girl.

"So, you're the young woman who has charmed my son." She bowed her head slightly. "You're as lovely as he says."

Cindra blushed and bowed her head. "You are too kind. I

wish we could meet under better circumstances, but I have a request for Your Majesties."

"Name it," the king laughed and Cindra warmed to him immediately.

Cindra took a deep breath, "My father has been lost at sea for many years. The magistrate says he will be declared dead at the end of the month. I know I sound heartless for this... but I need my mother's inheritance. If my father is declared dead before my birthday, I lose it all. I hoped you could sign it over to me... tonight."

The king snapped his fingers for a scribe, "Write down this woman's request and take her name. I'll have the papers ready and in order at the end of the ball." The king smiled as the feast was served.

Cindra had never seen so much food in her life. Winnie's eyes bulged to the plate of grapes set before her. Thessie tried to look bored and disinterested, but Cindra saw her eyeing a nearby pie. There was no talking for most of the first course as many people were more interested in the food.

"Tell me something about yourself," the prince insisted. "What were you doing in the woods so late at night?"

"Perhaps I was there to save you, Your Majesty," Cindra deflected. "I was visiting an old friend of my mother's."

The clock tower tolled just then, announcing the hour was past eleven.

Cindra looked to the prince aghast. "I have to go! I'm sorry, I want to stay." She leaped up and ran for the door, the prince following quickly.

"Wait!"

"I can't. I'm sorry."

The prince caught Cindra on the steps, "If you promise to come back, I'll ask no more questions of this."

Cindra removed one of her shoes and handed it to the prince. "This shoe is designed to fit only me. I'll come back for it."

Cindra climbed into her carriage and urged the horse on at great speed. She made it as far as she could along the wooded paths until the carriage could go no further. From there, she ran to the stone cave, unlocking the portal just before the clock struck midnight.

"That was close," Sloane greeted.

Cindra changed into a smaller dress for her journey back. "The king agreed to have the papers ready tonight. We'll finally be rid of this place."

"You're missing a shoe," Sloane observed.

"I gave it to the prince. He made me promise to return."

"Once the portal unlocks, you can come and go whenever you choose. No more of this mad dash every day. As soon as those papers are signed over and delivered."

Cindra shot to her feet. "No! I never gave my name or address. I've ruined everything."

Sloane nuzzled her gently. "Get it tomorrow when you see the prince again, but hide that slipper. Madame Bourguignon would lose her mind over a diamond shoe."

Cindra rubbed her forehead. "I better get back so Madame Bourguignon isn't suspicious."

Cindra hid the carriage behind the shed and placed the horse back in his stall. The diamond slipper and the orange were carefully tucked away under her petticoat. She slipped into the back door, locking it as she always did. So many years of practice made her quiet as a mouse.

"Well, here you are at last, Cindra. The way you left the ball, I thought you'd be here hours ago." Cindra froze as her stepmother's icy voice drifted through the darkness. Madame Bourguignon lit a lamp and sighed. "You really are an ungrateful creature. After all I've put up with, feeding you, clothing you, keeping a roof over your head, and you steal what is mine?"

"I've stolen nothing. My mother's inheritance is mine." Cindra groaned as her stepmother grabbed her by the hair and dragged her up the stairs.

"You ungrateful creature. You will not leave this room until I have what is mine."

"No--Madame Bourguignon, you can't!" Cindra gasped.

"The prince is coming tomorrow. He's looking for the girl the shoe fits. When he doesn't find you, I will have the fortune I deserve." Madame Bourguignon locked the door as she left. "Perhaps I can get him to marry Thessie. Her feet are almost the same size as yours."

Cindra charged, but only ended up hitting the door with her body. "Let me out! Release me. You can't keep me here like this."

Madame Bourguignon checked the lock and walked away with determined steps.

Cindra spent the rest of the night trying to break down the door or pick the lock. Overcome with exhaustion, she fell asleep just before sunrise.

It was almost noon when she woke, judging by the sunlight streaming through her windows. There was a loud commotion outside. Strangers at the door set Winsome into a state. The voice of the prince floated up.

"I'm looking for the woman who fits this shoe. Does it look familiar to you?"

Cindra hammered on the window with the palm of her hand, but no one seemed to hear her. She looked around for something strong enough to break the glass even as she heard Thessaly pushing her large foot into the tiny dancing slipper.

"The diamond slipper..." Cindra grabbed the other shoe and quickly cut a hole in the window.

"Up here, look up!" Cindra shouted, waving her hand through the window. But the light breeze carried her voice away.

The prince stormed out, and even at the great distance, Cindra could see he was livid.

"You knew this wasn't the woman I was looking for. How dare you waste my time?"

"The shoe looked her size." Madame Bourguignon gave a short charming laugh. "I thought perhaps it would fit."

Cindra reached into her deep pocket and found the orange. She took careful aim and tossed it out.

The small fruit rolled across the roof, down the gutter, through the drainpipe and landed at the prince's feet. Cindra held her breath as the prince examined it. She waved again, watching the prince carefully. He looked up and waved back.

"My lady! It seems I've found you." The prince said something sharp to Madame Bourguignon and waved a paper at her. Madame Bourguignon held her ground.

"My liege, I swear to you, she is nothing. Just a young orphan girl. Barely worthy of scullery work."

"I asked her name. What is her name?" the prince demanded.

"Cindra!" The answer came from Winnie, tucked away in a corner. "Cindra, come here!"

"Cindra? Is that you. my dear?" the prince called. Cindra nodded. "By order of His Majesty, the king, on this day, Cindra shall have the inheritance her mother left for her. And no one may question it." Loud thunder crashed through the cloudless sky as Sloane suddenly flew over the house. Thessaly and Madame Bourguignon screamed and ran inside as the large reptile landed on the roof. She reached one large claw into the window and lifted Cindra onto her back.

"I told you everything would work out," Sloane laughed as she gently placed Cindra on the ground.

"She's a friend; put away your sword." Cindra implored the prince. "It's because of her we have met."

She slipped the diamond shoes on quickly and looked up at Sloane. The prince bowed to the large beast and looked at the pair.

"He's very handsome, Cindra. I can see why you would wish to spend time with him," Sloane winked.

The prince cleared his throat. "Perhaps we should take a walk through the woods and talk?"

Cindra linked her arm in his and looked one last time at her stepfamily, then with the prince on her left and her dear dragon friend on her right, she walked off into her happily ever after.

ANSTICE BROWN

Anstice Brown has had her nose in a book and her head in the clouds for as long as she can remember. A geek/hippie hybrid with a love of all things retro, Anstice enjoys doodling, gaming, and raving about books on her blog, Curious Daydreams. She adores speculative fiction and is currently working on a science fantasy novel.

Anstice has a BA in Literature and Philosophy and currently works as a Literacy Learning Lead in a secondary school. She lives on the East coast of England with her wonderful husband and daughter and their mischievous cat, Magical Mr. Mistoffelees.

Her short story *Sea of Sorrows* appears in the YA romance anthology *Masquerade: Oddly Suited*.

FORGED IN FLAMES

Anstice Brown

*T*he night sky rang with the screams of burning men.

"Fall back, fall back!" Lord Fairmont led his remaining infantry away from the leaping inferno, his armor glinting in the firelight. Arrows glanced off the dragon's tough hide, noxious black smoke furling from her nostrils. She paced in circles, her long claws raking the ground.

"It's no good, sir, she's too strong. Shall I fetch the canons?" The captain wiped his dripping forehead with a bloody sleeve.

"And blast the bounty to smithereens? Fool! Bring the ballista."

"Yes, Lord Commander." The captain sounded his horn.

The dragon snarled and sent another blast of searing flame at them. A young soldier's terrified shrieks were swallowed up by the fireball that engulfed him.

"We have to retreat, sir!"

"No! She won't leave her nest unprotected. This is our chance."

The ballista rumbled to a stop and the engineer loaded the steel bolt and winched back the bowstring.

"Wait for my signal." Fairmont dismounted from his white stallion, swinging a leather pack over his shoulders. He ran forwards with his broadsword pointed right at the creature's belly. The dragon reared up, preparing to scorch him to ash when he screamed, "Fire!" and dropped to his knees. The ballista's bolt sped through the air and the broadhead found its mark, burying itself deep into the dragon's flesh. Dark blood spurted from the gash in her neck and her fiery breath petered into a strangled wheeze. She staggered before collapsing into the blood-soaked ground with a final, shuddering moan.

The soldiers peered through the dancing flames, none daring to utter a word. The silhouette of a man emerged from the billowing smoke coughing and spluttering. His men cheered.

"Retrieve the treasure." The men used ropes and planks to haul the colossal body onto the back of a huge cart. Fairmont wiped his ash-covered face with a silk handkerchief.

"Congratulations, my lord."

He flinched. Bony fingers gripped his shoulder.

"Where did you come from?"

A set of crooked teeth gleamed from under a hood. The hunched figure shuffled over to the cart and inspected the long, shimmering tail with her gnarled fingernails. "Most of the scales are still intact. There is enough here to make almost three bottles of elixir."

"Just three bottles? That won't last more than a few months."

"The teeth and blood are worth—"

"I don't care about coin. What about this?" He opened

the top of his pack to reveal a glint of gold. The old woman cackled.

"The gods were with you tonight, my lord. This prize will bring you a lifetime of glory, but you must act quickly. Bury it in the scorched earth and before morn, you shall possess the greatest treasure in all the kingdoms of Astrador." She glanced at the soldiers at the front of the cart. "None can know of this."

"Very well." Fairmont drew his blade and crept behind his men. He slashed and stabbed at their necks, their startled yelps dissolving into splutters and gurgles.

"What are you—" The captain's sword clashed against Fairmont's and he forced him backward, his eyes wide. He parried each blow until the sorceress swept behind him and he froze. His weapon clattered to the ground. She thrust her long talons into his ears until his round, glassy eyes gushed red. A murder of ravens scattered skyward, shrieking.

"He won't remember a thing." The crone's lips curled at the corners. "But that will cost you extra."

ON THE THIRTEENTH DAY, YASMINE AND VIOLETTE STOPPED crying. Zella refused to shed a single tear. If she cried, he was truly gone.

Her mother spooned oatmeal into her mouth, staring ahead at nothing in particular. Zella rose from the edge of the bed.

"I'll ask Lord Fairmont to call another day."

Yasmine's head snapped toward her, the spark in her eyes reignited.

"Oh no, you won't." She snapped her fingers at the dressing table and Zella hurried to fetch her robe.

"We're not ready for company, Ma." She draped the robe across her mother's shoulders. "Don't you think—"

"We need this, Zella. Now more than ever." Yasmine swung her legs out of the bed and teetered to her feet. She scrutinized her daughter's stained shirt, torn breeches, and bruised knees. Her nose crinkled. "He can't see you like that. You'll spoil your sister's chances."

Zella bristled. It would be scandalous for a nobleman to see her in something so immodest, but Ma didn't have to be so blunt. Her mother rifled through the armoire then thrust a black gown at her.

"You can wear this. Violette will wear the best satin."

Zella examined the fraying lacework adorning the bodice.

"Don't make that face, Zella. It's the only mourning gown that will fit you."

She gritted her teeth and dressed herself in the miserable shroud. This was all for Violette. She was staring at the gaunt stranger in the mirror when Violette returned from the yard with a bucket of goatmilk.

"You look beautiful, Zella. I'd best change too. Can you give me a hand?"

"Of course."

Zella tightened the satin bodice and unpinned her sister's brunette curls while Violette twittered away in her sing-song voice. The sisters looked nothing alike. Violette had inherited her mother's olive skin, rosebud lips, and captivating hazel eyes. Zella's pale complexion and androgynous features were plain by comparison.

Once Violette was preened to perfection, she insisted on braiding Zella's blonde tangles.

"For goodness sake, Zella. Your hair is like a nest of

serpents." The brush snagged on a knot at the nape of her neck.

"Ouch!"

"Keep still!" She yanked Zella's head backward. "Oh, I'm sorry. My nerves are getting the better of me. Everything is riding on today. It has to be perfect."

"You are perfect, Vi. And if Lord Fancy Britches doesn't think so, he's a fool."

"A fool with the power to save us or let us starve. How can you—"

A sharp rap at the door silenced her sister's admonitions. The sisters hastily arranged themselves on either side of their mother before Yasmine opened the door and a tall, striking figure loomed over them.

"Sir Louis Theodore Fairmont." The nobleman removed his feathered hat and swept into a low bow. "Dear Madame Bellefleur, how gracious of you to extend an invitation to me at such a tragic time. May I offer my deepest condolences. Your husband was a well-respected member of our community."

"Lord Fairmont," Yasmine dropped into a low curtsey. "What an honor it is to receive you. Please come in."

Fairmont strode over the threshold, his muddy boots splattering the polished floor.

"I'm sure you remember my eldest daughter, Violette." Violette curtseyed and offered her hand, which Fairmont brushed against his full lips.

"Charmed, my lady."

"May I formally introduce my youngest, Arizella." Fairmont's gaze traveled from the hem of Zella's dress and lingered at the tight bodice. She wished she'd remembered her shawl.

"Mademoiselle Bellefleur, you were but a child when we

last met, but you have bloomed into a rare and radiant flower. May I?" Zella offered her hand and he swept it to his lips with a dramatic flourish. Her face flushed. This wasn't the squat and unattractive man she remembered. How had she missed those cornflower blue eyes?

"Please allow me to show you to the sitting room." They proceeded into the modest lounge and Zella prepared the tea while her mother and sister made unbearable small talk.

She returned with a steaming teapot and their finest china.

"How have the raids been going, my lord?"

"Tremendously well, Madame Bellefleur. We managed to slay another Razortooth only yesterday."

Zella slammed the tea tray down. "And how many men did you lose?" She took a seat next to her mother, ignoring Violette's warning glance.

"Far too many, I'm afraid. It pains me that every day more families like yours are torn apart. But valiant men such as your father will be remembered forever as the heroes that helped to bring peace to Astrador."

"Really? We can't even afford a proper burial." Her mother's nails dug into her wrist. Lord Fairmont clenched his chiseled jaw.

"Leave it to me. I will see to it that your father is buried in the finest tomb imaginable."

"How kind of you." There was an awkward silence while Zella poured four cups of tea. "Of course, I'd rather no more men had to die for your cause."

"Zella!" Yasmine clapped a hand over her mouth.

"No, no, let her speak. I am curious to hear how she thinks she can save the town from dragon fire without an army." Fairmont folded his arms and leaned back in her father's chair. Zella steamed ahead, her words rushing out in one breath.

"Forgive me for speaking out of turn, but the attacks are almost daily now. The more you hunt the dragons, the fiercer they retaliate. The papers I've read from the Yeona in the North suggest that humans and dragons can coexist peacefully if we only make space for them. Perhaps if we stopped raiding their nesting grounds, they would simply leave us be."

Fairmont ran a hand through his fair curls and snorted.

"Leave us be? These are savage predators we are talking about, mademoiselle. The beasts won't stop until the town is reduced to ash. Is that what you want?" Zella opened her mouth to retort but her mother stamped hard upon her foot with the heel of her boot. She grimaced.

"I'm sorry if I offended you...my lord," she said through gritted teeth.

A rueful expression played across Fairmont's lips. "Not at all, Mademoiselle Bellefleur. Your naivety is most endearing." Zella balled her hands into fists between the folds of her gown. "The fairer sex is given to see virtue and beauty in even the dumbest and most brutish of creatures."

Not all of them, Zella thought.

"Madame Bellefleur, I understand that your family is going through a difficult time, so I will overlook your daughter's impropriety. I arranged this meeting to discuss your family's prospects and I am still willing to assist you."

"Thank you, Lord Fairmont. You are too gracious," Yasmine simpered.

"I am here to ask for your daughter's hand in marriage."

Violette beamed and their mother clapped her hands together, her face awash with relief.

"Why, of course, my Lord. What an honor! This is too wonderful. Violette has a modest dowry prepared—"

"No, not Violette. Arizella." Violette's face fell. Zella's heart pounding against the bars of her ribcage.

"I beg your pardon, sir, but Violette is the eldest."

"Forgive me, madame, but it is Arizella's exquisite beauty that has captured my heart. She is of age, is she not?"

"Yes, but—"

"I can't," Zella stood up and Fairmont mirrored her.

"What?"

"I mean, I won't. I won't marry you. I'm flattered, but no. No, thank you."

"Zella isn't exactly suited for marriage, my lord."

"No dowry is necessary, madame. I can offer you all lodgings at Fairmont Court and will arrange a suitable husband for Violette. I will also make a generous donation to your family purse. You will not want for anything under my care, you have my word."

"I'm not for sale."

"Please forgive my daughter. She was extremely close to her father and these last two weeks have taken its toll. We would gladly accept your offer."

"No apology necessary. Indeed, grief affects us all in strange ways."

A droning hum resounded through the house, turning her blood to ice water. Not again. Violette and Yasmine clung to each other.

"Forgive me, I must take my leave of you."

"Of course!"

Fairmont dashed to the front door. "I shall return on Wednesday at noon with a coach for you and your belongings. Farewell, madame, mademoiselles." He strode out into the rain and mounted his horse. Zella scanned the skies for signs of the approaching danger. Perhaps it was a false alarm. No. A black, winged shadow swept low over the hills.

"Don't be afraid, we'll bring down the monster!" He charged off for the hills, flanked by half a dozen cavalry.

"I hope that dragon tears him apart."

"Zella!"

Cannons thundered in the distance. She untied the goat from her tether and patted her round belly. "Come on, girl. It's not safe out here." She tucked the goat safely away in the barn then returned to the sitting room.

"Where's Violette?"

"In the bedroom. Leave her be for a while."

The warning hall blared on while they tidied away the tea things, then ceased abruptly.

Yasmine peered through the kitchen curtains. "Do you think they got it?"

"I hope not. The poor thing was probably only after a sheep or two to feed its young."

"How can you sympathize with them after what happened to your father?"

"They're only trying to survive, just like us. I don't blame them for Pa's death. If Fairmont hadn't drafted him into service..."

Yasmine let out a strangled sob and reached for a bottle from the shelf. She uncorked it and took several indelicate gulps.

Zella prepared the dinner in silence.

"Violette, are you coming to eat?" There was no reply. Zella sighed and ladled the broth into two bowls. She sat opposite her mother and stirred the broth round and round before taking a sip. The fresh vegetables and tender chicken breast tasted bitter in her mouth. She put down her spoon.

"This isn't fair, Ma. Violette should marry Lord Fairmont, not me."

Yasmine took another swig of ale. "I know things didn't work out as we expected, but we have to seize this opportunity. Without his money and protection, I dread to think what would become of us."

"We don't need him. You could make and sell your remedies again and Violette could join the seamstress' guild. We can manage."

"And what will you do? Open a dragon sanctuary, perhaps?"

"I could run the forge."

"Don't be ridiculous, Zella. Whoever heard of a maiden blacksmith?"

"I don't care what people think. Pa taught me everything I need to know. I'm an excellent welder. I could repair armor and weapons for the king's guard."

"You could, if you'd been born with more between your legs and less between your ears. You know that's not how the world works. Lord Fairmont is rich and handsome at least, you should count your blessings."

"But I could never love him, Ma."

Yasmine clanked the bottle down. "What's love got to do with it? You're not the first woman in the world to marry out of duty, Zella. Things could be a lot worse."

Zella put her head in her hands and rubbed her temples. She forced down a few more spoonful's of cold broth. She was selfish, worrying about her plight when Violette's dreams had been dashed.

After washing the dishes, she crept into the bedroom. The lights were out.

"Vi?" She undressed in the dark and slipped between the icy sheets.

"Vi, I know you're cross with me. I'm sorry, but I didn't ask for this happen. This is the last thing—" She choked back a sob, a wave of emptiness and despair threatening to drown her.

Violette's voice cut through the darkness, "Don't."

Zella rolled onto her side and the tears rolled down her cheeks, soaking her pillow. Neither of them said another word.

ZELLA AWOKE BEFORE DAWN, HER STOMACH CHURNING. SHE kept herself busy with the chores for most of the day, but after enduring a silent lunch with her family, the four walls of their cottage were closing in. She pulled on her clothes, swung a basket over her arm, and slipped out the back door.

She headed into Shadowmist Forest to collect wild mushrooms. She would make Violette's favorite soup for dinner. That ought to soften her a little.

Zella stepped over roots and animal burrows, weaving her way between the gnarled trunks of ancient oak trees. The woods were her sanctuary, far away from the bustle of the town center with no one except birds and scurrying critters to pass judgment on her. How often would Lord Fairmont let her wander outdoors on her own? After tomorrow, she'd be bound to the hearth and the marriage bed.

She bent down to gather a handful of mushrooms. A haunting whine echoed through the trees then sank into a guttural moan. A wounded animal, or perhaps even a woman in the throes of childbirth. Whatever it was, it was in terrible pain. She picked her way through the forest toward the otherworldly cry, which oscillated like a twisted version of whalesong.

She stumbled through a prickle of briars and her basket tumbled into the grass. A sturdy tower loomed above her, its spire hidden by the dense foliage. She searched for a door, but there was only a single window at the top. She circled the tower, running her hands along the brickwork. Her fingers found a rough seam where the stone jutted out. Someone had bricked up the entrance long ago.

A twig snapped and she ducked back into the trees instinctively. Lord Fairmont galloped into the clearing. What was he doing here? He rode to the base of the tower and shouted up to the window.

"Let down your tail, magnificent beast, that I may climb and you may feast."

The caterwauling ceased and a glistening tail slithered down the tower like a giant serpent, its tip almost reaching the ground. It had to belong to a dragon, but she'd never seen one with metallic scales before. Aurelian Leatherwings were rumored to have golden hides, but they were extremely rare.

Fairmont rubbed his hands together and hoisted himself up as if the tail were a rope. When he reached the window, he swung his legs inside. She could make out Fairmont's muffled voice, followed by ripping and squelching sounds. Perhaps the dragon had grown tired of small talk and decided to sink its teeth into Fairmont's flesh. If only.

The creature let out a panicked shriek and Zella flinched, retreating into the underbrush. After minutes of agonized wailing, the dragon's tail flopped out of the window. It was red raw and dripping with blood, many of its beautiful scales scraped away. Fairmont lowered himself to the ground and the tail coiled back up into the window.

She didn't notice the hooded figure emerge from the shadows. Fairmont placed a vial of blood and a handful of shiny flakes into her withered palm. Zella brushed a spiderweb from her face and crept as close as she dared, straining to hear their conversation.

"How long until the next batch is ready?"

"After the next full moon, my lord. I'm afraid that's the best I can do."

Fairmont thrust a drawstring purse at her, which she enveloped in the folds of her cloak.

"Tomorrow afternoon."

"Perfect. Tomorrow night, I take my bride. Tell me, wise woman, will she give me an heir?"

The sorceress clasped Fairmont's hand in hers and closed her eyes.

"The blacksmith's daughter will bear glorious fruit, but only from the seeds of love."

"What is that supposed to mean?"

"She sees through your glamor. Her soul will wither away in a loveless marriage, and with it, the destiny that I promised."

"Then make the potion stronger. I wish her to truly belong to me; not just in name, but in heart and soul."

"Then a potion is no good to you. A spell that strong requires a blood sacrifice. A heart for a heart."

Fairmont tugged at his collar. "Whose?"

"You must slay the dragon and bring the heart to me. I will perform the ritual on your wedding night to ensure that your bride is forever besotted with you, and you alone."

"Excellent. The deed will be done before dawn."

The sorceress coughed. "I don't believe in charity."

"Of course, name your price."

"I desire Oakwind Court."

"That estate has been in my family for generations."

"Then you must find another bride. Perhaps one of the lovely noblewomen bewitched by your façade?"

"No, no, I must have her. The moment I laid eyes on her lustrous hair, I knew she must be mine. It's been agony waiting for her to come of age. I didn't go to the trouble of dispatching her father for nothing."

Zella sucked in a sharp breath and the witch's eyes locked on the trees beside her. She shuffled backward. She couldn't hear what they were saying now. It didn't matter. She tasted bile in the back of her throat.

She sprinted through the forest, her shirt snagging on low branches and bile rising in her throat. When she reached the dirt road, she doubled up and retched against a tree stump. Though the idea of marrying that pantomime villain had horrified her yesterday, she would have endured it for her family's sake. But to lose her heart and soul to Pa's killer was unthinkable.

Zella raced home, white-hot tears blurring her vision. She nearly bowled Violette over at the front gate, flinging her arms around her and wailing.

"Zella! What...?"

"Fairmont killed Pa!"

"What are you talking about?"

"He murdered him so he could marry me. I overheard him admit it." The color drained from Violette's face.

"No! It can't be true. Pa was killed defending the town."

"Fairmont used the dragon attack as a cover. There were no witnesses, remember?"

"I...I don't understand."

"Pa loathed Fairmont. He would never have let either of us be bullied into marriage, no matter how desperate our situation. Fairmont wanted me to think I had no choice."

Violette shook her head. "Poor Pa. I can't believe I let Fairmont pull the wool over my eyes. I was so angry at you for spoiling my chances. I'm sorry, Zella."

"It's not your fault. He's been taking a potion made of Aurelian Leatherwing scales to make himself appear handsome and charming. It's all a glamour."

"Aurelians? I thought those were myths."

"I saw the poor thing myself, golden scales and all."

"What? Where?"

"He has it locked in a tower in the middle of the forest. That's not the worst of it. His sorceress plans to use the dragon's heart to bewitch me into loving him. If that happens..."

"We can't let it happen."

"What can we do? Report him to the authorities?"

"We can't prove he killed Pa? No one will believe us without evidence."

"I could show them where he's keeping the dragon. Maybe they can get the truth out of the sorceress who brews his potions."

"It's not illegal to capture a dragon. And Fairmont would probably have her tried for witchcraft before she could betray him." Violette cupped her sister's chin in her hands. "You must run away."

"I can't leave you and Ma."

"We'll survive, Zella. What you said to Ma was right. We can take care of ourselves. Fairmont is dangerous. We have to make him believe you're dead."

"What?"

"He'll never stop searching for you otherwise. You must flee tonight. I'll plant your clothing at Ophelia Falls, make it look like you drowned yourself. You can escape in the opposite direction, though Shadowmist Forest and up into the mountains."

"And then what?"

"It's only about a week's hike to the Yeona settlement. I know you can make it."

"But what about you?"

"I'll be fine, but we can't tell Ma any of this. It's safer for her if she doesn't know."

Zella nodded, tears welling in her eyes.

"I'll help you pack while she's resting."

Violette stuffed Zella's clothes into their father's satchel, then snuck into the larder to find some supplies. Zella headed outside to the forge. She breathed in the familiar scent of rusted iron and coal dust and for a moment she could hear the whoosh of the bellows and the clang of the anvil as Pa taught her how to draw, shrink and bend the metal. She wandered between the workbenches, pocketing tools that would come in handy for her journey: a hammer, chisel, and pocket knife.

The gleam of a steel blade illuminated in the afternoon sun caught her attention. The last sword Pa ever made. She slipped it down from the hook and ran her finger along the smooth, cold metal. The gilded hilt was inscribed with the weapon's moniker: Chrysaor. Before she could stop herself, she grabbed the top of her plait and cut through it with one swift slash. Her locks landed in a coil on the floor. She kicked the plait under the workbench and sheathed the blade, tucking it into her belt.

Violette met her in the garden and handed her a loaf of homemade bread, a pouch of goat's milk and a ham wrapped in cloth.

"Thank you, Vi." She stowed the food in her satchel with the tools and slung it over her shoulder then shook her head, relishing the cool breeze on the back of her neck.

"What?"

"You look like...you. I approve."

The sky glowed orange and soon the forest would become dark and treacherous.

"I can't."

Violette stroked her cheek. "You can, Zella. You're a Bellefleur, and we are survivors. Don't you worry about me and Ma." She squeezed her sister, then nudged her firmly. "Now, go and be who you were meant to be."

Zella said nothing. She turned away from her sister, away from the cottage and away from everything she ever knew. Without glancing back, she ran.

HER CALVES BURNED AS SHE TRIED TO OUTRUN THE encroaching darkness. Once night fell, it would be easy to lose her way in the dense undergrowth. Once clear of the forest, she could fill her skein at the river and camp at the base of the mountains until morning.

She stopped to rest against a tree, panting. Their dragon's tortured wail gnawed at her conscience. At least it would soon be put out of its misery. Her stomach twisted. To return to that tower would be beyond foolish, it would be nothing short of madness. She must have lost her mind then, for her legs carried her back to the tower against her better judgment.

She stared up at the window. "Hello?"

The dragon fell silent. What had Fairmont said? "Let down your tail... magnificent beast, that I may climb...and you may feast." The dragon didn't stir. It was for the best. It was none of her business what Fairmont did with the creature and she had no desire to become its supper.

The tail descended and Zella gasped. The swelling and blood had vanished, leaving no evidence of Fairmont's torture. She brushed her fingertips against the gleaming scales and the dragon flinched at her touch. She jumped up and wrapped her legs around it. The dragon heaved her up and the ground receded. Golden sparkles danced in front of her eyes and she forced herself to fix them on the window. When she reached the top, she grasped the stone sill and hauled herself inside, tumbling onto the wooden floor.

The tail snaked itself around its owner, an immense yellow dragon wrapped in a tangle of chains, tethered to the floor with a metal stake. A leather harness bound its enormous wings and its strong jaws were locked in an iron muzzle. It strained against the chains, amber eyes wide and fearful.

"It's all right, boy," she made an educated guess based on the dark frill around his neck. "I'm not going to hurt you." The dragon snorted and a shower of sparks flew from his nostrils. She stamped them out with her boots. "I don't blame you. I wouldn't trust me either. You must be terrified of humans after how you've been treated. I'm not like him, I promise. I want to help you."

"Let down your tail, magnificent beast!"

Zella's stomach lurched. What had she done?

"That I may climb and you may feast."

The dragon narrowed his eyes.

"Don't let him up," she whispered. "Please. Trust me." The dragon twitched the end of his tail.

"I'm waiting!" Fairmont bellowed. "Let me up, beast! Or perhaps you'd rather starve to death?"

The dragon pricked up his ears but Zella shook her head. "Ignore him. We're safe up here. I won't let him hurt you again."

"Dragon! Let down your tail at once, I command you! This is your last chance!" He was met with silence. "Fine! I'll make my own way up. Make the most of your last precious moments." The sound of galloping hooves faded into the distance.

"I think he's gone, but we must hurry." She unsheathed her sword and approached the dragon. He snarled and gnashed his teeth against the muzzle, his throat glowing like embers. "Don't be afraid," she said, unsure of the words were meant for the dragon or herself. "I'm going to get you out of here."

She reached forward and grabbed a loose chain from across the dragon's back, raising her sword. The dragon flinched. She swung the blade at the weak spot where two links joined. The chain snapped and slithered to the floor. The dragon strained to stand, still bound fast. He whimpered impatiently.

The hammering of hooves against damp earth filled her ears. Fairmont had brought company. Something heavy rumbled across the ground toward them.

"Now!"

An ear-splitting boom rocked the tower. Zella stumbled, crashing into the dragon's belly.

"Again!" Fairmont roared and something crashed into the base of the tower once again.

"Does he want the whole tower to crumble?" One by one, she destroyed the chains and the dragon clambered to his feet. He paced up and down, his talons rapping against the floorboards while the tower juddered again and again. When the last chain clattered to the floor, the dragon rose onto his hind legs and Zella backed against the wall to avoid being flattened.

"Easy, easy! Hold still. I need to reach your wings."

The dragon lowered himself down as she unbuckled the harness that bound him. It slid to the floor and the dragon unfolded his crinkled, iridescent wings. He screeched and flapped wildly, forcing Zella to duck for cover. The worst quake yet rocked the tower with a thunderous crash. Fairmont and his men cheered and clattering footfall reverberated against stone.

Zella grabbed the hammer and chisel from her bag and reached for the dragon's muzzle. He hissed at her and shrank back.

"Come on," she extended a shaky hand and he sniffed it tentatively. "That's right. Now, hold still." She fumbled with the padlock with shaking hands. Sweat dripped from her cropped hair.

Fairmont burst through the door flanked by two of his men, his mouth falling open.

"You! What is the meaning of this?"

The padlock cracked open and the dragon drew up to his full height, letting out a triumphant roar.

Fairmont held up his hands and retreated into the doorway, signaling for his men to back up.

"Arizella, my love. What are you doing with my dragon?"

"He's not your dragon!" Zella spat. "And I will never be your love."

"We'll see about that." Fairmont lurched forward, brandishing his broadsword. "I raised this dragon from a hatchling. I've trained it to obey my every command. Now, come to me, my little fawn, before you hurt yourself."

"You disgust me."

He smirked and held a hand to his heart. "Your words cut me to the quick. So, you saw through my glamor and couldn't bring yourself to marry such an ugly brute, eh? How dreadfully shallow."

"It's not your appearance that repulses me, it's your cruel heart! You killed my father!"

"What a fanciful imagination you possess, Mademoiselle Bellefleur. A dragon just like this one incinerated your father. It was a tragedy."

"Liar!"

"It doesn't matter. You'll soon be mine. Now get out of my way."

He pushed Zella aside and thrust his blade at the dragon's chest, missing by inches. A puff of steam rose from the dragon's nostrils. Zella snatched up Chrysaor and met Fairmont's blade with her own. She struggled against him, but Fairmont overpowered her easily, forcing her to the floor.

The dragon snarled and the frill around his neck flared into a dark halo. He belched a stream of fire at Fairmont, who leaped out of the way. The wooden floorboards were set alight and a blistering inferno ate its way toward them.

"Fairmont, get out of here! Look around you. This is madness!"

"This is your doing, not mine. You had to meddle in business you don't understand. In a moment, I will have that beast's heart, and then I'll have yours too!"

Fairmont hurled himself across the gap in the burnt floor, his eyes gleaming yellow in the firelight. He pierced the dragon's shoulder with the tip of his sword. Fairmont cowered behind his shield before the dragon howled and ignited the floor around him. He rolled out of the way and stabbed at the dragon again, slicing into Zella's forearm as she tried to fend him off.

They backed up against the window. Hungry flames licked at Zella's boots. She clambered up onto the dragon's back, her arm throbbing and dripping blood. The dragon bristled, but didn't buck her off. He leaped onto the stone window ledge, braced like a cat about to pounce.

The crackling blaze threatened to devour Fairmont.

"Climb on!" He reached for the dragon's hide but he snapped at him and shuffled to the edge of the window ledge. Zella leaned forwards and wrapped her arms around his neck.

"Are you sure you know how to fly?"

The dragon decided there was only one way to find out. He leaped out of the window and they plummeted downwards headfirst. Zella squeezed her eyes shut, bracing for impact. None came. She opened her eyes and found herself hurtling upwards. Zella clung on with all her strength. A strangled cry followed by a sickening thud tempted her to risk a glance at the ground. Fairmont's crumpled body lay face down in the mud. His men raced forwards to help before realizing it was too late and pointing their weapons skywards.

But they were already beyond the reach of arrows, swooping through wispy clouds. Soothing liquid sizzled against her wounded arm and the pain evaporated. The dragon's eyes sparkled with tears. She buried her face into his frill.

"Thank you, friend."

The dragon beat his resplendent wings and together they flew beyond the horizon.

DENISE RUTTAN

Denise Ruttan is a writer, editor, photographer and legal assistant based in Corvallis, Oregon. She holds a BA in creative writing from Eckerd College and is turning full circle back to fiction after a seven-year career in small town newspaper journalism. She has been previously published in Danse Macabre's DM Du Jour. She blogs at dnruttan.com.

In her spare time she enjoys knitting, playing flute, is learning guitar, and yoga. Her fiction is mostly speculative but also covers themes of crime, historical, and contemporary.

Above all else, she is interested in exploring the human condition and what circumstances make us change.

Find her on Twitter at PassageofSpace and on Instagram at quillandlens.

DRAGON GIRL

Denise Ruttan

*I*n the darkness of the courtyard, the guard Tomlinson tightened his grip on the hilt of his sword. The noises of rustling fabric and softly padding feet roused him from deep thought. Alert, now, to the possibility of danger, he studied the shadowy shapes of the rhododendron bushes and onyx flowers. Carthan honor guards were renowned for their finely attuned senses and Tomlinson was no exception to this reputation. But this was a dull post, and it was easy to grow complacent. He freed the cobwebs from his brain as every muscle tensed.

Then Tomlinson made out the figure of Queen Anne in the shadows, and the stiffness immediately melted away. Queen Anne, an insomniac whom Tomlinson suspected was often kept up late by her worries about her kingdom, often took to the courtyard for nightly strolls. She was a fiercely protective queen, a true Queen Mother. She preached to her subjects and to her command post the imminence of war and the importance of battle-ready posture. Cartha had witnessed a century of peace since its last fierce conflicts, but Tomlinson believed her with a bright sense of pride. He imagined she must stay awake at night, lying in bed, fragile in her white shift, dreaming of blood and death. He wondered if it was difficult to rule a kingdom as a female without a man to guide her. Still, his loyalty to his Queen Mother was unwavering.

Tonight, however, Tomlinson was sure it was not her duties as queen that kept Queen Anne up tonight, but her duties as a mother. Her only daughter, Katharine, known to everyone as Kit, was saying goodbye to her home and her family this week. Princess Kit was getting ready to embark on a long journey to marry a prince in a far-off land. These could be the last few days that Queen Anne ever spent with her only daughter.

Tomlinson watched her pace the courtyard. She seemed lost in thought, her long, thick braid of blonde hair descending down one slender shoulder, the frizz fraying at the edges like wisps of ghosts. He never disturbed the Queen on her nightly strolls; it would be unseemly for a guard to talk to a queen for anything but an inspection of the regiment. If he could talk to her, he would say a comforting word, perhaps put a hand on her shoulder, perhaps tell her of the wedding day of his own daughter, Yaris.

Queen Anne sat on a bench and stared to the side for a moment, a flinty look of resolve hardening her eyes. The queen took off her sandals, so that her bare feet shone white in the moonlight. Tomlinson would be lying if he claimed his pulse didn't quicken. He looked away.

But then the queen slid a knife from a holster on her leg, and Tomlinson returned his gaze to her. It was a long, thick blade, worthy of a warrior. Tomlinson couldn't help but look. In one swift motion, the queen sliced her fingers with a knife, carving blood from skin. Queen Anne's face remained remarkably placid. Tomlinson winced, ready to come to her aid, but something told him to wait, some instinct.

Then the queen squeezed her fingers, causing the blood to drip onto a lacy handkerchief, staining the delicate fabric. She took a bandage and wrapped her hand with the dexterity of a wartime nurse. Then she returned the knife to its sheath on her leg, put the bloody handkerchief in a clear bag, and slipped the bag into her pocket.

In the darkness, then, her bright eyes met Tomlinson's, and she knew that he had been watching when he should have turned away. Nerves tightened his throat. But she smiled and put a finger to her lips, as her hazel-brown eyes gleamed in the darkness, matching his. They now shared a secret.

Then she fled the courtyard, as if she had never been there. The insects buzzed again, breaking the stillness. Tomlinson's heart pounded.

There were rumors that Queen Anne was really a witch.

For the first time, Tomlinson wondered if the rumors were true.

HER WHOLE BODY WAS STREAKED WITH SWEAT AS PRINCESS Kit tried to get her breath under control. She smiled at Caleb, the chief honor guard, who had spent the last couple hours sparring with her. Caleb had always shown a special interest in Princess Kit's training, as much as her Queen Mother would have preferred Kit learned to cross stitch delicate patterns and play beautiful piano sonatas instead.

Kit's unruly brown hair was plastered close to her head in tight, elaborate braids. It was the compromise Kit had made with her mother - she wouldn't cut her hair short if she could still pull it back like this. Height-wise, she was a little over five feet tall, with a slender, petite figure. Fighting made her feel strong, empowered, not just a grown-up little girl inside a fragile body. Right now, for instance, confidence and adrenaline coursed through her veins as she breathed hard. Today she wore a simple black tunic, grey tights and ankle-high boots. The dust from the arena rose in clouds around their feet, making her eyes sting.

"Nice form today, princess," Caleb said. "Just think about working on what we talked about, and you're getting there."

He knew she was leaving, too, but he had adopted Princess Kit's attitude about the whole thing. Maybe if she ignored her imminent departure, she wouldn't have to leave.

"Thanks, chief." Her mother might refer to the guards by their given names, but Kit felt it disrespectful to gloss over their titles. He didn't have to spend so much time with her, even if she was a princess.

Today was a warm spring day in the middle of the week. Only a couple of days left before the departure ceremony. The flush of heat added weight to her sweat. Kit knew she was supposed to pack for her travels, but she felt childish about having to leave this place, the only home she had ever known, to go marry some prince. She was in the same mood she'd been in when she was ten and her mother said she was too young for dragons; that she should play with blocks with the nursemaid instead, or sit beside her mother and learn to sew. So, Kit had run to the dragon stalls without her mother's knowledge, and talked to the dragons in secret at night. She befriended the dragon guards and the servants who kept watch over them and eventually, bringing the dragons raw hamburger meat from the kitchen turned into training them.

Kit still didn't know how to cross stitch or sew or play the piano. She didn't know how to keep a house, manage servants or to cook. But she could fight, and she could train and ride dragons. That was what mattered, in the end. And anyway, nothing happened on the palace grounds without the Queen Mother's approval, as much as Kit had thought she was getting away with a secret, back then.

Kit grabbed a towel from the hallway leading into the arena, where, during gladiator games, warriors would gather to wait to fight while they announced the roster to thundering cheers. She wiped her face, the scratchy towel coming away with dark grime, and tossed it into a laundry bin hanging from the wall. As she left the arena, a servant handed her a glass of water, which she glopped down and handed back with thanks.

The dragon stalls, in fact, were her next destination. Maybe she could use a shower, but she still had to say hello to Falada. As she handed the water glass back to the servant, she thought the servant wrinkled her nose at her. Kit grinned. Maybe another royal would see that as impudent, but she didn't care. She stunk, after all.

Leaving the arena, Kit was immediately assaulted by the noises of market day on the palace grounds. Warmth rose in her chest that was something other than the spring weather as she saw the farmers' stalls lined up in neat rows and the crowds of people milling around. Queen Anne could have kept her palace grounds closed and private at all times, but she liked to be a queen for the people. She liked to invite them in. Once a week during the spring and summer seasons, the farmers from around the valley came here to sell their wares. At this time of year there was not much produce, but there was fresh sourdough bread, anjave fruit, meat, and animals for sale, as well as artisan crafts, jewelry, baskets and needlework.

Goats and sheep meandered in the dust as minstrels played lively tunes on their yama pianos, trumpets and drums.

Dressed like this, sweaty and nasty from sparring and wearing only a simple tunic, Princess Kit could slink through this boisterous crowd without anyone knowing her. In any other event like this, a sighting of a princess would have caused everyone in the crowd to grow silent and bend a knee as she passed. She was glad for the lack of recognition; she didn't need that kind of attention. Some days she wanted to pretend she was not a princess. She really wanted to be a dragon honor guard. But even if she were not a princess, women could not become honor guards, based on an old law. In wartime, or so the stories foretold, women had to stay home and raise babies, while the men had all the fun.

Grimacing, Kit made her way through the crowd, trying not to bump into anyone. She passed goats and cats and stalls full of trinkets, where artists called to her, "A pretty bracelet for a pretty lady? I give you a good deal."

Soon enough, she had pawed her way free of the crowd and made her way on down to the dragon stalls. She found her heart racing, and it wasn't just from her recent physical exertion. Crowds like that always bothered her. The crush of people, tightening like a noose around her neck. They made her want to hide. There was always, always a chance that she would be recognized, and today she got lucky. Her mother would go apoplectic if she knew Kit had been to market day without a guard in tow. But she had gotten in and out, and nothing had happened.

Kit paused outside the dragon stalls to collect herself, standing with her back against the wall. She breathed slowly, working on the breathing exercises that one of the dragon trainers had shown her. A dragon can always sense your fear and your anxiety, he had told her. A dragon always knows your pain. You can't ride a dragon with that demeanor and have it respect you.

She sank to her haunches, flopping her arms over her knees, and let the pause linger. Moments like this, moments to herself, were moments she lived for. But they were usually moments fraught with doubt, flush with sweaty palms, racing heart, the headache crawling at her temples and the fire rumbling in her belly.

As she sat there, she saw two servants pass by. They were talking and laughing, gossiping as servants do. One was a chambermaid, a new one; Kit couldn't remember her name. She was talking to one of the stable hands. The chambermaid's hair was short, her curly blonde hair cropped close to her head, and she wore the standard black cap and black and white uniform with ruffled sleeves of servants assigned to menial tasks. The stable hand wore a simple white tunic and black pants, also the standard uniform for her station, but her dark hair was long, tied back in a ponytail. Kit envied the chambermaid's haircut, and hated herself for the thought.

"Did you hear my new assignment? You won't believe it," the chambermaid said, her voice breathless and tinged with rage.

"No, tell me," the other servant said, eagerly conspiratorial.

Kit noticed how the other girl hung on the chambermaid's every word, as if she couldn't wait to report back the gossip to her real friends.

"I'm to ride with Princess Kit in three days' time," the chambermaid said. "I suppose it's because I can ride, but I don't know why they picked me at all. I'm just a chambermaid, and I'm new, at that."

"No, you're not serious," the servant gushed. "What an honor! You should be proud. Aren't you proud?"

"Not in the least," the chambermaid said. "I don't know much about this palace yet, but I don't like that girl. She might as well be a boy, the way she's always fighting with the chief guard and hanging around the dragon stalls. She has no manners. She seems rude and full of herself. Can you imagine spending a month with her, on the road? What a nightmare!"

"Come on now," the other servant said, stifling a nervous giggle. "Don't talk like that. She's not so bad. I don't think I'd want to be a princess either. All that curtseying and piano playing and all those rules, you know. Would you want to be married off to a prince you've never met?"

"It's just selfish," the chambermaid said, her voice hot with indignation. "If I had that kind of power, I wouldn't want to waste it, that's all. Come on, let's go. We have chores to do. We're not princesses after all."

The other servant's nervous giggle turned into an honest laugh as they linked arms and left the dragon stables, disappearing into the market crowd. They never noticed Kit. The chambermaid stole a glance over her shoulder, and she met Princess Kit's eyes. It was a startled, swift look, but then her stare firmed into a neutral expression.

Kit's eyes smarted. And not because of the dust this time.

A SERVANT BRUSHED KIT'S HAIR AFTER UNDOING THE complicated braids that flattened it to her head for sparring practice. The ivory brush tore through the frizzy snarls of Kit's mop of unruly hair, and she tried not to wince. She was not a little girl who cried when her hair was brushed anymore, so that only her mother could brush it.

Now, her mother left her cross stitching on her chair and put a hand on the servant's shoulder. "You may go, Mabel," Queen Anne said in an imposing voice. It was a voice that reminded Kit of her childhood, when she was afraid of everything, including her mother, the queen. "I will take it from here."

Queen Anne's hands were gentle as they ran through Kit's hair, massaging her scalp. Her head still itched at times these days, like it had when she was little. When Kit's mother worked the brush through her hair, however, it was with forceful motions.

"We need to talk about your impending departure," Queen Anne said, the firmness still in her tone. Kit fought disappointment. "You can't avoid it forever."

"Yes I can!" Kit said petulantly, feeling childish even as she said it. "You don't have to make me go!"

"Not this again, Katharine," Queen Anne said. "You're not fifteen any more. You are the proper age to marry. And our kingdom needs this alliance, to keep the peace."

"It's Kit, for the last time. And your kingdom needs this alliance," Kit said. "And what war? We've been at peace for a century."

"Your given name is Katharine, and it's far more befitting a princess than Kit. You know I never liked that nickname. You're old enough to drop it by now," queen said. "If peace is so secure, then why do you learn to spar with Master Caleb?"

Sometimes Kit wondered that very question. She wondered why she was not happier with cross stitch or playing piano. Sometimes it was a matter of defiance against a mother who wanted a daughter who wanted those things.

"You never approved of me fighting," Kit said. "You always wanted me to learn the domestic arts. You wanted a more ladylike daughter."

"That's not true," Queen Anne said. "Nothing happens on palace grounds without my knowledge. I have always approved of your fighting. I want a Warrior Princess, after all, for a Warrior Queen Mother."

"You're just saying that because I'm leaving," Kit sighed.

"I'm proud of you... Kit." Queen Anne swiveled the chair so that Kit faced her mother. She tasted the nickname gingerly. "My only daughter."

Tears pricked Kit's eyes. She found she was crying a lot lately, this last week of her departure.

"There's something I wanted to give you when nobody was around, a rare occurrence in this palace." She took the bloody handkerchief from her pocket and handed it to her daughter. Kit looked at her skeptically.

"What's this?" she said, very carefully keeping her hands still. She wasn't curious about it, but her hands trembled.

"It's a charm," Queen Anne said. "Oh, I know, you'll have a chambermaid and treasures and riches on your journey to meet your prince, but I wanted you to have this. In case anything goes wrong. It will help you when you most need it."

Tentatively, Kit took it, and felt the lacy texture stained with her mother's blood in her fingers. She didn't want to hold it. Her hand burned with nerves.

"Is it true what they say, that you're a witch?"

"No," Queen Anne said. "But I've learned a few things from witches."

She smiled, turned Kit back around to face the wall, and continued to brush her daughter's hair.

THE HONOR GUARD FRAMED THE COURTYARD IN A NEATLY ordered row, the warm wind blowing the tassels in their dress uniforms. There were dozens of them, all encircling the premises. Every last one of them looked solemn, sincere, and Kit appreciated that. She knew all their names. She would miss them the most. They were her only friends here, as the conversation the other day between the chambermaid and the stable hand had made clear.

Kit stood at the dais facing the courtyard wearing an emerald green dress and gray mink shawl, her hair in ornate clusters of curls under her crown for the occasion. The people of the kingdom stood in the streets, and watched in the courtyard, and crammed in everywhere they could find a place. They didn't get many chances to see Princess Katharine and this would be their last. Normally, this was the spot where market days were held. Now, Kit was the spectacle. She wished she could be riding Falada instead.

Finally, after the speeches about happy marriages and wonderful journeys, and the music from the flute and tambourine orchestra and the gaba player, Queen Anne took the stage. A hush fell over the crowd, which had been murmuring and laughing in nervous anticipation and impatience.

"My fellow citizens, what a momentous and sad day," Queen Anne said. Her voice boomed into the wind. "I am sad because my only daughter is leaving me, and I will miss her dearly. But I am also honored and proud. As you know, Princess Katharine is promised to marry Prince Geoffrey of

Firedell. Firedell is one of many kingdoms that threaten the peace of our good nation. They thirst after our resources, after our dragons, after our happiness."

At that moment, Kit spotted in the crowd the chambermaid who was to accompany her. The girl wore a simple black dress and smart black Mary Jane shoes, a servant's finery. Kit learned since that day that her name was Nell Duran. And Nell had a reputation for a surly attitude. Nell met the princess's gaze, a glint of defiance in her eyes.

Kit's stomach flipped, as she was suddenly overcome with the stark reality of her imminent goodbye. Just some more speeches and rituals. The bright colors of the banners and the vivid pop of the fine clothes of the crowd blurred together. The dragons were saddled, the provisions were loaded in a carriage that each would drag behind them. The dragons would spend much of the journey walking. The kinds of dragons that had made Cartha famous took to the air for tricks and stunts, but their ability to stay alight was limited.

Falada, too, waited with the honor guard, at the end of the line, his chin held high, watching her protectively. People gave the two dragons a wide berth. Dragons were unpredictable and dangerous, after all. Kit bit her lip. She would not cry.

Her mother droned on. Some more impassioned pleas about the importance of alliances and the fragility of the peace. Kit had always wondered why the Queen was so paranoid. But she knew nothing of life outside Cartha. She barely knew life outside the palace. Beyond the palace, the city was encircled by walls. Only farmers were allowed beyond the walls. Citizens were restricted from traveling except for designated trade missions approved by the queen. Information to and from the city was monitored by palace censors and anything amiss was reviewed by the queen. In short, Cartha was a bubble. A bubble of safety and ignorance.

Thinking of this, Kit's mindset began to shift. She almost didn't notice the change at first. This would be the first time she was allowed outside the palace. This would be the first time she was allowed outside Cartha. Her heart started pounding in her chest as nerves mixed with excitement. Maybe she was looking at it all wrong. She wasn't forced to leave the only home she had ever known. She was going on an adventure.

And maybe she could find a way to not marry a prince.

THE ADVENTURE WAS NOT VERY EXCITING AS THEY SET DOWN the road. Kit was not used to riding Falada for longer than an hour or two. The dragon's stubby wings bit into her legs and the saddle made her legs sore. And Nell was getting on her last nerves.

"It's so hot," Nell said, behind her. "Why does it have to be summer so soon? And look how long we've been riding. I'm tired of sweating."

"I thought you were supposed to help me," Kit said with a frown.

"Yes," said a small, brash voice behind her.

"You can help me by quitting your whining," Kit grumbled. "Never met a servant with such a mouth."

"I'll be more than a servant one day," Nell said quietly. The warm spring wind almost tore her voice away.

"What did you say?"

"Nothing. Can we at least stop for a water break?"

Kit suppressed a sigh. Falada gave her a knowing look.

"Might as well," she heard him rumble in her mind. She shook her head and clutched the reins tighter, hurting her fingers. Then she pulled up and brought Falada to a halt. Behind her, unsuspecting of her intentions, Nell and her dragon almost ran into her charge.

"We're stopping now?"

"What does it look like we're doing?" Kit said. She stroked Falada's muscled neck with its green mottled skin, thick and crusty with age and texture. Falada sensed her emotions at once and sent warm thoughts to her. She smiled for the first time since leaving Cartha. "There's a shady grove over there, it's a good spot to stop."

"What do you know about good spots to stop?" Nell said. "It's not like you've ever left the palace."

Kit felt her face burn. The cheek of this girl. She must have learned her royal etiquette from a pig sty. Kit dismounted Falada and tied him up in front of an oak tree in the shady grove she had described. They left the wide dirt road and entered the grassy meadow in the forest beyond. Nell followed suit. The sound of birds and insects around them would have sounded musical if Kit could hear them over her thrumming temper.

Kit brought two sandwiches out of the provision case and handed one to Nell with a sour look and a water canister. Nell returned the sour look with one equally piercing.

"Listen," Kit said, once they were sitting cross-legged on the ground, eating tuna with lettuce and whole wheat. "I don't know why you have a problem with me, but traveling with you is going to be a pain in the rear if you don't quit it with the attitude."

"Who said I have an attitude?" Nell mumbled over a mouthful of bread.

"You've been complaining the whole time, and you haven't once let up on giving me a piece of your mind," Kit said, meeting her servant's eyes with a clear stare. "I know you probably have a problem with royalty, or you think I think I'm better than you, or something, but I wouldn't mind being your friend."

Nell laughed. "Friend." She talked while eating. "We're not equals and you want to be friends."

Kit sighed. "That's fair. I would be happy to just get along."

"An accident of birth puts you there and me here," Nell said with a sigh of her own. "I've never been happy with that arrangement. Not like they say we are supposed to be happy with it."

"It's not fair," Kit admitted. "I recognize that. I never wanted to be princess."

Nell leaned her back against the oak tree and sighed as a breeze rustled her hair. "I always wanted to be a princess," she said quietly, taking a sip of water.

They stared at the road and the dust settling in the path, not looking at each other this time, each lost in thought. It was strange they had run into no other travelers on this road so far, Kit thought.

"What about your parents?" she asked. "What do they do?"

"They're dead," Nell said. "But my mum was a seamstress. Pop shoed horses."

"I'm sorry," Kit said. She reached out her hand and touched the fabric of the blanket she had put down to set their picnic lunch on.

"No skin off my back," Nell said. "Pop was a drunk and mum ignored me."

Kit felt herself soften toward Nell then, as she brushed

her hand back. Nell was looking out into space, her eyes carefully blank, but then her arm extended, and she grabbed Kit's hand. Kit felt her pulse pounding in her throat, and she didn't know why her heart quickened like that. But the touch was the first gentleness that Nell had shown her the whole trip so far, and she found she wanted it. Their hands lingered like that for a little too long than was proper, before Kit withdrew her own hand and began clearing the picnic things.

"I'll do that," Nell said. "That's my job."

"Oh, now you want to do your job?" Kit said, a teasing inflection in her voice that surprised her.

Another first for the trip: Nell smiled, and Kit was startled to find her smile radiant. Nell, with her short, curly blonde hair and her ruddy cheeks, a few inches shorter than Kit in height, slender, petite-shouldered. Kit felt herself inexplicably wanting more touch, and she reached out to touch Nell's hair before the other woman could react.

"What are you doing?" Nell said, the moment of softness broken. She grabbed her wrist. Kit froze.

"Your hair," Kit said, smiling and shaking her head, feeling foolish even as she said it. "I am jealous of your hair. I always wanted mine short like that, and my mother would never let me. She said it was unbecoming of a future queen."

"That's a silly rule," Nell said, her hand still around Kit's thin wrist. "Who gives a fig how long a ruler's hair is?"

"Oh, there are all sorts of silly rules like that for rulers," Kit said, moving her hand back to her side and already regretting it. Then confusion replaced the sudden bloom of warmth in her chest. She couldn't understand why she felt so giddy, so exhilarated. Just a moment ago, she hated this girl.

The smile faded. "We should get back on the road," Kit

said. "We need to make tracks before dark. As my mother has always said, it is not safe outside Cartha."

"We haven't seen anybody on this road all day," Nell said, shaking her head.

"Maybe the bandits emerge at night," Kit said. Nell packed up the blanket and the water and snorted as she cleaned up.

The two were riding the dragons again, steering them down the road once more in no time. When Nell paced behind her some distance, Falada took the opportunity to talk again.

"What's going on with you?" the dragon said, his voice disparaging.

"Nothing," Kit said. "I'm glad we're finally not at each other's throats, that's all."

"You do realize you're supposed to get married, girl?"

Kit felt her face flush. "It's nothing like— what?"

"You were looking at her like when you saw your first seven-tiered atani cake when you were four," Falada said.

"But that's impossible," Kit whispered fiercely. "She's a woman."

"So? Just because people don't talk about it doesn't mean it's impossible."

Kit sighed. "It's not possible," she insisted. "I'm getting married. Stop making up lies, dragon."

"As long as you understand your mission," Falada said.

Behind them, Nell picked up the pace as she fought with her mount, a disgruntled dragon who did not talk named Kara.

"What are you two talking about?" she said. Kit's face flushed and Falada gave her a warning look. Kit could hear Nell wrestling with her dragon, who was wanting to buck. "I'm having the worst time with this stubborn creature."

"Try sweet talking her instead of giving her lip," Kit said. "That works with me."

"Does it?"

Nell finally got her dragon to behave, and rode side by side with Kit, with the road just wide enough to take them. She glanced at her furtively, with her mouth curved. Kit felt her heart thumping again, and looked to the sky, cursing her sudden rush of feeling.

AT NIGHTFALL THEY STOPPED AND SET UP CAMP, AND FED AND watered the dragons, who were tied up to a tree and established a canvas tent. Nell got the fire started and they sat around it, roasting deer sausage with buns and marshmallows for dessert. Nell kept burning her marshmallows, the white fluff searing with soot and making Kit laugh every time. On the third marshmallow, Kit suddenly got very quiet. Nell tossed hers into the embers of the fire and looked at her.

"What's wrong?" Nell said.

"You know," Kit said soberly. "I can't remember the last time I laughed so much."

"You know," Nell said. "You are nothing like I thought you would be."

"Oh? What did you think I would be?" Kit looked at her toes, at the fire, everywhere but meeting Nell's eyes.

"I thought you'd be a spoiled, entitled brat," Nell said, shrugging. "You are a little spoiled, but you're..."

"I'm what?"

"You're turning my best-laid plans into disasters, that's what."

"Your plans?"

"My attitude wasn't an accident," Nell said matter-of-factly. "I had a plan. I was going to kill the dragons, then scare you into taking my place. I had a plan to marry that prince instead of you."

Kit's heart pounded in her chest, but this time not with the rush of emotion from earlier. It was more like fear.

"I don't want to marry him," she said solemnly, her voice almost unrecognizable.

"I know that," Nell said. "It was just... a silly plan. I don't want to stay a servant forever. But there's nowhere to go for me."

"You could..."

"Spare me," Nell said. She stood up, trailing her marshmallow stick in the dirt. Her thin tunic flapped in the lick of the night breeze. "You don't know what it's like."

Kit stood up and walked closer to Nell. The glow of the fire reflected in their faces. The night sky above twinkled with stars. She didn't even know what impulse propelled her forward, but she knew she had to be near Nell. Kit stood behind her, not daring to touch again, but feeling like she almost could. Her voice was soft, like a child's, when she finally spoke.

"Tell me."

Nell's shoulders sank. This time, Kit reached out and touched her left shoulder. She felt Nell's muscles tense under her hands. Then Nell turned around and placed her hand in hers. She leaned forward, searching Kit's eyes. Without thinking, without even questioning her urge to do so, Kit took a risk and brushed a light kiss on Nell's cheek. Her ears were on fire as she immediately regretted it.

But then Nell framed Kit's chin with her hands, and kissed her back. Their tongues met, and Kit tasted burnt marshmallow and smoke. The warm feelings that had started blooming earlier became a flame in her chest. But she drew back, confused, uncertain now.

"I'm getting married," Kit said, sighing. She walked away, pacing in front of the campfire. "Women don't do these things with each other. You're my servant."

"I was going to flip that, remember?" Nell said. "We're equals now, in the dark, in front of this fire. You said yourself, you don't want to marry him. And women do... do this."

With that, Kit turned back to her, distress and longing and music all crammed into her expression. Nell kissed her again. This time Kit didn't stop it.

PRE-DAWN LIGHT DAPPLED THE HORIZON AS KIT, BLEARY-EYED, stretched her arms. Then, with a start, she thought about what she did last night and her heart shot into her mouth. She closed her eyes, breathing in deeply, the ashes from the dead fire, the scent of the pine in the air, Falada's ever-wakeful, ever-judging large eye.

Next to her, under the blanket, Nell stirred, but did not wake. Kit looked once more, because she could, at her luminescent skin, and finally got up, moving quietly so as not to wake the other woman. Thinking about their nighttime bedding, she felt the giddiness rise in her throat again, the sudden flush of happiness. She hastily put on some clothes and approached Falada. He still stared at her reproachingly.

"Stop it," Kit sighed. "I'm just... this is just... experimenting. No one has to know."

"You stop it," Falada said. "You're getting married, or have you forgotten?"

"You sound like my mother," Kit said.

"Your mother would not like this either, and you know it."

"Oh Falada," Kit said, shaking her head and sinking into the dragon's rough hide. The dragon, despite himself, embraced her with his wings. "Always the dutiful one, aren't you?"

"Aren't you?"

"Point taken."

They stayed like that a moment too long, Kit marveling at the sense of contentment she felt at this moment. She didn't want that to go away.

"I guess I should make breakfast," she said. The dragon didn't respond, but she felt his hackles go up. "What's wrong?"

Her touch revealed fear, anxiety. Kit grabbed the sword out of her pack, suddenly alarmed, and touched Nell's shoulder, who stared at her with heavy-lidded curiosity.

"Get dressed," she whispered. "Something's wrong."

Nell put on her clothes and took some water from the water canister, as well as her own blade. "Robbers?"

At that, five horses suddenly crashed into view, carrying five riders, tall men with large shoulders, wearing the leather and iron of highwaymen. Kit stood ready. They thought they had the element of surprise, but she claimed that when she swiftly killed their first attacker, using the techniques she had learned from the fighting ring. Nell helped her subdue a second, but it didn't take the other three long to overtake them, despite Kit's skill. Nell looked at her with admiration, then fear.

One of the men went after the dragons. Kara did not put up much of a fight, and was killed almost instantly. Falada, though, was a fighter.

"Wait!" Kit said. "Don't kill him! He could be valuable to you!"

"Then make him behave," growled the man.

Kit tugged on her captor's hold, glaring, and walked over to Falada. She put a hand on the dragon's hide, steadying him. Her lips grazed his textured skin. "Shh. Shh now." She put all her mental energy into willing him to obey. And the dragon stilled, rearing his head back and snorting. He scared the horses, one of whom reared in kind and screamed.

Once everyone was deadly quiet, the men securely tied Kit's and Nell's hands and legs. "This one," said one of the men, his charcoal-black hair wild around his face, as he looked at Nell with glowing eyes. "This one I'd like to take." Even as Nell met her look, Kit spat on him. The man only laughed.

"Banno," one of the other men growled. "No sampling the merchandise."

Banno looked visibly disappointed. "Boss."

"Which one of you is Princess Katharine?" the boss asked.

Even before Kit could speak, Nell struggled against her bonds and raised her shoulders back in as regal of a posture as she could muster. "I am."

Kit looked at her imploringly, willing her to take it back. But then Nell met her eyes again, and her look brooked no contest.

"Very well, Princess," the boss said. "Prince Geoffrey will pay us a handsome ransom for your safe return."

He grabbed Nell's shoulder, and the two of them mounted his horse with Nell riding in front. Kit felt tears prick her eyes, and blinked them back. Falada, meanwhile, gave her a knowing look. As only a servant now, she would walk beside one of the other mercenaries.

Maybe the real world really was as dangerous as her mother feared.

THEY RODE HARD FOR SEVERAL MORE DAYS. KIT PLOTTED escape at every opportunity, but there were few opportunities, and they were treated roughly. One night, she and Nell tried to escape with Falada, but this time, the men really did overpower and kill the dragon. Kit remembered the shock at the gushing blood, her tears, Falada's obsidian eyes. Remembering her mother's charmed, bloody handkerchief, she begged them to let her keep Falada's severed head, as a trophy. It was superstition, she told them. They would be haunted otherwise. Amazingly, they bought the story. They had her walk with the head in her pack.

It didn't take long after that for them to reach the kingdom of Firedell. The capital city was walled, just like her own. Runners spotted them up ahead and brought word back to the king. A party came out to meet them. There were members of the king's guard, heavily armed. Not an army, just ten men. They'd been told of hostages.

"We're here to see King Philip," said the boss, whose name was Henry. "We have his son's bride, and we want to be paid for our trouble."

Far above, Kit spotted the archer from her vantage point. She stayed quiet. She didn't want to meet Nell's eyes, to give them away. But she stared at the small of the other woman's back, instead. She felt such conflicting emotions now. Was Nell just play-acting, rehearsing for the role she thought she wanted, and they would run away together after all this? Or was she still scheming, her original plan? Kit's breath flip-flopped in her throat. But then the archer loosed his arrows, and Denny fell, his expression stunned.

Kit sprang into action, her training kicking in. She grabbed Denny's sword since he was closest to her, while Henry had his knife at Nell's throat. Nell looked frozen, deadly calm, as Henry's grip tightened.

"You want to kill any more of my men, she's next," he yelled, the wind seizing his voice. But he didn't see Kit behind him, when her blade slammed into his spine. Nell jumped away and Prince Geoffrey's guards joined them in the fray, the other men falling next. Bloody, grimy and dirty, Nell and Kit looked almost indistinguishable. Princess and servant, which one was which?

A man emerged from the gates, as his guard parted for him. Kit realized with a start that it must be Prince Geoffrey. He walked as a prince would, his posture regal, his head thrown back, his delicate features, his blonde hair shaved, his ice-blue eyes blistering. He stared at them both, calculating.

"Princess Katharine is a skilled swordswoman, her mother told me," he said, his voice clear as a bell in the sudden stillness as his kingdom's protection watched. "But both of you are skilled, so which is which?"

"I'm Princess Kit," both Nell and Kit said at once, and Kit felt a stirring in her chest as she looked down at her feet, her chin depressed, suddenly ashamed. Nell wanted this. She wanted Nell. But she could give Nell what she really wanted.

"I'm Nell," Kit said, her voice creaking. "The chambermaid."

She stepped away and dropped her sword, her shoulders sinking. She didn't see Nell's probing look, the concern in her eyes. She whispered, so that only the two of them could hear: "It's what you wanted. I don't need it."

"But this is your destiny," Nell whispered.

"It's yours now, through a strange twist of fate," Kit said, concealing her smirk.

Prince Geoffrey held out his hand, and Nell hesitantly stepped forward, adopting the pretense of the regal bearing from before. But then she started to believe in it, and she clasped Geoffrey's hand with her own. Kit felt a swell of pride. Any sense of betrayal she had felt before washed away, scalded by something else, something deeper, that she could not name.

"There were supposed to be dragons," Prince Geoffrey said, clearing his throat as he smiled at his new bride.

"The bandits killed them," Nell said. "But my maid still carries the head. Perhaps you'd like to put it on a spike on the walls of this city, to show the people outside that no one can touch us."

This time Prince Geoffrey's grin turned devilish. "I like the way you think."

Kit looked at them both, and the feeling of pride quickly dissipated. These feelings. They were of no use to her now. They just got in the way.

THE FIELD WAS MUDDY, AND KIT WAS ETERNALLY MUDDY. MUD in her fingernails, mud streaked on her skin, mud in her eyelashes, goat dung in her toes. But surprisingly, she found she liked the work. It was simple. There were no expectations. She worked by herself, no bosses, no abuse. The sunrise swelled in the sky with its shock of pinks and purples. This was not the life she would have dreamed of for herself. But it was different.

In the distance, she heard the goats call, and her Border Collie, an anxious dog she had named Sammy, leapt to her side and begged for touch, burying his head in her stomach. She laughed and stroked his head.

Every day she thought of Nell. Some days, the thoughts faded. It was too painful to think about, some nights, remembering their only night together, the feel of her skin under the rough blanket, with the stars shining overhead, her reach for her. That was her old life. A life in between that was never meant to be.

The days passed. She traded for books at market days and read them in the hearth in her the shack that passed for her house. The work was hard, but, another surprise - good for her. Every day when she went to market, she saw Falada's head on the wall, looking over everything, victorious in his ghost life. She would study him at times, reflecting. She still had the handkerchief. She wondered what the charm would do.

One night, she snuck away from the farm and climbed the wall, being careful to be quiet. Her feet were bare and scratched the stones. She held the bloody handkerchief firm in her hands. Once face to face with Falada, his judgmental almond eye staring at her mercilessly once more, she wiped the sweat and blood from his matted head with the cloth, and found herself weeping silently. She left the cloth there. The magic was just a story.

But it was not just a story, after all. Falada's head began to talk. It began to talk to whomever would listen. It talked of the goat girl who was really a princess. And people listened, and they started to talk.

WHEN THE SOLDIERS CAME FOR HER, KIT WAS SITTING IN THE mud with her back against the fence, her eyes closed. Her goats crowded around her, their feet inches from her legs, anxious for their food. She breathed in their odor, the sweat, the hay. Sammy started barking in a ferocious way. She hoped it wasn't a wolf.

But it was a wolf.

"Princess Katharine?"

SHE MET THE KING IN HIS CHAMBER, ALL THE FINERY SPREAD before them. The king and queen sat in their thrones together, solemn. The prince stood near them. Their court watched, their games at rest for now, watching the game currently in play. Such riches. Kit wondered if Geoffrey was cruel.

The hall of steel and mirrors was cold. There was the sound of water dripping off in the distance. Some guards brought out Nell. Kit's heart caught in her throat. Even now she didn't feel betrayed. But Nell would not meet her eyes. Her head was shaved, and there were scars along her back, blood on her delicate face. Kit fought the sudden swell of emotion that threatened to overtake her, and remembered her training. She only stared at the Prince. Her bridegroom.

"What do you want to do with her?" Geoffrey said. His voice was soft. Not the flinty tones that Kit expected. "We could kill her for this betrayal, and it would be well within your rights as my future Queen." His eyes turned obsidian, the color of Falada's when the dragon was angry.

"No," Kit said. The guard made as if to slap Nell, even

though the girl was cooperating. Kit raised her chin and summoned up all her experience, all her mother's bearing, all her mother's ardent paranoia. "You won't hurt her. She will be my lady-in-waiting."

A gasp sang through the court. The Prince studied her.

"Such an honor for a traitor," Geoffrey said. A cruel man would have insulted her. Instead: "Why?"

"She was trying to protect me, not betray me," Kit said. "I trust her with my life. And she gave me the greatest gift I could have asked for. A life. A taste of a real life."

Geoffrey laughed then, and calmed himself. "Herding goats? A life?"

"Now I can relate to the people," Kit said, meeting the flint that entered his gaze. "And the people will love me for it."

"Very well," Geoffrey said. He flicked his hands, and the guards released Nell. She gasped. Kit fought the urge to run to her, to take her in her arms.

"Thank you for the wedding gift, my liege," Kit said, and for the first time, looking around at the court, watching the people watching her with awe, fear and respect, she wanted to be queen.

In her bedchamber, later, Kit let Nell undress her. The other woman's delicate touch, removing her clothes, unbuttoning and unclasping. They were alone here. For the first time in months, Kit had cleaned all the mud from her pores.

Then Nell faced her. Her eyes were deep and sad. Kit remembered Falada, and she grew sad as well. "You're getting married," he would have said reproachfully.

Nell kissed her, a lingering caress of the lips, then stepped back.

"You know I can't stay," she said, her voice tight.

"But you're not a chambermaid anymore," Kit managed, once she found her voice. But she knew what Nell would say next.

"You're getting married," Nell said. "And soon he will be in your bed."

"But we could have separate bedrooms," Kit said, her voice growing desperate. "We would have so many private moments together."

"Not as Princess, then Queen. You rarely have private moments," Nell said. She touched her cheek, her fingers grazing a scar from the fight with the robbers.

"But..."

Nell put a finger on her lips, then kissed her again. She tasted like woodsmoke.

"Just promise me this," Nell said. "Own your power. Don't take it for granted. Help people. Use your position for the greater good. Lift up people like me. Then you will honor me more than you can ever know."

"But you wanted this," Kit said, her voice a whisper.

"Not like this."

Kit couldn't say what she wanted to say next. Instead, tears pricking her eyelids, she touched Nell's hand and said, "As you wish."

Nell's eyes said goodbye, and then she disappeared into the night beyond the safety of the room, as Kit's future spread before her, bright and luminous like the stars above them on their last night together, like the shade of Nell's skin in the dark.

S.O. GREEN

Simone Oldman Green lives in the Kingdom of Fife with husband, John. They have been published by Dragon Soul Press, Otter Libris, Rogue Blades, Storgy Magazine, L Ellington Ashton, Iron Faerie, Eerie River, Zombie Pirate and Black Hare Press. They also won 3rd Place in the British Fantasy Society's Short Story Contest 2018 for the feminist post-Apocalypse piece, *Travesty*.

Writer, vegan, martial artist, gamer, occasionally a terrible person (but only to fictional people). They thrive on the unusual, which might explain why there are so many cats. Find them at thebasementoflove.blogspot.com or as a Twitizen @SOGreenWriter

THE DRAGON'S HEART

S.O. Green

*T*he Dragon Queen was bored.

It happened, once every century or so. When it did, cities burned and kingdoms fell and humans died by the hundreds. Anything for a little entertainment.

She conserved her energy like any good reptile. She wore the soft and slender form the humans favored, kept her horns tucked up under a hood of ebony silk. To the untrained eye, she appeared armored. No. Her skin was dragon scale, black as midnight. And sensitive to pleasure despite it all.

Her palace was a spire of black stone, a jagged, obsidian crown upon the tallest peak. She'd had her slaves mine the stone and drag it there. Many of them were buried in the foundations. Her throne was made of tributes from the far reaches of her realm. Gold and precious stones and the bones of a hundred sacrifices, the most beautiful among her subjects.

The fairest of them all.

Trophies were her only company. The bracelet made of

king's crowns that she wore in her dragon form that jingled so merrily. The great, iron doors of the dwarven city, Baux, buckled and blackened by her very own fire. She had laid siege to them herself. Burned their king in his throne room.

She looked at them and sighed. That had all been so long ago.

"You are restless, Your Majesty," the man in the mirror said.

"Always so insightful, my faithful servant."

She rose from her seat, stretched as far as her limited shape would allow. She could have filled the throne room, knocked down its pillars, smashed through its roof as she took flight. She could have turned the golden throne into a pretty puddle with a breath.

What was the point of power with no one to match it against?

The mirror was just another trophy. A polished shard of black glass, shaped like a knife. He had been hers for centuries. Once the most powerful man in the world until she had given him a choice - death or servitude. No doubt he regretted his decision.

He had been a handsome soul, but now he was just a shadow on the glass. Featureless and openly, deliciously resentful.

"Perhaps you are feeling merciful, my lady."

The queen laughed. "Merciful enough to free you, is that it? Why would I ever want to let you go when you are so very amusing?"

"You might find another who is more amusing than I."

She arched a brow. "You have my attention."

"You have conquered peoples and cities and nations. But you have never conquered a heart."

"Not impressed so far," she muttered, studying her claws.

He didn't have the features to scowl, but it was in his voice when he said, "Behold."

He showed her a kingdom. An unimpressive, dull little kingdom in the snow. A rock on a white rug. She could have crushed it in her hand, scattered its dust into the wind.

"They call it Snowden. It is the northernmost of the human realms, beset by constant blizzards. They are at the mercy of the elements. Yet they prosper."

Didn't humans always prosper for a time? They were brief things. They and all their works could be forgotten in the blink of her eye.

Or snuffed out with a pinch of her fingers.

"This is their leader," he said, and showed her beauty.

She sat on the throne with her chin propped on her fist and the queen would have recognized that boredom anywhere. Armed and armored, she was ready for combat. In her mind, she was a thousand miles from there.

Doing what? The queen wanted to know.

"Lips red as blood, hair black as ebony, skin white as snow."

"Yes, yes. She's very pretty. What's your point?"

"She has promised her people an end to dragons."

The air in the palace shuddered. Servants trembled in their hiding places. It had been so long since the queen had been surprised.

"Is that so? And how does she hope to deliver this miracle?"

"She has already begun."

The girl's hand rested on the hilt of an obsidian blade etched with symbols that had been lost to the world for lifetimes. The queen knew them by sight. What they signified.

Dragonsbane.

"I could turn her to ash with a sigh. I could crush her under my thumb. Why should I be concerned with this *girl*?"

"You *could* crush her," the mirror said, and now she could hear it smile. "But look at her. She despises your kind. She wants to wipe them out. Her heart belongs to her people. It is cold as the snow that smothers her realm. How rare, how strange a thing this girl is. Could you ever hope to win her?"

"Of course, I could," the queen said. "No one can resist me. You couldn't."

The surface of the mirror rippled. She had touched a nerve.

This girl would need to be ever-so amusing if she was to take his place.

But, perhaps, this challenge was just what the queen needed.

"Yes," she said softly, and a smile came to her black lips. "She's perfect."

THERE WERE STILL TOO MANY DRAGONS. IT DIDN'T SEEM TO matter how many Snow hunted down and decapitated, there were always more.

The map was littered with red flags. Each one represented another bloody dragon. She only had one life to give, one sword to wield. How was she ever going to get the job done?

And the ones she'd killed weren't even dragons.

Wyverns really. Drakes at best. Small fry. She was wasting her time with winged rats when there were bears out there. Giant, fire-breathing bears.

The other realms weren't going to help. She'd made her peace with that. They thought her campaign was doomed to failure, a waste of time and resources and manpower. The moment she began to irritate the High Dragons, she was done for. They'd incinerate her. Maybe Snowden too, if she'd *really* annoyed them. A message to the others.

At best, they called her a fool. At worst, a heretic.

What was more human than bending the knee to a tyrant?

Worshipping dragons as gods. It made her sick. They were bullies and that was all. Scaly, flying, gold-grubbing bullies and, so help her, she was going to kill as many as she could before her time in the world was at an end.

"Lady Snow?"

She flinched at the servant's voice. "Gods, what is it now?"

"A messenger, my lady. From the Dragon Queen. He has brought you another gift."

Snow considered. "Tell him to piss off."

"He was really quite insistent."

"Fine. I suppose I've nothing better to do. I'm not trying to govern a realm or persecute a war or anything."

This was the latest wrinkle in the quest to rid the world of dragons. One of the High Dragons - the Highest, in fact - had asked for her hand in marriage.

Awkward, considering Snow was in the middle of a war to exterminate her entire species.

It wasn't difficult to reject the offer. The Dragon Queen's cruelty was legendary. She had her own lands, her own humans to rule over, but she demanded a tithe from each and every other dragon in the world and all of them paid up, without question. And, when she squeezed them, they squeezed the world. Tyranny by proxy.

Snow traded the cold, stone war room for her cold, stone audience chamber. A man in a black robe was waiting to greet her. Unbearably pale and there was frost on his eyelashes, just like the others. He bowed low before she could ask him not to.

"What do you want?" she demanded. "You didn't come to bring me another corset, did you? Please tell me it's not another comb. I have enough of the damn things already. I'm not a doll. I'm a busy woman with things to do."

"It is none of those things, my lady," he said, and reached into his robe.

Snow's hand wrapped around the haft of her sword, drew the first two inches of blade. It had occurred to her several times that each of these messengers could be an assassin sent to put an end to her Dragon War.

Gods, she'd have been ecstatic. If the Dragon Queen herself sent an assassin then it meant she was *really* giving the High Dragons something to think about.

She'd have died a happy woman.

Instead of a dagger, he produced a box. Heart-shaped, fashioned from black wood, ornamented with gold and studded with rubies like drops of frozen blood.

"You're not going to die if I take it, are you?" she asked. "All the others died."

"The queen is presenting you with a magnificent gift as a token of her undying affection," he said. "She hopes you will accept it in the manner in which it is intended and cautions you against rejecting it. You stand to lose a great deal if you do not act wisely."

"Oh good! It's not just a present; it's a threat! My favorite!"

He placed the box in her hands and met her sour expression with one of giddy delight.

"With this task complete, I am released from her service."

And he dropped dead. Just like that. Just like all the others. With a big, beatific smile on his frostbitten face.

Who was the Dragon Queen that her servants seemed so much happier in death?

Snow looked at the box. Some deeply buried survival instinct screamed up at her not to open it. Except that she was the first person to kill a dragon in a century. She'd been ignoring good sense her entire adult life. Most of her childhood too.

She thumbed the catch on the box and lifted the lid.

There was an apple inside, cupped in the crimson velvet. An ugly, bruised apple, skin black and shiny, covered in thick, emerald protrusions, like veins. And it was throbbing.

It wasn't an apple. It was a heart.

She snapped the box shut and swallowed bile.

Then she marched to her bedchamber and tossed each and every single gift the Dragon Queen had ever given her onto the fire.

Heart-box included.

SHE WOKE IN THE PALE NIGHT TO THE GENTLE MURMUR OF THE blizzard outside her walls and the ashes of the Dragon Queen's 'gifts' in the hearth and a sudden feeling of terror.

Her heart ached. It *burned*. It hammered at her ribs so hard she gasped.

"Were you dreaming of me?" a voice asked.

"By the hairy gods!" Snow screamed.

She was out of bed in a single thundering heartbeat. A shift white as the boundless snow preserved her modesty. She ripped a sword black as the shadow at her bedside from its scabbard. The Dragon Queen smiled at her with glowing eyes.

"I pity the human reliance on sleep but I envy your capacity to dream. Dragons can only wonder what you see beyond the veil."

"Maybe you'll find out when I kill you," Snow snarled.

"You are sweating. Feverish. Do I warm you?"

"You piss me off. All those gifts. All those dead messengers we had to bury. You really don't understand courtship, do you?"

"I am learning."

"Maybe you should try learning to take 'no' for an answer."

"I'm the Dragon Queen, dear. 'No' is an answer for other people."

She was everything that Snow had expected. Looming, magisterial, frightening. Covered from head to toe in supple, black scales, save the cold and regal pallor of her face. A crown of ornate horns curled from her temples, wrapped in a hood. Her cloak billowed behind her like wings.

Snow stared at her across the royal bed, gulped down the knot in her throat and tried to focus on the anger. This *thing* in her bed chamber was a monster. A world-eater.

Beautiful or not.

The Dragon Queen prowled towards her. Snow levelled Dragonsbane.

"Stay where you are or I'll gut you. I swear to the gods."

"Such fire for the ruler of such a cold realm. Have my

gifts done nothing to win you? I suppose I should have expected that a human could not truly appreciate their value."

"Corsets and combs," Snow spat. "What am I supposed to do with those?"

"Perhaps you could have made yourself presentable for me. Though you are perfectly lovely as you are."

If she hadn't needed to keep both hands on her sword, she'd have covered herself. Maybe grabbed the robe from beside the bed. Her realm for a suit of armor or even just a tunic.

"Shut up," she snapped, face burning.

"The gifts weren't important, my dear. It was the *materials* that I wanted you to notice. Bones. Teeth. From my own kind."

"What are you talking about?"

"Every gift I sent you was another dead dragon, slain by my hand." She laughed at Snow's surprise. Musical and malevolent. "Did you think I would try to court you without knowing your heart?"

"I can slay my own dragons."

"Perhaps. But you're so bad at it. Look at you. So soft and helpless. No claws, no scales. You can't fly and all you breathe is wind. Let me help you. All I ask for in return is your love."

"If you take another step, what you're going to get is my sword!"

How had she ever thought she was safe? How had she ever thought she could win? She was an ant hiding in the dark, waiting for the dragons to kick over her rock and burn her to a crisp.

Even that would have been preferable to this.

"You don't want to help me. You want to control me."

"Wouldn't you like to be controlled?" The queen's lips curled. A sneer. An invitation. "I have found that humans often do."

"Not me."

She lunged, thrusting Dragonsbane. It plunged through the queen's chest. So did Snow. She stumbled, almost tripped, recovered and swung around. The queen watched her, smirking.

"You're not really here," Snow growled.

"Of course not. I would have taken you in my arms from the first moment if I were."

"What are you? Not a ghost. I'm not that lucky. An astral projection then? An illusion? A hallucination?"

"A dream. You burned my heart and breathed me in. Filled yourself with me. I'm inside you now. In your lungs and your heart and your blood. Can't you feel me? The heat of me?"

"You poisoned me."

"Lovingly."

"What happens now? Will I die? Is this your victory? Did you come to gloat?"

"On the contrary. You will live. For a very long time, unless I decide otherwise. No, I have come to deliver an invitation. I want you to join me at my palace. Become my bride. I have given you the fortitude to make the journey. The heart was my final gift. It was supposed to be a talisman. I wasn't expecting you to ingest it but... Well, you've been full of surprises so far."

"And if I refuse?"

The question hung in the air like a blade over Snow's neck. The Dragon Queen stepped towards her and she grew, limbs stretching, teeth lengthening, eyes glowing. A phantom she might have been, but terrifying all the same.

When she spoke, smoke poured from her mouth. "Then I will come to collect you myself. I will burn your precious city to the ground and all your subjects with it. Are the lives of your people not a fitting dowry?"

She reached for Snow's face, claws elongating. She flattened herself against the wall, twisted her face away. Dragonsbane lay forgotten at her feet.

"This is a dream," Snow gasped. "And if it's a dream, I can..."

She woke to the whirl of the blizzard and the first light of dawn. Her shift, her sheets, her mattress, all soaked in sweat. Her heart felt swollen. Too small for her ribcage. And hot, like it was on fire.

Dragonsbane was on the floor, out of reach. Where she'd dropped it in the 'dream'.

She took a breath and gasped as the pain took hold.

She knew what she needed to do.

"YOU'RE LEAVING, AREN'T YOU?"

Snow looked up, her knapsack half-packed. She wondered if it was the rough travelling clothes or the sight of her putting all her possessions in a bag that had given the game away. Leon stood in the doorway and watched her like a thoroughly-kicked puppy.

He might have been the closest her realm had to a handsome prince, even though he was technically neither. She liked his easy smile and his kindness, his concern for his subjects. And the way he always voted with her at council meetings.

He'd been the heir. Next in line to rule before she'd come along. Yes, it was an elected position but his father and his father's father, and a whole lot of fathers before them, had all been elected to the post.

Then Snow had wandered into town, soaked in dragon's blood and holding a blade thought lost to time and, suddenly, the voting priorities had changed.

They wanted a leader who could keep them safe from dragons. Well, she'd done a marvelous job of that.

"I don't really see that I've got much choice."

"You always have a choice. Are you sure you're making the right one?"

"She'll burn the city down if I don't go. And then she'll take me anyway. It's not really a great case for staying."

"It was just a dream, Snow."

"No," she said, stuffing an engraved torc she didn't like to talk about into her bag, "it wasn't."

"We'd fight her. For you."

"I'm not going to ask anyone to do that. Besides, I don't think the other members of the Council would share your passion."

She kept raising taxes. It turned out Dragon Wars were expensive.

"Hang the Council. The people would stand with me."

"Yes, and you're all adorable and I'd give you the biggest hug but do you think I want that on my conscience?"

"You're our protector, Snow. Maybe the Dragon Queen won't come looking for you if you go but what about the others? You said yourself, they'll never stand for a free humanity."

"I know." She took a deep breath, took the scabbard from beside her bed and held it out to him. "That's why I'm leaving Dragonsbane with you."

Just for a moment, she wasn't the only Snow White in the room. "What?!"

"They're going to elect you to be leader once I'm gone, Leon. That means it'll be your duty to keep them safe. You don't have to finish my war but the people are going to look to you for protection and guidance. Whether you like it or not."

He was going to have to get used to it, just like she had. When she'd first arrived, all she'd wanted was a fast horse and directions to the nearest dragon eyrie. Instead, she'd been handed a key to the city and more responsibilities than she could juggle.

"You can't protect them without Dragonsbane."

"You can't protect *yourself* without Dragonsbane. It's the only weapon that might make a difference against something like the queen of dragons."

"I'm sure I'll figure something out," she lied.

He finally took the sword. He held it with his fingers, like it was going to bite him. She *really* hoped he got over.

They'd have probably gotten married one day, if she'd stayed. Political, mostly, but she didn't think she would have minded it. She just wasn't ready yet.

"You're really going to do this?" he asked. "Ride north to the End of the Earth? Marry the Dragon Queen?"

Snow laughed. "Who? Me? No, I'm going to ride south."

It was less of a smile and more a snarl that formed on her face.

"If the Dragon Queen wants me so badly, she can come and get me."

IT WASN'T EXACTLY THE KIND OF TRIUMPHANT DEPARTURE they'd sing ballads about. Sneaking out of the city in the dead of night, wrapped in a travelling cloak like a bandit.

Riding a horse that wasn't hers, carrying a sword that wasn't hers, her entire life packed into a single bag.

The folks who saw her, the stumbling drunks and night-watchmen and the guards on the gate, probably didn't think it was their ruler vanishing into the darkness, never to return.

She left it up to the Council's discretion to break the news. She hoped they wouldn't be stupid enough to tell everyone she'd run away. Nothing quite inspired panic like learning your fearless leader had galloped out of the city one night in the middle of an unwinnable war.

She hoped that, if they knew the truth, they'd understand. Legends of the Dragon Queen had been passed down for centuries. Some said she'd crawled out of the deepest, darkest hell and the other dragons had taken to worshipping her like a living god. Others said she'd usurped her husband's throne or that she'd clawed her way up from humble beginnings after hatching somewhere in the Elderloom Mountains.

Whatever her origin, she'd carved a bloody swathe through human and dragon kind alike ever since. She was a distant figure of folklore. A nightmare. A threat and a warning.

And now, apparently, Snow's fiancée.

The horse carried her out into the white void beyond Snowden's walls. She'd charted a course but all she was looking for was a place to leave her mount. Once she was far enough from the city, she'd stable it and head out on foot.

The queen had said she was undying. It was time to test that.

She could still feel the burning in her chest. Even with the barbed wind raking at her cloak and the frost catching in her eyelashes, the warmth was there. Dragon fire in her heart. A touch of darkness. Something insidious and frightening.

She should have expected that the queen would know exactly what she was doing. That she'd know exactly where she was.

The shadow passed over her like a hand smothering out the sun. Snow shuddered but not from the cold. A huge, black shape cleaved through the clouds on immense wings and banked, crashing down less than a league away. Blocking her path.

The queen's dragon form was long and sleek. Its scales shone with rainbow colors, like oil on water. Every claw was longer than Snow was tall. Its tail could topple buildings. Its wings could flatten regiments.

The other dragons she'd fought - feral, no better than animals mostly - had rampaged. They'd charged at her, breathing fire and roaring, and she'd known exactly what to do.

The queen just stared at her, eyes alight with savage amusement. Entertain me, little fly. Buzz for me.

Snow realized she was doomed.

The horse skidded to a stop. She clung on as it reared. Then it stood, staring at the monster ahead, stomping its feet, breath steaming in the cold air.

She leaned forward in the saddle, towards the horse's quivering ears. "Ride back to Snowden as fast as you can."

She leapt down, sending up a puff of snow as she landed. Her hand clapped the horse's flank and it broke into a full gallop. And she sprinted in the other direction.

The dragon watched her. She thought it might have been laughing at her. Then it burst into the air with one beat of its wings and Snow was swallowed by a fierce, new blizzard.

She kept running. Somewhere above, the Dragon Queen was circling. Playing. Enjoying the sport.

How did you fight a dragon? Simple. You used the enchanted sword you'd stolen to absorb its fire and pierce its heart.

What if you didn't have an enchanted sword? Then it was probably best to kneel and pray for a quick death.

The queen landed behind her. The ground pitched like a ship's deck in a maelstrom. For a second, Snow was airborne. Then she landed and stumbled to keep her footing. She heard the slow, menacing intake of breath, smelled sulphur in the air. She dived into the snow just as a roaring rush of flame cut a trench through the white and scorched the earth beneath.

Careful, my love, a voice whispered. It echoed in her mind. *I don't care for burnt offerings.*

Snow considered her response, then turned and flicked her a V. The voice just chuckled.

She started running again and wished she hadn't neglected her legs. She heard the queen take to the air again and spun, sword drawn, hacking at her underbelly as she passed low overhead.

But she wasn't wielding Dragonsbane. She scraped sparks off those armored scales and then cried out as the blade snapped in half.

The queen's tail whipped at her as she passed. Such a casual move but powerful enough to break every bone in her body. She leapt, instinct driving her, and narrowly avoided the clubbing blow. Instead, she tumbled down a slope, gathering snow as she went, and realized she couldn't stop.

She grabbed a jutting root and jerked her body to a halt just as she reached the edge of the chasm she hadn't even realized was there, hidden in the deceptive and blinding white of the snowfield. She dangled into the abyss and, for the first time in her life, started to seriously question the life choices she'd made up to this point.

Something grabbed her wrist. Something with claws.

"It appears that I have saved your life," the Dragon Queen said, human form restored. And smiling. Always bloody smiling. "How will you show your gratitude?"

Snow considered.

"Like this," she said, and rammed her half-sword into the other woman's throat.

It didn't pierce. It deflected off her scales and nicked her cheek. Snow had a half-second to celebrate the knowledge that she was the first being - human, dragon or otherwise - to actually hurt the Dragon Queen in a millennium.

Then she was doing a *lot* of falling.

A hell of a lot of falling.

SOMEWHERE, BETWEEN THE HEART-STOPPING PLUNGE AND THE river of icy water, Snow passed out. She knew she wasn't dead. It would have been too much like mercy and her luck had run out the day she'd attracted the attention of the Dragon Queen. The hot pulse in her heart, the pressure of the queen's avid attention, stayed with her even in sleep.

She wasn't surprised when she woke up. She was surprised at *where* she woke up.

Carved stone walls. Miner's iconography. The clang of hammers on anvils and the tang of molten metal being worked. The inescapable sense that there was a lot of stone between her and the sky.

"Welcome to Adamant, upsider," the grey-haired woman sitting beside the bed said. "City of the dwarves."

Snow sat up. Then she lay back down. No, that wasn't a good idea.

"How did I get here?" she asked. Her voice was rough as pumice. She felt swollen. Waterlogged.

"You came out in our underground stream. The washer women were very surprised."

"Yeah, I'll bet."

"We emptied a lot of water out of you, human. Is that normal? I didn't think humans breathed water."

"We don't. I'm... special."

Wasn't that the truth? Snow, Chosen of the Dragon Queen. Undying puppet of the cruelest being on the planet. You special girl, you.

"I'd tell you that you're welcome to stay here as long as you need but you don't really have a choice about that, being half-dead and all."

Snow reached out, exploring the space where she was lying. A slab of sculpted stone, more like an altar than a bed. The mattress was stuffed with spongy moss and the sheets were coarse. She wasn't in any position to complain.

Her host ground petals in a mortar for a while, measured in some water, then came back to pour the whole mixture into Snow's mouth. It burned. Not nearly as hot as her heart.

"Are you the physic here?"

"Aye. The doc, you might say. Call me Medea. I suppose I'm the closest this city has to a leader as well."

"You don't have a king or queen?"

"We were slaves of dragons for centuries. When we made our exodus, we decided. No gods, no masters. We live in the spirit of community and not one of us is higher than another. Even so, the others ask my opinion more often than not."

"Makes sense. You know what's best for their health."

"How do humans choose a leader?"

"In my country, by popular vote."

Medea's snub nose crinkled. "That doesn't sound very safe."

"They elected me so you're probably right."

"Why? What did you do that was so bad?"

"I started a war against the dragons."

Whatever the concoction had been, it was working. Snow sat up laboriously and looked around. This was definitely dwarven architecture. She'd seen it before. A long time ago. Before Snowden. Before she'd killed her first dragon.

"Is that how you ended up here?" Medea asked. "Running from the consequences of your actions?"

"Kind of. Have you ever heard of the Dragon Queen?"

Medea looked at her as though she was stupid.

"Right. Well, she might have asked me to marry her. And I might have snubbed her."

"That's... admirable. In the way that madness sometimes is."

Snow didn't care for the pitying look in the other woman's eyes. She swung her legs out of the rough sheets and stood up. Her head brushed the ceiling and she realized she'd stood up too fast. Thank the gods for below average height.

"I left my realm to save my people from the queen's wrath. I'm not going to bring her right to your door too. I'll leave as soon as I'm able."

It took all her resolution to say it. Then she needed to sit down again. She put her head in her hands and tried to still her trembling. Medea lay a small hand on her shoulder.

"Dwarven doors were built with dragons in mind, girl. If you need to shelter here, we gladly welcome you."

"Thanks, but..."

She couldn't stay. She *knew* she couldn't stay. But she couldn't stop shaking. She couldn't stand. She could barely move.

Just like Medea had said. She didn't have a choice.

"If you're having dragon trouble, I might make a suggestion. Once you're on your feet, go and visit Dour. He can teach you what dwarves know about killing dragons."

"You think he can tell me something that'll help against the Dragon Queen?"

Medea smiled. "I told you we were slaves. The dragons didn't give us our freedom," she said. "We had to take it."

IT WAS A WEEK BEFORE SHE COULD STAND WITH ANY confidence. The burning in her chest turned molten. She imagined the queen rampaging across the frozen wilderness above, searching for her.

Did she know she was down here, among the dwarves? Did that just make her angrier?

The first time she was able to stoop through the infirmary's doors, she took Medea's advice. She went in search of Dour.

She found him yelling at a gaggle of younger dwarves outside a tunnel they were excavating. Is that how your mother taught you to swing a pickaxe? Who put that prop there? Have you even seen a piece of stone in your life before, boy?

The pipe in his mouth gave him a strange lisp. Snow tried not to laugh.

She stepped close. He held a hand up at her until he was done with his lecture. Then he turned his glare on her.

"Aye?"

"You're Dour?"

"Not polite of you to say, upsider."

"No, I mean, you're the dwarf *named* Dour?"

"So, what if I am? What do you want?"

"Medea said you could teach me to fight a dragon."

"No."

Snow blanched. No easy feat when you were already white as they came. "What do you mean 'no'?"

"I can't teach you to fight dragons because you're human. Your kind don't have the right stuff to fight dragons. Do you know how long the Subjugation War lasted? Two hundred years. It took two centuries for the dragons to break the collective will of the dwarves. They held us down for generations. We built their palaces, sculpted their thrones, smelted their crowns. We mined gold and jewels for their hordes. Then we threw them off our backs with pure, unadulterated violence. Did you ever hear about a Subjugation War between humans and dragons?"

"No, sir, I didn't."

"That's because there wasn't one. Humans never even *tried* to resist dragons. You fell on your knees the moment they descended from the dark skies. Or you built temples to them and worshipped them like gods. So, no. I can't teach you. Some things can't be taught."

He tried to walk away. She grabbed him by the shoulder and dragged him back. He went to swat her arm away but she held firm.

"I've killed dragons before, Dour. I stole Dragonsbane

right from under Maladgar's nose and plunged it into his shriveled, black heart. I've painted myself in the blood of wyverns and drakes. Now I've set my sights on no less than the queen of dragons and I won't rest until she's bones in the snow. I'm going to face her whether you help me or not. But I figure I stand a better chance with the knowledge of the dwarves at my disposal, don't you think?"

Okay, so maybe she'd employed a little creative license but what she'd said had *mostly* been true. And the kind of warcraft that could emancipate an entire people sounded very useful.

Dour finally shook her off. He raked his fingers through his long, dark beard.

"Fine. I'll teach you what I can. We all will. But don't be surprised if you get burnt to a crisp."

Snow grinned. "At least I won't be surprised for long."

He just grunted. Apparently, he didn't do jokes. She'd need to keep that in mind.

DOUR PUT HER TO WORK HELPING WITH THE EXCAVATION. SHE didn't complain. It was part of her rehabilitation. Recovering what she had lost when she had washed up, mostly dead, in Adamant. Giving back a little of what she was taking from them by staying there.

Every night, she fell onto the slab they'd prepared for her, limbs turned to water, and slept the sleep of the dead. Every morning, she woke to the feeling of the Dragon Queen's hand around her heart, squeezing.

After another week, Dour took her to Bright. She was Dour's antithesis. Maybe his wife? She took Snow's measurements and began to forge her a suit of dwarven mail to wear.

"It's going to be the biggest suit of armor I've ever made," she beamed. "Well, the tallest anyway. Dour's is the widest."

"I don't like to wear armor," Snow explained. "I like to be able to move."

It wasn't like steel was going to help if a dragon hit her, except that it might keep her in one piece for when they buried her. Speed was the key when fighting a dragon. That and the magic sword she was seriously regretting leaving with Leon.

"This is dwarven armor, girl," Dour growled. "Supple as leather. Strong as steel. And, most importantly, it's fireproof."

"Really? What do you make it out of?"

Bright's eyes lit up. "Dragonhide."

THEY MADE THE CLIMB INTO THE UPPER REACHES OF Adamant. Surface tunnels that none of the other dwarves ever bothered to visit. As far as they were concerned, those tunnels could collapse and seal them off from the surface. Let that be the end of it.

Only one dwarf still lived up there, in that darkness.

"Shem was the greatest tactician of the exodus," Dour explained, as they reached the top of yet another steep incline. "He's the reason most of us were able to escape to Adamant. A hero of the people."

"Then why does he live so far away from everyone?"

"He's ashamed. I said he was the reason *most* of us escaped. He's also the reason some of us didn't. Sacrifices had to be made. People had to be left behind."

Snow had never been able to ask her people to make those sacrifices. She'd wanted them to prepare, to be ready for an attack but, more importantly, she'd wanted them to live. So, she'd fought the dragons herself, alone.

She'd known she was fooling herself. How many could she kill before her luck ran out? And then what?

She'd been trying to fight a war for humanity's freedom and she'd never asked for help, all because she hadn't wanted their deaths on her conscience.

She hadn't wanted to end up like Shem.

He was sitting on a stone block in an empty corridor lit by a single candle. His grey hair was long and tangled and dirty. He barely stirred when they approached.

"No one's come yet, Dour."

"I know, Shem. You'd have told us if they did."

He nodded. "Aye, that I would." He turned his head. It seemed to take real effort. "Who's the lass?"

"I want to learn how to fight dragons."

"And you want my advice?"

"Yes," she said, "please."

"Don't."

"I beg your pardon?"

"Don't fight dragons. You'll lose too much."

"I don't have anything to lose."

Not really. No realm. No title. No husband. No enchanted blade and no horse. Not even a torc she didn't like to talk about anymore.

He laughed humorlessly. "They can always take more from you."

"That's her plan," Snow said. The Dragon Queen had made it pretty clear that she wouldn't stop until everything Snow had was hers. "My only choice is to fight. I need to know how. Please, Shem."

He looked at her. Stared her in the eye. She saw the fire and felt her own candle flicker in recognition.

"You want to get their attention, you challenge them," he rasped. "They can't abide a challenge unanswered. They like to make war out on the open plain but you lure them into a tight space, make them change into a smaller form, and you take away their advantages. It'll still be a fight but... There's always a chance. There's always hope."

"What else?"

He peered out from under hooded eyes. "Someone needs to make a sacrifice."

"Yeah, don't worry. I think I drew that straw already."

"THE THING ABOUT DRAGONS," THE CHIEF ALCHEMIST SAID, "IS that they can fly."

Snow nodded. "I'd noticed."

His name was Gezund and he was the only dwarf she'd met, including Medea, without a beard. Or eyelashes for that matter. He opened his mouth to clarify his point, hesitated, then whipped out a handkerchief and sneezed explosively.

"The only way to stop them flying," he said, inspecting the black stain on his hankie, "is to put holes in their wings."

"I've done it a couple of times," Snow told him. "I used a bow and arrow."

"Then you already know that's a *terrible* way to incapacitate a dragon."

She couldn't dispute it. Hers wasn't the steadiest hand or sharpest eye for archery but, even if it had been, arrows were too slow to catch a speeding dragon and too brittle to pierce their hide.

"What would I use instead?"

"This," he said, and placed a steel tube attached to a wooden handle on the worktable in front of her. "We call it a pistol. We created them during the emancipation."

"What does it do?"

"It's kind of like a crossbow."

"What's a crossbow?"

"By the stone, you humans are backwards."

"At least my nose is clean."

"I'll have you know that this is a hazard of working with black powder and I-I-I-"

He sneezed again. His poor, overworked handkerchief reappeared.

"I can show you how to work the pistol. How to load it. We can give you powder and pellets but you'll need to work on your aim. One thing you'll learn about invention. It can only augment skill, not replace it."

"Fine. I'll practice."

Snow rolled one of the lead balls between her fingers. She tried to envision it blasting out of the pistol's tube, flying through the air to meet the Dragon Queen's outstretched wing.

"Won't it just blow up in my face?"

"Not if you use the right amount of powder. Dwarves have been working with it for centuries. We know how to use it."

"And you only made these weapons a few years ago?"

"Because it's always been sacred to us, girl. Show some respect. Our ancestors called it a gift from the earth. We used it for blasting. Mining and excavation only. The dragons *made* us turn it into a weapon when they took our freedom."

She understood. Having your freedom taken from you

made you redefine what was sacred. You did things you didn't think you'd ever do.

"The dragon I'm hunting has pretty big wings. I don't know how many shots it would take to bring her down."

"That's where Som comes in. He's our poisoner."

"You have a poisoner?"

"Of course. Just in case someone needs poisoned." Gezund turned and gave the other dwarf in the workshop a friendly kick. "Som, wake up. The upsider's here."

Som lifted his head off the table. There was moss and petals tangled in his ginger beard, like flowers growing in red vines. He blinked up at them both and then raked his sleeve across his eyes.

"What time is it?"

"Never mind that. I'm teaching the girl how to kill a dragon."

"Dragon? Well, that's simple. You poison it."

"Poison?" Snow asked. "What kind of poison works on a dragon?"

"Any kind, assuming the dosage is right," Som said. "A high enough dose could send any creature, big or small, straight to..." He yawned expansively. "...sleep."

"Did you poison yourself again?" Gezund demanded. "You're hopeless."

"That's another thing about poisons, upsider," Som said, turning his watery eyes on Snow. "In the correct dose, they can be medicines."

A black-powder pistol and a potent poison. A plan was beginning to take shape in Snow's mind. With Dour's training, Bright's armor and Shem's tactics, she had a better chance than she'd ever had before of resisting the queen's amorous advances.

There was really only one more thing she needed.

Courage.

SHE RETURNED TO HER ROOM. SHE'D REALLY BEGUN TO FEEL at home there. Perhaps more than she ever had in Snowden. The labor was honest, the dwarves companionable. She felt understood and appreciated and no one ever asked her to tell them what to do.

One of the women was tidying when she entered. A younger dwarf with fair hair and wide, blue eyes. She was mute, as far as Snow knew, and tended to wander the city in a daze. The others called her Addle and never asked anything of her.

"Thanks for cleaning up," Snow said.

Addle nodded graciously. She hovered, like she was waiting for something, only Snow didn't know what. She cast around for something to say.

"Actually, I've been meaning to ask. I... had a knapsack with me when I fell. I was wondering if they found anything with me in the river. Some jewelry maybe?"

Addle shook her head. Snow's aching heart sank. It was stupid to even miss the bloody thing. It didn't signify anything good. She should have thrown it away a long time ago. Or sold it, since it was made of gold. She'd never have the chance again.

She'd carried it with her all this time. Now she was pining for it. What did that mean? What did it say about her?

"You're better off without it."

"Wh-what did you say?"

Addle smiled at her. "You're not a slave anymore. None of us are."

"How did you-?"

"You have a decision to make. The choice will be yours, even if you feel like your hand is forced."

Her hand was small but her grip was strong as she clasped Snow's fingers.

And again, she said, "you're not a slave anymore."

Snow just gaped at her. Medea had told her that Addle hadn't spoken since the emancipation. Now, suddenly, she'd spoken like a scholar with a woman who wasn't just a stranger. She wasn't even the same *race*.

She didn't have time to question it. Addle bowed and departed, leaving Snow to her own company.

She felt the burning peak in her chest and knew it could only mean one thing.

The queen was closer than ever.

SHE'D FELT IT BEFORE, THAT NIGHT IN HER ROOM IN SNOWDEN. The eerie, otherworldliness of waking in a place that should have been familiar but instead was strange.

Adamant was silent. The hammers and picks had fallen still. The muffled rumble of powder blasts was absent. There were no voices. The room was dark and the only light was blue, like she was underwater.

Like she was dreaming.

The Dragon Queen was sitting at the end of her bed. Snow flattened against the wall and groped for something to defend herself with.

She found nothing.

"I suppose I should have seen it before, shouldn't I?" the queen asked. Something was dangling from her fingers, catching the sinister light.

A golden torc.

"Why didn't you tell me that you were a slave?"

Only one answer occurred to her. "Because I'm not a slave anymore."

"Who was it? Xeron? Maladgar, perhaps?"

"Does it matter?"

The queen clenched the torc so tight she warped the metal, left impressions of her slender fingers in it. "Yes."

"It was Maladgar. He kept me in his horde with all his other favorites. The golden orb, the ruby bigger than my head, the crown of the last king to stand against him."

"And Dragonsbane."

"His second biggest mistake was that he didn't lock it up."

"His *second* biggest?"

"His first was that he didn't kill me when he had the chance."

The queen laughed. "An emancipated slave takes it upon herself to rid the world of dragons and then falls madly in love with the queen of dragons herself. How delightfully romantic."

"Only if the story ends with true love's first kiss."

Which it wouldn't. She'd rather die than be a slave again. For any dragon.

"My only regret is that you killed him already. I'd have ripped out his beating heart for ever having touched you."

"I told you before, I can kill my own dragons."

"Yes, and I'm sure the dwarves of Adamant are teaching you all their best tricks, aren't they?"

Snow felt what little courage she'd rediscovered drain out of her, along with her voice. She wanted to shout. She wanted to threaten. She wanted to goad. She couldn't find the strength to even speak.

When she did, she begged. "Leave them alone."

"Why should I?" She turned her glowing eyes on Snow, leaned forward, lay a taloned hand on her thigh. "Give me a reason."

There was only one reason. Only one thing she could offer.

"I'll come to you," she said. "I'm through hiding anyway."

"I'm glad." The queen cupped her cheek but it didn't feel of anything. No contact, no pleasure, no pain. Just cold. "I can't bear to be apart from you for another moment."

Snow closed her eyes and felt the dream disintegrate around her. She woke to tears on her pillow. She knew she'd made the right choice - her own choice, just like Addle had said - and it felt terrible.

But there was a flicker of defiance in it, even now.

She'd said she'd come out. She hadn't said she would submit.

SHE DIDN'T TELL ANYONE THAT SHE WAS LEAVING. THE dwarves were there all the same. Medea, shaking her head. Dour, scowling. Bright, a touch of sadness in her smile. Som and Gezund, trying to tell her more about poisons and powder, as if distilling those last drops of knowledge would save her. Addle was there too, but absent, staring at things that weren't there.

Shem met her in the surface tunnels, grim and grey as ever.

"I'll wait for you to come back," he said, as he showed her the route to the snow and sky.

"I'm not coming back. I'm sorry, but there are others up there who need me."

"Then I'll pray it's your choice to make."

"Thanks."

The surface beckoned with a talon-tipped finger. Snow began the long walk to the surface. To her meeting with the queen. Dour had gifted her a sword of dwarven make. It wasn't Dragonsbane but, when she held it, she felt invincible. On her other hip was Gezund's pistol and a bag of Som's poisoned pellets. She had Bright's armor, Medea's grudging blessing and Addle's courage burning bright in her mind, overpowering the searing in her chest.

Shem had taught her how to defeat a dragon. But the queen wasn't just any dragon.

The blizzard called to her down the tunnel, howling and wailing. She'd have thought the queen was having a tantrum if she hadn't been about to get exactly what she wanted.

She stepped back out into the bleak winter. White flecks swiped across her cheeks. The wind tossed her hair. She'd almost forgotten what it felt like to be cold.

The queen was a dark shard in the snow-blind whiteness. Even at a distance, she could see the smile on her face. And the torc in her hand.

You're not a slave anymore.

Snow drew her sword. Drew her pistol. The queen started laughing.

And then she changed.

Snow ran as the immense dragon form took flight. She lifted her head, aimed the pistol, tracked it as it wheeled overhead. The downdraft blew her over, sent her tumbling through deep drifts. She rolled back to her feet and took aim again, peering between spinning snowflakes.

The wing. Puncture the wing.

The pistol erupted like thunder in her hand. Weeks of practice and she still wasn't used to it. Her hand went numb with the recoil and she watched the pistol ball vanish into the darkness above.

She tried to reload but she'd only trained to do it within the confines of Adamant and there were no blizzards underground. The wind blew the black powder, her frigid fingers fumbled the pellets. She swore and tossed the pistol away.

The dragon swooped low overhead. She tucked and rolled, avoiding its grasping talons. Then it slammed into the ground. A less graceful landing than usual.

There, in its left wing, was the smallest tear. Had she actually *hit* the bloody thing? Didn't that make her the finest pistolwoman who'd ever lived?

"How are you liking the poison?" she asked. "Is it making things interesting for you?"

She wondered if the queen could hear her over the howling wind. Then the dragon spun around and roared so loud there was no doubt.

What had Shem told her? Challenge them? Because they can't abide a challenge unanswered.

Snow spread her arms. "Come at me, bitch!"

She turned to sprint across the open field, gratified when the queen loped after her and didn't take to the air again. It looked like the pistol and the poison had done their job.

And ahead was the crevasse where she would make her stand. All she had to do was reach it.

She heard the rushing intake of breath again, felt the heat of the flame on the back of her neck. She yanked her hood up and kept running. Time to trust in dwarven craftswomanship.

The queen unleashed her fire and Snow kept running. She waited for it to engulf her, to roast her alive and leave her a charred husk on a patch of scorched ground. Instead, she felt the heat bending away from her, repelled by the dragon hide. Magic that wouldn't fade, even when the dragon itself was dead.

The queen was just as surprised as Snow. She roared and leapt into pursuit and Snow could feel the lead she'd created for herself vanishing as the monster chewed up the space between them.

It was too late. She was in the crevasse now, running deeper and deeper, and it didn't matter that the queen's jaws were reaching out to bite her clean in half or that she could feel the heat of its breath on the back of her neck.

The dragon form's shoulders hit the sides of the narrow chasm and it jerked to a stop, jaws snapping shut, cutting Snow's cloak to rags. She skidded to a halt and spun, sword raised. The dragon wriggled, trying to get closer. It managed an extra yard. She chopped it across the snout. It recoiled with a hiss.

Then it collapsed, folding in on itself. Taking on a smaller, more mobile shape. Just the way Shem had said it would.

The queen stepped out from the cloud that had once been her dragon form. It clung to her like black ribbons, snarling around her arms and legs. There was blood on her flank, oily and opalescent, and a dainty scar across her nose. Even so, she looked as proud and poised as ever.

Snow knew the poison must have affected her. She just wasn't showing it.

"Don't you find this dance tiresome, my love?"

Snow grinned. "I could go all night, sweetheart. How about you?"

The queen smiled thinly. Snow backed up, pointed her sword squarely at her heart. Dragonsbane or not, she'd run her through.

"You can't defeat me with that blade, no matter how pretty it is."

"I think I'd like to try. Just to be sure."

They slashed at one another, sword and claws. Sparks flashed between them. The queen was slower, clumsier than usual. Snow saw the opening and struck. She thrust.

Down.

The point of the sword broke the scales on the queen's thigh and pierced deep. It stopped her in her tracks, dropped her to one knee. Snow pulled the blade free and swung to deflect a swipe of claws. She hacked the other woman's fingers off.

The queen didn't scream. She didn't make the slightest noise. She met Snow's eyes as she brought the point of the sword up under her chin.

"I win."

"Indeed, you do." The queen didn't look defeated. She looked pleased. "But I have one more gift for you. Freedom."

Snow's eyes narrowed. "I *have* freedom."

"The freedom of another. The man you left behind. You are fond of him, are you not? I found warmth enough for him in your heart. I must admit, it made me jealous. You have nothing but contempt for me. So, I took him far away, to my palace, and I placed him inside a mirror from which there is no escape. A prince in a glass coffin."

Once upon a time, Snow was sure she'd had patience. Not anymore. She grabbed the queen by the throat and held the point of the sword at her eye.

"Why? Why would you do that?"

"Because I'm curious to know what you will choose. You refused my proposal and burned my heart. You tried to flee to the end of the earth to escape me and yet you came to me when I called out to you. You reject a life with me but, when I dangle his life before you, you will surrender your freedom. Won't you?"

Snow nodded slowly. It was Shem's most important piece of advice.

Someone needed to make a sacrifice.

"You'll let him go?" she asked, "if I submit?"

"Of course." The queen's lips curled into a sly smirk. "What use would I have for him if I had you?"

It was the hardest thing Snow had ever done. She drove her sword into the snow.

"What do I need to do?"

"Take my hand. And let this story end as it is supposed to. Like you said. With true love's first kiss."

Snow did as she was instructed. The queen rose to her feet, all injuries forgotten. She dragged her close, enveloped her in her arms, and Snow felt the burning in her chest hotter than ever before.

The queen's lips were cold as ice.

THE DRAGON QUEEN WAS BORED.

Bored of dwarves. Bored of humans. Bored of other dragons. She was bored of trophies and tributes and being immortal.

She wanted to be in love.

She rose from her throne, crossed her palace and stood before the mirror. She placed her hand upon the glass. The girl glared at her. She tugged at the torc around her neck. Her skin and the gold, marked by the queen's fingers. Now the glass coffin was hers.

"Mirror, mirror, on the wall," she whispered, "you are the fairest of them all."

Her black lips curled into a satisfied smirk.

"And you're mine."

DAMIEN MCKEATING

Damien Mckeating was born and a short time after that he developed a love of fantasy and the supernatural. After studying screenwriting at university, he worked for a time as a radio copywriter, before becoming a teacher for children with special educational needs. He has written for radio, comics, film, prose, and worked as a lyricist and bass player for a peculiar folk band. He has short stories included in different anthologies, ranging from modern takes on Irish mythology to SF adventures for young readers. He is fond of corvids, writes daily, and is currently the oldest he has ever been.

NANSI AND THE DRAGON

Damien Mckeating

*T*he mountain stood at the heart of Evergreen, the land that the people had called home for as long as they could remember. Vibrant forests of rich greens and browns stretched from the mountain and formed a ring around a verdant grassland. Deer and buffalo roamed there, birds soared in the cloud-tossed skies, and the soil of Evergreen was rich with growing plants and vegetables.

Nansi stood at the base of the mountain, perched on an outcropping of grey rocks surrounded by green ferns. The wind pulled at her clothes, whipped her hair, and was filled with the scent of damp wood and soil. The rains had paused, but the clouds were full with more to come. Nansi breathed deeply and smiled. She felt like the whole world was hers.

She looked up at the mountain. They called it Dragon Peak, after the creature that guarded its summit. There were secrets in the mountain, and Nansi aimed to discover them. A switchback trail led halfway up to the peak, but after that, the going would be tougher. She would have to climb and scramble. Others had tried the climb and the only ones who had come back had been the ones who gave up. The dragon did not take kindly to visitors.

Behind her, Akra swore and wrestled with the tent. Nansi looked at her husband and sighed. He was a homebody and did not enjoy traveling. He would rather be at home, surrounded by the rest of the people, and sleeping in a comfy bed in a proper house. He would complain all night and then moan all morning about the bad night's sleep he'd had in the tent. The ground would be too hard, the night would be too cold, the animals would be too close and too dangerous.

"Let me help," Nansi said.

"No, you go back to posing on your rock. I'm fine," Akra teased.

"I was admiring the view," she said as she started to clip together the supports for the tent canopy.

"So was I," he replied with a smile.

Nansi smiled in return. This was her thing, this journey, this quest, and she had told him, quite honestly, that she did not mind if he stayed behind. That he had come with her anyway meant everything.

"We'll have to huddle for warmth tonight," she said.

"Might as well be warm before the dragon eats us."

"The dragon doesn't travel down the mountain."

"The dragon hasn't traveled down the mountain *yet*."

Despite his worries and his complaining, they slept soundly, nestled into the warmth of each other's bodies while the wind and rain lashed at the tent.

Nansi started them early the next day. As she had predicted, the first part of the climb went quickly. The ground was rocky and uneven, but not difficult if you paid attention. Halfway up the mountain, they gazed across Evergreen and saw their people's land laid out like a glistening jewel. The Winding River cut the land into pieces, a dazzling streak of blue amidst the greens, yellows and browns.

"It's beautiful," Akra said.

Nansi didn't reply. Her gaze was fixed beyond the Evergreen. On the horizon was a dark smear stretching as far as she could see, surrounding the Evergreen like an invading force. It was the Fallows. The land there was barren, dead and poisoned. Nothing grew. Any animal taken from it and eaten made you sick. If you traveled the Fallows, you became weak and died. It sucked the life from everything and every year, it took a little more of the Evergreen from them.

"The dragon will have the answers," Nansi said. "We'll turn the Fallows away."

"So you say," Akra mumbled, although not too loudly. He wanted her to be right, after all.

They climbed. Nansi found herself smiling as she scrambled, jumped, and hauled herself up the rocks. It felt good. She felt alive. Her muscles ached and sweat glistened on her skin. Akra complained and lagged behind.

"Look," Nansi said, pointing out strange arrangements in the mountain. Bits of metal, impossibly big, stuck out from the mountain like bones piercing skin. There was no sense to where they appeared. It was as if something was buried in the mountain. That was what Nansi believed. That was where she believed the answers were.

"They're just stories," Akra said.

"Everything is just a story," she replied. "But some stories are true."

They had agreed that she would make the last part of the ascent alone. She would be faster and it would be safer for both of them.

They kissed and then kissed again, this time with a fierceness that replaced their unwillingness to risk saying goodbye.

The dragon waited.

Nansi went on alone. She loved Akra, but was glad he was waiting for her. On her own, she felt capable and strong. She didn't have to keep looking out for him. Deep in her soul, she knew he would wait for her as long as he had to.

It grew colder as she neared the top. The sun sank, the shadows grew longer. There were patches of snow in the shadows of rocks. The trees were sparse.

She was surprised to find a path leading up to the last rise of stone, a slab of grey rock that rose up from the mountain like a wall. Nansi frowned, looking for a way to climb it, before she realized she didn't have to. She wasn't looking at a wall: she was looking at a door.

Now that she'd seen it, the door was obvious. Its grey metal and clumps of rockfall helped to disguise it, making it part of the mountain. Looking around with a new frame of expectation, Nansi saw more bits of metal protruding from the stone. What she had taken for a boulder was a round, metal device, beaten and weathered. On its otherwise clear surface flickered a red light.

Nansi studied it. The light was a circle that floated above the surface of the metal. Nansi reached out and passed her hand through it, watching the red glow ripple over her hand. The light chirruped, like a happy bird, and Nansi pulled her hand back.

The mountain rumbled and a cascade of rocks drew her attention to the summit. There were ripples of movement and the oiled scrape of metal on metal. From beneath a layer of snow, dust and rock, the dragon began to reveal itself. Coils of metal, wrapped around and around the summit, began to shift and unravel. The serpentine body revealed itself as the dragon uncurled itself from the mountain and snaked its way down towards Nansi. Claws longer than she was tall gouged the stone.

The dragon descended.

Its face was made of jagged, sharp angles. Its hinged jaw snapped open and close, revealing metallic teeth and tiny jets of steam. Tendrils, like whiskers, snaked around its face, each emitting a glow that cascaded from red to green to blue and back again. Blue eyes blazed on either side of the head, their gaze fixed on Nansi.

Nansi stood her ground as the mountain shook under the giant, metallic serpent's approach. It vibrated through her, a rhythmic counterpoint to the fear that made her tremble.

Its head hung in front of her while its body curved away, stretching back up the mountain. She would never have believed anything so vast could exist.

"Identification," the dragon said. It was a voice of screeching metal. Steam erupted from its mouth as it spoke.

"I am Nansi Ashani," she said.

"Designation not recognized. This area is classified delta. Trespassers will be terminated."

"You are the great dragon," Nansi said and swallowed her fear. "I need your help."

"You have ten seconds to leave the area. If you do not comply, you will face irreparable organic damage."

"The Fallow is killing us," Nansi said. She pointed towards the dark horizon. "I believe you can help us. Everything is dying."

The dragon looked at the horizon. Nansi saw its eyes

swivel, saw concentric circles within its eyes expand and contract.

"The protocol is failing," it said. "Analyzing... multiple systems offline."

"You know how to fix it, don't you?" In her excitement Nansi took a step towards the dragon. "The answers are in the mountain. I want to know. I want to know all of it."

"Further information is required to adjust protocol parameters to optimal levels."

"What does that mean?"

The dragon studied her. Its eyes blazed and a blue light washed over Nansi. "Designation: Nansi Ashani," it said. "The protocol requires DNA samples and environmental extracts. If the parameters are adjusted, a system reboot may be initiated."

"And that will save the Evergreen?"

The dragon hung motionless. "Calculating," it said. "An environment conducive to existing life forms can be re-initiated, within a zero point zero, zero, zero, one margin of error."

"I don't understand what you want. I don't know what it means."

"We will show you," the dragon said.

One of the floating tendrils by its mouth flared into green light and arced towards Nansi. She reached out to touch it and was surprised by how warm it felt. The dragon wrapped its claws around her waist and lifted her into the air. The green tendril snaked around Nansi's neck, curling around to the back of her head where it slid under her skin.

Nansi gasped.

Her mind flooded with images, numbers, letters, sounds, formulas; fleeting impressions that built on each other to create a view of the world in Nansi's mind that she had never anticipated.

The dragon showed her a swarm of mosquitos. It focused in on one of them and took it apart, dissecting the creature into its constituent limbs, before going deeper and showing her its blood vessels, its molecules, its DNA.

On a vast plain, it showed her a metal box, lying bent and broken in the grass, surrounded by the big cats that hunted there. It showed her components in the box; wiring, processors, and the target of her search: a memory drive.

Deep in the Fallows she saw a stagnant pool of water. Its surface was slimy with rainbow colours and foul bubbles popped on its surface. Next to it lay the bones of a long dead animal.

And it showed her the people. It took her deep into their bodies, plucked them apart like it had the mosquitos, and revealed the final component.

Nansi was sitting on the ground when she came back to her senses. The back of her neck hurt and she clamped her hand to it.

"Your interface is missing," the dragon said. "There will be no permanent damage."

"Those things you showed me," Nansi said, her mind still reeling. How long had that taken? Seconds? "If I bring you those things, you'll give me the stories inside the mountain?"

The dragon whirred and steam hissed. "Yes," it said.

THEY FOLLOWED THE WINDING RIVER, NANSI LEADING THE way and Akra close behind. When she'd descended the mountain, he'd wept and then become caught between concern and anger when he saw the wound on her neck.

"You could have been killed," he said as he swept her hair out of the way and cleaned the injury.

"We're all going to die one day," Nansi said.

"That doesn't mean we have to hurry it along."

"I was talking about the Fallows, but I know what we need to do to stop it."

She had tried to explain what the dragon had shown her and what they needed to do. The words were unfamiliar on her lips, the concepts vague in her mind. The dragon had given her knowledge, but no context. All she knew was to take the next step in front of her.

The river would lead them to the Flats; an area of marshland where there were plenty of mosquitos.

"What does the dragon want with bugs?" Akra said.

"Their biology is extraordinary," Nansi said as they trekked over sodden ground, moving further into the Flats. "The way they store and convert the blood they feed on makes them walking DNA repositories. By analyzing them, the dragon can develop an intricate history of the Evergreen's life forms. It's what they were designed to do."

"Designed? You mean by the Creator?"

Nansi thought for a moment. She could feel the answers forming in her mind, but it took control for her to understand them. When she was tired her mind buzzed with information, making her head hurt. "A creator, yes," she said at last, "but not like you mean. Not like the people understand it."

They found a dry patch of high ground and camped near the river that night. It was a clear and cool night. As the herons nested on the riverbank, Nansi lay on her back next to Akra and stared at the stars and the moon.

"What are the stars?" she asked Akra.

"The eyes of the Creator," he said. "The gleaming lights of other dragons, high up in the sky." He caught something in the tone of her question and turned his head towards her. "What do you think they are?"

"Other worlds. They're like this one, but so far away that all we can see is a tiny speck of light and it takes millions of years to get to us. There are other suns out there. There are other moons."

"Other Evergreens?"

"I believe so. There is so much that we haven't seen. The Evergreen was supposed to be bigger than this; it should cover the planet. Something went wrong." Nansi turned to smile at Akra and saw that he was crying. "What's wrong?"

"That's not what you think," he said. "That's what you know. You *know* these things now, don't you? They're not just stories."

"Everything's a story."

"But some stories are true."

She wiped the tears off his cheek. "It changes some things, but some things it doesn't change at all. We're still the people. The Evergreen is still ours; it was made for us. And I still love you."

"I love you," he replied.

They held hands and fell asleep looking at a sky twinkling with distant worlds.

The next day they travelled through the Flats proper. They had to wade often, but they traveled on higher ground when they could. Crocodiles liked to hunt in the Flats, and the people told many cautionary tales to their children about wading in rivers.

Early in the afternoon, they saw a single tree growing on

a hill. It was surrounded by still water, and the tree was blurred by a swirling haze of insects that buzzed around it.

"A swarm," Akra said. "If we get too close to that, they'll eat us alive."

"But just imagine what information they're carrying," Nansi said.

The mosquitos in the cloud buzzed around each other, moving from the tree to the water and back again. The fruit of the tree was small, red berries, and the insects would eat them when blood was scarce.

"We have to get closer," Nansi said.

Akra shook his head. "We should look for some others. Sometimes they feed on the crocodiles." That was true, and the thick skin of the crocodiles meant the big beasts often didn't notice what was happening.

"You want to meet a crocodile?"

"More than I want to meet them," Akra jutted his chin towards the swarm. "They're not just going to pop over and follow us back to the dragon."

"They might," Nansi mused.

She sat for a while, watching the bugs and thinking through the idea she'd had. One mosquito was all they needed, but more would be better. Too many, of course, would be dangerous.

Nansi settled on her plan. She took one of their empty water jugs and set it down on the ground. Using a knife, she pricked one of her fingers and let drops of blood fall into the jug and onto the rim. She cleaned the knife and her finger, sat back and waited.

She did not wait long.

A mosquito came to investigate. It tasted the blood on the rim and then flew inside the jug. Another followed. And another. Soon there were a dozen or more, buzzing around in the jug and making it hum.

"That's enough," said Nansi, with one eye on the swarm. She scuttled forward, crouching low, and popped the cork back into the jug. She picked it up and felt the buzzing through the clay walls. "See?" she grinned.

"Just don't drop it," Akra grumbled.

Nansi wrapped the jug in a blanket and stored it in their pack. Her skin tingled as she thought about the information contained in there. She carried a miracle with her, one that no one in the people had ever conceived of.

Nansi grinned as she felt the world opening up around her.

THEY TRAVELED WITH THE SETTING SUN, MOVING TOWARDS drier land, and finally to the great Open Plains. Miles of wild grass grew and rippled in the wind. Deer and buffalo grazed, the big cats hunted, snakes slithered, rabbits burrowed, and crops sprouted from the rich soil. It was sometimes called the Plains of Plenty, for it held everything the people needed to survive.

Nansi savored the breeze on her face, only to realize she had been thinking about ways to harness the energy of the wind. These new thoughts often intruded in her mind, appearing as if out of nowhere. They didn't feel like her own, but there was only her to think them.

"There's a tribe nearby," Akra said. "We could stop there to spend the night in a house with walls, speak to some people, and see what news there is."

"A tent has walls," Nansi teased.

"Proper walls," Akra asserted. "The kind that a big cat can't tear through."

The wild cats of the plains were bigger than a man, with wickedly curved fangs that rose up from their lower jaw. They tended to be solitary, but even one cat could devastate a whole group of hunters.

"No, we keep going," Nansi said.

The journey across the plains was peaceful. Most of the wildlife avoided them and Nansi and Akra knew how to stay away from the ones that were dangerous. It was, in many ways, calm, but Nansi drove them onwards with a nervous energy that worried Akra.

"You don't sleep," he said to her one day.

"I sleep," Nansi said. She knew she slept because she dreamt.

"Not real sleep. You don't stop moving. You twitch. Your fingers move like you're whittling at wood. Are you dreaming?"

"I don't remember," she said.

It was half-true. Her dreams were confusing and messy. Images and ideas clashed and collided in her dreaming mind. It was a kaleidoscope of information that left her nauseous if she dwelled on it. She was learning to let it lie and trust that the knowledge would appear when she needed it.

That was how she located the memory drive. Throughout the day she would stop, scan the horizon, and wait until the knowledge came to her. She would just know where it was. She took them west, making small adjustments to their path as they went.

Before the drive they were seeking had gone offline, she knew that it had been collating information about weather patterns, air pollutants, rainfall, temperature, humidity, soil acidity, atmospheric pressure and a dozen more criteria. If she concentrated on a concept, she could begin to understand it, but it never lasted long. Once it had given her a nose bleed, which she had hidden from Akra to stop him from worrying more.

They followed a tributary of the river, circled around a herd of buffalo, and eventually stood on high ground, looking down at an expanse of scrubland. There was a rocky outcrop with a scattering of trees. The drive was down there. Lying asleep under the trees was a big cat. It dozed in the shade, its tail sometimes flicking at the flies that buzzed around it.

"It gets worse," Akra sighed. "At least death will be quick."

"Are you volunteering to sacrifice yourself while I get the drive?" Nansi raised an eyebrow.

Akra laughed. "You'd be lost without me."

"If we wait, it will go and hunt."

"You haven't seen the carcass, have you?" Akra pointed. Beneath one of the trees was a large buffalo carcass, partially eaten. The big cats had prodigious appetites, but once sated, they would happily lie in a post-meal stupor for a day or two. This cat had enough buffalo left for another meal, assuming another predator or scavenger didn't come along to try and steal it.

"So, we wait a while," Nansi suggested, knowing that they couldn't. Either the cat would realise they were there, or something else drawn to the dead animal would.

"If we'd gone to tribe, we could have persuaded a few hunters to join in."

Nansi shook her head. "We can't fight it. But we can't get the drive while it's down there guarding it."

"Guarding it?" Akra chuckled. "My love, it probably

doesn't even know it's there. It's not guarding it, it's just bad luck this is where it's decided to take a nap."

"You're right," Nansi said, a smile lighting up her face. She'd given the cat too much credit. It wasn't guarding the drive; it was just in the way. "We just need to find a way to move it."

"And stay alive."

Nansi sat and watched the cat while Akra made them a simple supper. This close to the cat, he was too afraid to light a fire and cook in case the smell woke it up.

"We can't outrun it," Nansi said. "We can't fight it, but we're smarter than it is. And we can get help."

"The hunters?"

"Buffalo."

Akra snorted. "Something else bigger and stronger than us."

"And afraid of us," Nansi said. "If we go back to the river, we can make a noise, get the buffalo scared. One of us in the north and one of us in the east will drive them this way, along the river, and into the pass between the hills."

"They'll stampede right at the cat," Akra said.

"And the cat will move."

Akra nodded. "Okay. Will the thing we're after survive?"

"It's survived this long. I think it has protection enough." Nansi thought about the drive and winced as the statistical information about the unit's composition and protection flashed through her brain. "It will be fine," she grimaced.

"But will you?"

Nansi smiled at him. "I'll be fine too," she lied. She knew better.

They were up with the dawn. The big cat had not moved. Nansi and Akra went quickly, moving in a slow, loping run that carried the people great distances. They found the buffalo herd had moved a little, now close enough to the pass for their plan to work.

Nansi went north and Akra went east. They signaled to each other and made as much noise as they could, whooping, hollering, bashing sticks or pans together. At first, nothing happened. Slowly, beast by beast, the buffalo started to pay attention. Nansi hoped they decided not to stampede at the noisy interlopers, but her worries were unfounded. All the buffalo wanted was to get somewhere quieter.

The great herd began to shuffle and turn, their assembled mass starting to drift across the plains, away from the river and the noise and towards the pass. A cloud of dust rose up into the air and within moments the herd was gone, moving too fast for Nansi and Akra to ever keep up.

Akra laughed and leapt into the air. He hugged Nansi and kissed her. "My brilliant wife," he said. "You did it."

"We did it. Without getting trampled," she added.

"Let's see if our big cat has been roused from his slumber!"

They followed in the wake of the stampeding herd. The dust cloud billowed on the horizon and Nansi and Akra could taste it in the air as they went. When they reached the outcropping, there was no sign of the cat and one of the trees had been knocked over and trampled.

"A rude awakening," Akra said.

"Keep a lookout, in case he comes back," Nansi said. She ran across the rocks, following the unerring signals that arrived in her mind without conscious thought.

When she found the spot where the monitoring station should be, it wasn't there. She panicked and began to search. Time and herds of buffalo had left their mark. The station was several yards away, battered and half buried. Nansi fell to her knees next to it and used her hands to sweep away the dry soil.

The station was a metal box, designed to withstand intense environmental pressures – much more so than the Evergreen presented. Nansi's hands moved automatically, finding and pressing the release catches to open up a plate on the station's front. The circuitry she saw inside was astounding. A few days ago, it would have been the most amazing thing she'd ever seen, now it was part of a collection of miracles that were re-creating her view of the world.

She saw the station as a circuit diagram. She let herself react to the information and, without her making any conscious effort, she found the memory drive and plucked it free.

"Is that it?" Akra said, looking over her shoulder.

In her hand rested a black, plastic rectangle, with a row of gold teeth along one edge. It looked like nothing, but Nansi understood that it was priceless.

"This is it," she said, and put the memory drive in her pocket. "It holds more information than a billion mosquitos."

Akra nodded, looking doubtful. "If you say the mosquitos were designed, then the big cats were designed too, yeah?"

"I suppose so," Nansi said. She searched her mind for the information and stumbled upon fragments of ideas. "The world needed to work to exist," she frowned. "A viable food chain, self-sustaining and self-correcting."

"Everything has a purpose," Akra concluded.

"Yes."

"Even the people."

"I think, maybe, the people *were* the purpose. To make sure we survive."

Akra was thoughtful. "You need more than to just survive. Everyone needs purpose. You have your quest. And I have you."

Nansi smiled. "There is one more thing we need to get."

She looked off towards the horizon at the dark landscape where the Fallows waited.

No one knew when the people discovered that the Fallows meant death, but everyone knew that if you went there, you would get sick. Sometimes you saw animals stray into that blighted landscape and sometimes they came back with their fur gone, their skin melting, their eyes blind, and other horrors.

The Fallows destroyed both flesh and land. It was a poison that took more and more of the Evergreen every year.

"This will kill you," Akra said.

"The dragon can save me. I'll be fine," she turned away from him as she spoke, nervous that she might giveaway the half-lie in her words.

She stared at the Fallows. She had never been this close to it before. The start of that barren landscape was only a few hundred yards away. Even here the grass around them was shorter, sicklier, sparser. The sickness was seeping under their feet.

"I'll be there and back in a day," she said.

"That's too long."

"It's got to be far enough inside for the sample to be valid. The dragon needs to see the poison at its fullest." She turned back to Akra. "We don't give up now. Not after what we've done."

Akra didn't say anything. He pulled her to him and held her tightly. She held him back. The two of them took a deep, nurturing comfort in the warmth and feel of each other. Nansi had once heard a poet use the phrase "My shape will comfort you," and she found it suddenly apt.

"Wait right here," she said. "I'll be back by sunset."

"You'd better be, or I'm coming after you."

Nansi took only a small vial to collect a water sample with and left everything else behind. She needed to travel fast and light. Any food or water she took with her would become contaminated. She had to travel as far as she could on her own and get back as quickly as possible, before the sickness destroyed her.

She left the Evergreen and Akra behind, and went out into the Fallows. It consumed her, wrapped its barren world around her, and sucked her in. Its atmosphere was heavy. Nansi felt it as a physical weight on her shoulders and in her chest. The Fallows hated life. It felt conscious, as if it was aware of her and hated her for living.

Logically, she knew that wasn't true. There was no demon living in the ground, as the story of the people said. The dragon had shown her the poison that was at work, the failure of the protocol to promote the Evergreen beyond its current boundaries. When her work was achieved, the dragon had shown her the processing towers that would be returned to operation. The air would be cleaned. The world would be made whole.

Nansi became aware of the silence. There were no birds. No animals moved. With no trees to move through, even the wind was silent. She couldn't bear the thought of the

Evergreen becoming like that. The idea of it stabbed at her heart.

She traveled quickly and calmly. The sun was warm and sweat trickled freely down her face and back. She licked at her dry lips and tasted the dust that caked them. When she got back to Akra, they would find the river and she would dive into it.

She could smell the waterhole before she could see it. The stench of damp and decay washed over her. It left her skin feeling greasy, like the poison in the wasteland was coating her body.

Nansi gagged and covered her mouth with her arm. She edged closer to the water and now she could taste it on the air as well as smell it.

The stagnant liquid stretched out ahead of her. The bones of long dead fish crunched under her boots. She was looking at the remains of what must have been a large lake; the dead trees behind her must have marked the shoreline. The water that remained was brackish and dark. A bubble formed and popped.

Nansi crouched at the dead-lake's edge. She tied a leather strap around the vial and dropped it into the water, holding the strap so her skin wouldn't touch the liquid. She lifted the vial out and stuck the lid on.

She held the strap and watched the vial spin gently as it dripped dry. The liquid inside was dark and sediment swirled around it.

A ripple blossomed on the surface of the water and spread out towards her.

Nansi tensed and stared.

There was nothing moving. What could have done it?

She watched the ripple-circles spread.

The world was silent.

The lake ahead of her exploded and Nansi scurried backwards. Water rose into the air and thick, black mud erupted with a sucking *squelch*. In the midst of the violent upheaval was a crocodile. It was the largest Nansi had ever seen and she did not understand how it was still alive.

Its skin sloughed from its body, revealing rancid bones and muscles. Its eyes were bloody hollows. From its elongated maw rose a mess of wicked teeth in stages of decay. The jaws snapped and some teeth broke and fell.

The beast crashed back down into the mud, rivulets of filth streaming down its undead body.

Nansi stared in horror. She knew that she was going to die. The crocodile was too close. She couldn't outrun it. She couldn't fight it.

But the beast collapsed into the muck and didn't move. A sickly gargle came from deep inside its throat. Its sides rose and fell erratically as, despite everything, it breathed.

Cautiously, Nansi crawled away from it. When the beast still didn't move, she got up and started to run, looking back over her shoulder once to see if it was following.

It wasn't.

The rush of adrenaline and the flood of terror were her last clear memories of the journey back to Akra. There was a pain in her throat and chest. Her vision started to blur. Her head hurt; the sun was too bright and even simple thoughts escaped her and left her confused.

Where was she going?

She had lost her sense of purpose, but knew only that she had to keep moving.

Keep going.

One step.

Then another.

Back to the dragon.

WHEN SHE WOKE, IT WAS DARK. THERE WAS A CLEAR NIGHT sky above her, filled with stars and a waxing moon. The air was cool and clean. She breathed deeply and savored it. Her breath startled her. There was a pain in her ribs and she could hear herself wheezing. She struggled to sit up and collapsed with the effort.

"It's okay," Akra said as he scurried over to her. "Don't try to move. You've been very sick."

Nansi turned her head and her vision came in and out of focus. She saw their tent, a campfire, their packs. She saw the mountain, rising up as a shadow in the night that blotted out the sun.

"The dragon," she whispered.

"That's right. You said the dragon could fix you, so I brought you back to the mountain. Gave you some chala root for your fever, got you some fresh water, made you some soup. You haven't eaten or drunk much, but some. Enough?"

Nansi sighed. "Yes."

Akra held her hand and she did her best to squeeze it back. In truth she had no idea if her hand had moved at all.

"Tomorrow, we'll go up the mountain," said Akra.

"You can't carry me."

"Stop talking. Save your strength. You should never have gone into the Fallows. Should have sent the dragon if it was so important."

"The dragon protects the mountain."

"We did what it wanted. Now it can save you."

Nansi smiled. "No. Not me. I'm going to save you."

"Stop talking. You're delirious."

Nansi felt a cool cloth press against her forehead. She closed her eyes and drifted into an uneasy sleep.

There were dreams. She thought they were dreams.

She was on the mountain, high up the path, where the wind turns cold and you can taste frost in the air. She was lying on a pallet and she saw ropes trailing from it to Akra, who stood with his back to her. The fool had dragged her up the mountain.

"Hey!" he shouted and waved his arms. "We're here! We did it! Come and help us!"

Nansi's world went dark again.

She saw the dragon, snaking its way down the mountain, towering over Akra, reaching for her with its clawed hands.

Then the cold air was rushing past her. There was metal all around her. She could hear the whirring and hissing of the dragon as it carried her. She heard Akra screaming and swearing.

Another gap... another darkness...

The world was warm again. Nansi came awake with a sudden clarity and urgency. She sat up on a bed she didn't recognize. Her body ached and threatened to drag her down again, but her mind was clear.

She was inside the mountain.

The room around her was bright, clear and clean. There was a bed and... things she didn't recognize... until the knowledge started to come to her... there was a drip in her arm, a computer next to the bed monitoring her vitals and through a nearby door that was a shower and toilet.

She gasped.

There was so much that she knew.

Her blood... they had changed her blood, cleaned it, given her blood that wasn't hers. Akra had carried her to the dragon and the dragon had brought her to the mountain. They had all of the samples, all except the last one...

Nansi hauled herself out of bed. She clung to the wall for support and forced her way out of the room.

"Where is he?" she asked, remembering that the facility had voice activated systems. "Where is Akra?"

"Hello, Nansi," said a gentle, female voice. "Akra is currently at Laboratory Prime. I can guide you there."

"Do it."

Lights in the hallways flickered, leading Nansi deeper into the facility. She started to assimilate some of her new memories. The facility had been designed as a terraforming plant. It should have transformed the planet into one, vast Evergreen, capable of supporting a huge array of life. The people would have been educated by the hardware within the facility. But it had failed. They had been living a life half-lived. The samples she had procured would have kickstarted the process again, except they still needed the last sample... one of the people. The facility needed to assimilate and process the primary life-form to integrate any changes that had occurred while offline.

Nansi had meant for it to be her.

Akra had beaten her to it.

She found him in the processing lab. He lay on a bed, with countless tubes and wires leading from his body to the computer system arrayed around him. Blood, flesh, brainwaves, heart, DNA – everything and anything about him would be integrated.

"Hello, Nansi," he said.

"This was supposed to be me," she said.

"No, it wasn't." He smiled as he spoke. He was calm and almost serene, despite the web of technology that was wrapped around him. "You couldn't die here. You wanted the stories, and now they're yours." He held her hand and gave it a squeeze. "They're in your head now, aren't they? I saw them doing that while they fixed you. You know, fixing in this place looks a lot like killing."

"It was a blood transfusion."

"Well..." he tried to shrug, but lying down amidst the wires and cables it didn't work. "I don't know about such things."

"You found the dragon. You brought me back."

"You tell your stories. You always wanted these stories, Nansi, and now you can share them with everyone else."

Nansi held his hand and sat with him. Around her, she felt the facility sparking to life in the heart of the mountain. The world would be healed. The Evergreen would grow. Nansi saw how it would happen. She would teach the people what she had learned:

The world was full of stories and some of them were true.

ANDREA J. HARGROVE

Andrea Hargrove is a librarian from Eastern Pennsylvania with two previously-published short stories (a fairy tale called *The Fairy Maze* and a Western murder mystery called *Naomi*, both in anthologies by Zimbell House Publishing). She has always felt a connection to dragon tales and legends, partly because she was born in the Year of the Dragon and partly because they often take place in nature, where she likes spending her free time.

She's spent many happy hours hiking and reading outdoors. (Majestic views and cozy forests are equally welcome.) Besides that, she's recently begun studying kenjutsu and iaijutsu at a local martial arts dojo.

You can find her on Twitter (@AndreaJHargrove), and you can visit her new website (andreajhargrove.com), which is all about reading, writing, and the literary life.

THE GOLDEN ARROW

Andrea J. Hargrove

*S*unlight glinted off the golden arrow as Aidan nocked it against the coarse bowstring. Before he drew it back, he fought the tremor in his hands by taking a deep breath. The trembling subsided, but his mind and body still buzzed as he stared at this great treasure.

He turned his attention to his target – a simple wooden circle that he'd set up at his favorite spot by the lake. Ripples on the water glittered almost as much as the gold, but he was used to that distraction, at least, and nothing else in the little valley pressed for his attention. The lush hills around the lake afforded him a rare sense of privacy, and the familiar birdsong in the air, coupled with the almond-like scent of meadowsweet flowers, soothed rather than distracted. Any visible animals moved languidly, including his own horse, which grazed nearby.

Aidan honed in on the painted red and white rings on the target across from him – faded and peppered with holes that mostly clustered around the scarlet center. The wind picked up, but Aidan kept his eyes glued forward and recalculated the arc of the arrow as he finally pulled back the string of his longbow. The delicate strands of the fletching – also gold – tickled the corner of his mouth as he held the arrow steady against the weight of the draw, elbow tilted up and feet comfortably wide.

His horse, Rory, began to snort and pace. Aidan checked on him and found him head up, ears swiveling, and nostrils flaring. He couldn't find any reason for Rory's distress, so he soothed the horse and patted him on the nose until he settled in place.

Then it was back to the target. After two more deep breaths, Aidan let the arrow fly, but just as he released his fingers, a hot burst of air swept through the valley. Rory bolted with a scream, and the arrow veered wildly off course to point straight at the lake. Down it plunged, tip careening into the sparkling water as Aidan dropped his bow and called out, "Rory!"

He sprinted after the chestnut stallion, heart pounding, until a low rumble stopped him cold. He jerked his head up and around until he found the source of the disturbance:

A snow-white dragon lay on top of one of the hills, surrounded by a thick tangle of grass and wildflowers. These short plants did little to conceal the massive body, which stretched longer than two horses, even without the head and neck or the spiked tail that curled around the body. Two bat-like wings wrapped around it, too, at least at first. The creature unfolded itself and swooped down at Aidan, who bolted for his bow and arrows. Rory was long gone, disappearing

A massive shadow passed over his head, and then the creature settled nearby, all scales and teeth and claws. Aidan moved by instinct, fitting an arrow and whirling around to face his opponent. The main thing Aidan noticed was the toothy grin that stretched across the dragon's mouth, and then the pale eyes that danced above it. The dragon rumbled again, and this time Aidan identified the sound as a laugh.

He licked his lips and cleared his throat before addressing it. "I am Aidan, prince of Greenhaven." He swallowed hard between sentences to keep his voice from cracking. "What do you want, fiend? Did you blow my arrow off course?"

"I did. And I would apologize, but I meant to do that."

The voice, not as low as he would've guessed, also came with an unexpected softness. He realized that this dragon was a female, though he wasn't sure what to make of that. Before now, he hadn't considered the differences between male and female dragons, if any, much less what they would mean to him. In any case, the dragon confirmed his suspicions by following up with an introduction of her own.

"I'm the Princess Cara, and you have no idea how long it took me to find you."

"I suppose I don't." He shot his arrow straight at the dragon's eye, but she merely closed her eyelid and let it bounce off.

"None of that, now. You'd need a magical arrow, like that golden one you just shot into the lake, to take down a great dragon like myself."

"I... I... I'm sorry for shooting you."

"No, you're not, but never mind that. We're both in a position to help each other, and I'm anxious to get started. What do you say?" She batted her short eyelashes at him, mimicking humans in a way that made Aidan curl his lip and draw back.

Cara, the possible princess, watched him carefully, letting her long head loll from side to side as she tracked his progress. He paced around his quiver, tapping his fingers against the yew bow and staring right back at her, albeit with wider eyes. "I've never heard of a Princess Cara. Who are you, and how do you think we can help each other?"

The dragon dropped onto its massive haunches. "Oh!" she cried. "I suppose you wouldn't know much about me. My father's kingdom, Windmere, is far to the north. We're small but proud, and we've resisted invaders for the past hundred years, mostly with our magic. Unfortunately, the worst threats usually come from within. In this case, my father's sister thought she'd take me out of the line of succession by turning me into a dragon."

Aidan thought he was following the story. "You used to be a human?" he blurted. She nodded, and he continued, "And you're looking for someone to defeat your aunt?"

"Oh, no, she's been arrested, but she says she doesn't know how to reverse the enchantment."

"So, *that's* what you're looking for. And you've heard the rumors that some old wizard made Greenhaven's castle so that it could break curses." There was a whole town around the castle, also walled off, that might do the trick, but the castle itself was focal point.

"You've got it." Cara nodded encouragingly. "Are the stories true? All your neighbors say so."

Aidan bit the inside of his cheek as he racked his memory. "I don't really know. I'm not sure if anyone does."

"Regardless, I've been searching the world for a year, and this is the best lead I've gotten so far. Do you mind if I stay in the castle for a little while to see if that'll do the trick and break the enchantment?"

"Maybe. You said we can help each other."

Cara jutted her chin toward the lake. "I can get your arrow back for you."

"The one that *you* blew into the lake."

"That's the one," she said brightly. "I couldn't risk you shooting me with it, but I'll get it back if you promise that we can be friends, and that I can stay in your castle for a little while." When Aidan hesitated, Cara added, "It looked like an awfully *important* arrow."

Aidan's shoulders slumped. "It belongs to my mother, the queen. She entrusted it to me, and I came out here to practice with it." He tore his eyes away from the dragon to stare out at the lake. After all, she could snap him up at any moment, whether he was watching her or not. "Do you really think you could find one little arrow in there? It's deeper than it looks, with a mess of plants and things at the bottom."

Brushing away his concerns with the sweep of one clawed hand, Cara said, "But of course. I'm a dragon, and dragons are drawn to gold and magic."

"Okay." He scrunched his face, but her whole body perked up and her wings spread out to the side. "We have a deal then? I'd shake your hand, but..."

She waved one hand, and again, a flash of white sliced across Aidan's vision. "N...no, that's okay," Aidan said. "We have a deal."

Cara didn't need any more encouragement. Her muscles coiled, then she leapt up. She shot into the sky, her flexible wings beating noiselessly to take her higher and higher. When she looked like a cloud against the bright blue sky, she dove for the lake with a wild laugh.

At that speed and angle, she would've slammed right into the lake floor, but she pulled up so her belly just skimmed the water, arching her body back and maneuvering into a wide loop that slowed her momentum. Her scales rippled as she flew, and Aidan thought he saw some colors in them after all.

He got a better look when Cara made it all the way over and took her second run at the water, this time shallower and slower. She had that same iridescent shimmer as she moved, and it hypnotized Aidan as she plummeted into the lake. Water furrowed around her body as she descended, and even when she disappeared completely, she left a large wake.

Parts of her poked up as she ferreted around in the lake, and sometimes the tip of a wing or tail would briefly emerge. Often, a large cloudy mass floated just below the surface of the water, wiggling this way and that as Cara swam around. She darted from side to side and bobbed up and down, until one final dive that resulted in triumph.

She swam back up, breached the water in a heavy shower, and climbed onto the shore. Her teeth clenched the shaft of the golden arrow, with the fletches poking out like she was a farmer chewing on a tiny stalk of wheat. Cara trotted over to Aidan, bent her neck down, and deposited the arrow into his hands. "That's it. Let's go!"

Aidan froze. "Go?" he asked. "You mean to the castle?"

"That's right. You promised."

"Sure, but if you come *right now*, the guards will think you're chasing me, and they'll shoot you down. There are other weapons there that can hurt you besides this one arrow. And you'll scare all the people inside."

Cara cocked her head then nodded. "All right. I'll come after sundown. Do you have gardens or somewhere for me to land?"

"Sure. There's a big courtyard on the south side. Meet me there. I'll make sure no one shoots you. That is, as long as I can make it back in time."

The dragon grinned sheepishly, in another unsettling facsimile of human mannerisms. "Oh, right. Your horse ran away, didn't he? That part I am sorry for, since I'm sure he only ran because he smelled me."

Aidan sighed and collected his bow and quiver. "That's alright. I'm sure I can catch him." He forced his legs to start moving again. They wobbled below him but didn't give way as he dashed after Rory. If he could just get away, he might be safe. If he could get back to the castle before nightfall, he could have his mother order all the soldiers to surround the south courtyard with arrows and spears and swords and any other enchanted weapons they could find. Maybe he'd be there, too, with his own bow and the golden arrow.

The head was still wet, so he wiped it against his breeches, trying to get *her* off of it. She had to go, as soon as possible.

Luckily for Aidan, Rory was loyal and well-trained, and even a dragon scare couldn't make him run too far from his master. In fact, he was trotting back in the direction of the lake when Aidan spotted him. "Easy, boy!" he said, seizing the reins and burying his face in Rory's neck as he stroked the fine hair. "Are you ready to go?" murmured the prince. "I hope so, because we have a dragon to kill."

THE QUEEN WELCOMED HER ELDEST SON WITH OPEN ARMS, and Aidan fell against her, burying his head against her shoulder.

"There's a dragon coming, Mother," he sobbed as she held him tight.

"Where is it?" she asked. "Is anyone in danger?"

"Not yet. She's coming here because she wants to live in the palace."

"Why would she want that?" As she spoke, she ran one

of her soft hands over his short red hair. He wasn't sure what answer she expected to hear, but as his tale spilled out of him – the lake, the arrow, and the bargain – he felt her stiffening in place. When he concluded with a tearful plea for assistance, she asked, "Do you think that a member of the royal family is justified in breaking a promise?"

As Aidan turned his face up to her, feeling like he was six again instead of sixteen, tears blurred his vision. He wiped them away and sniffled. "Not usually. Not when we promise things to people, but here, I was just tricking a monster."

The queen placed her hands on Aidan's shoulders and stepped back, running her eyes up and down the length of him. He wished he hadn't come like this, with his hair and clothes all rumpled. He'd layered a simple leather jerkin over his doublet, both of which sat askew on his skinny frame, and his breeches and boots were scuffed beneath them. "Why should we keep our promises?"

The answer came automatically. "Because it's the right thing to do."

"Why else?"

This time, Aidan considered before answering. "It sets an example to the people around us?" It was something she often told him about the good or bad behavior of the court, and she was glad the lesson was in his mind, if not his heart.

She searched his eyes, and he guessed she'd see fear in them, even if her own were inscrutable. "Do you think it's a good idea to break your promise to a dragon?" she asked.

Aidan stiffened and shook his head. "No, you're right. Do you think I should let her come here and try to be her friend?"

"Do you?"

"That's what I promised her, so I guess so."

"I'm proud of you, Aidan. Remember that you'll have plenty of knights around you in case you run into any trouble. After all, we don't want to endanger our citizens. On that subject, please find out what dragons eat so that we can provide enough to keep our guest satisfied."

He sagged more as hope flew out of him, leaving him weak at the knees. It was decided. He'd have a dragon for a guest after all.

AIDAN WAITED UNDER THE OVERHANG AROUND THE courtyard, his mother at his side and a pair of guards flanking them. He wanted to tuck himself behind one of the columns, but his mother stood as still as one of those old stone structures, and he couldn't hide if the queen didn't. He couldn't stop himself from shifting from foot to foot and plucking at his cuffs, but he held his ground.

Deep shadows flowed over the castle walls in the last few moments before sunset, plunging the field before them into near-darkness. This space, with its trampled, patchy grass and collection of varied targets, usually served as a training area, even this late in the day. Aidan had never seen it so deserted, or even been anywhere near it without the shouts of men, the clanging of swords, or the neighing of horses carrying over the din of castle life.

Now, the silence set him even more on edge. His mother hadn't wanted to scare the visiting princess -- though Aidan doubted that would be a problem -- so she'd ordered most of her men to clear the area. A few lurked around the perimeter, some with barely-effective torches and some out of sight.

Cara swooped in with the dusk. Bats usually circled

overhead, but they'd all vanished for the occasion. "Good evening, Your Majesty. Your Highness." She addressed the queen and Prince Aidan respectively, with a bow to the queen. "Thank you for having me."

"It's our pleasure. You know, I was privileged to meet your charming father once on a state visit to Windmere. I'm sure your presence here will be as much of a delight." She turned meaningfully to Aidan, who took a step forward.

"Welcome, princess," he said stiffly. He couldn't think of anything else to say, so he left it at that.

After a moment, his mother continued, "We've emptied a room for you to use near the doors here, since some of our hallways might be a tight squeeze."

"I'd hate to go around knocking torches into tapestries," Cara laughed, "though I can get around better than you might think from looking at me."

"That's excellent. Aidan can take you on the grand tour tomorrow, and you can meet my other son and more of the court while you're at it. Tonight, he can show you to your chambers, unless you need to eat first." This was the first time Aidan detected a hint of anxiety, but he her voice sounded a little more constrained than usual, Cara didn't comment.

"Oh, no, I ate before I came, though if you could bring me a cow or a couple of sheep every few days, I'd appreciate it."

The queen relaxed just a hair. "I'm sure I can arrange that."

"I don't suppose you have a guess at how long I'll be here before I know if your curse-breaking castle works for me?"

"I've consulted my council, and they agree that three days is the typical amount of time needed to break spells. If this castle really is your cure, we should see results by then."

"Thank you so much!" As the queen left the courtyard with one of the guards, Cara bowed again, tucking one arm underneath her and folding over with her long neck and head curving down.

Butterflies swarmed in Aidan's stomach when she straightened up and locked eyes with him. Hers glowed faintly in the darkness.

"Would you care to follow me?" he asked her, though he'd much rather walk behind her as they passed through the great oak doors and into the castle.

"This'll be so much fun!" Cara said. "We'll be together for three whole days!"

Three. Whole. Days.

The presence of the guard, a beefy fellow with a puckered scar across his forehead, was the only thing that kept Aidan from bolting. Instead, he turned to the princess, smiled with gritted teeth, and said, "I can't wait."

THE NEXT MORNING, THE CASTLE TOOK ON AN ANTICIPATORY buzz. Half the staff took elaborate measures and routes to avoid the dragon while the other half found excuses to catch a glimpse. A handful of nobles spoke with her about their respective countries, with varying degrees of enthusiasm.

The children of the castle held extremely polarized views, with some weeping at the mention of the great serpent and others clamoring to get close to her. Aidan's brother, Finn, was in the second category. As a sheltered seven-year-old, his only concept of danger came from stories he'd heard, and the one time he fell from a hawthorn tree and broke his arm.

When Finn saw Cara, his eyes became saucers, and his

little mouth formed an O-shape. He beelined straight to her, despite Aidan vainly grabbing for his tunic and briefly catching a fingerful, and he hugged Cara around one of her ankles. His arms didn't make it all the way around, no matter how hard he squeezed. "Hello, Princess Cara," he said belatedly. "It's nice to meet you. Can I have a ride?"

"No," his brother exclaimed. "It's rude to ask, and you might fall off."

"The princess wouldn't drop me."

"Of course not," Cara assured them, "and I'd be delighted."

Aidan pursed his lips. "Remember, Mom only let you start riding full-sized horses last year. I can't imagine her letting you fly."

Finn sighed in martyred resignation. "You're right."

The win was short-lived, since Cara quickly jumped in with a compromise. "What if I lay down and you climb onto my back?" she proposed. "Then you can *pretend* we're flying."

With barely a glance at Aidan, who offered a reluctant nod, Finn scrambled up to perch between the two wings. Aidan gave him a boost and for the first time leaned against the warm body. He shrank back as though the fire in her belly would burn through skin and scales.

Finn whooped and began sliding up and down the back. Then he sat in place, stretched his arms out wide, and swayed back and forth as he pretended to fly. "It's so pretty up here!" he said. "Aidan, come up here with me!"

"No, I don't think we'll fit."

"There's plenty of..."

"I said no!" Aidan crossed his arms and turned away. Finn fell quiet, and it wasn't long before he slid down again.

"Maybe I could give you the castle tour now," Aidan suggested, his face reddening after his outburst.

Cara's voice dropped into a more guarded tone than usual. "That would be lovely, thank you. Finn, maybe we can talk more later. Would you like that?"

"Yes, please! Bye, princess." He waved his fat hand as Aidan led Cara away.

They rambled through the stone corridors together, Aidan pointing out statues and coats of arms and such when he knew the history behind them, but otherwise focusing on the rooms themselves. The castle had been built piecemeal over time, so there was no discernable pattern, and it was easy for newcomers to get turned around. Cara, however, took it in stride, once pointing out a window at a perpendicular wing and asking, "What's on that pediment above the library window?"

The curtains were drawn shut, so she couldn't have seen the books and scrolls inside. "It's just some weird face. Nothing real."

"They're pretty."

Since the faces were pulled into grotesque expressions, with wild eyes and hair and sometimes horns, Aidan suspected her opinion had to do with the fact that they were gilded heads. Aidan had caught Cara eyeing anything gold that they passed, from sconces to mirror frames. "You know your way around really well, don't you?" Aidan asked when they got going again.

"I think it's another dragon perk. I was good at reading maps before, but now I always know where I am."

"It sounds like there are an awful lot of good things about being a dragon. Why do you want to change back?"

Cara balked. "For my father's kingdom, of course. Only humans can rule Windmere. My aunt probably thought she was doing me a favor by turning me into a dragon instead of killing me, but my father... Well, never mind."

"What about your father?"

"He really wants me to rule. It's what he's been training me for. And he thinks that this enchantment business is hard on me. I think he's taking it worse than I am."

Aidan nodded. "I see. Well, I don't see, exactly. My mother can take anything. It's me who'd be a mess if anyone in this family turned into a dragon." He didn't mean to blurt all this out, but Cara smiled softly and admitted,

"I am, too, sometimes." Then she cleared her throat and brightened up again. "Come on," she said, "race you to the south courtyard."

ON THE SECOND MORNING OF CARA'S VISIT, AIDAN KNOCKED less tentatively on her door. She responded with a sleepy "Come in!" and a roaring yawn.

He tugged on the front of his shirt and marched in, prepared for the sight, or so he thought. Instead, he found himself in front of a dragon sprawled atop a carpeting of shiny treasures. Most were gold, but some silver and gems graced the small pile, as well as some less valuable things. Aidan recognized most of the treasures from around the palace, and he jabbed a finger at the mess, "What is this? What are you doing?"

"What, this?" Cara rolled onto her back, stretched, and raked her fingers through some cups, which jingled against her claws. "This is nothing. I'm just sleeping on a pile of..." She jerked up and righted herself. "Oh, Aidan, I'm so sorry. I collected these things last night. I don't remember where I got them all from, but I can put them back, or someone can, if they must. I'd really, really rather you didn't take them away. Maybe it's another dragon thing, but I just like having them around." She gave a quick, almost hysterical laugh. "You know how these things go."

No, he really didn't know. But he still found himself choking out some intelligible words as he backed for the door. "We certainly want our guests to sleep comfortably, princess. Let me find my mother. Maybe she'll agree to let you sleep on some or all of these things while you're here. Would you wait here while I get her?"

"Of course." Cara smiled weakly, but she was soon out of his sight.

As soon as Aidan shut the door, he fled to the throne room, since his mother always started her morning business there, and she would've long-since finished her breakfast. The guards didn't stop or even slow the prince when he threw himself into the room calling for his mother. "It's Cara!" he said, stopping the whole room cold. "She took some treasures from around the palace to sleep on, and I told her that might be okay, but I'd have to check with you."

The queen had half-risen from her throne at his first cry, but she sank back down and said, "I'll trust your judgement in this, my son. I can send a servant to make sure she hasn't taken anything irreplaceable that we need elsewhere. Do you foresee a problem?"

Aidan started to pace before the dais with the raised marble throne. "I don't know. She seemed off. Like she didn't know what she was doing. And if a dragon can't control its actions..."

"*Her* actions."

"Her actions," Aidan agreed. "I just don't know what she'll do, and I'm not sure she knows, either."

"Is she a danger to us? Was she threatening you or anyone else?"

"No, that is, I don't think she *wants* to be a danger, and she wasn't acting like one *right now*, but I just don't know what to think or what to do."

The queen folded her hands in her lap. "Do whatever you think is best for your people and for your guest. As I said, I trust you to take all necessary precautions and not to overreact."

Aidan nodded slowly and sighed. "I'll get Cara out of the room so you can send someone to look at whatever's there."

His mother dismissed him, and he dragged leaden feet on the way back to Cara's room. He rehearsed a few excuses to dislodge her from her makeshift horde, but they all fell flat in his ears. She would know what he wanted, whatever he did.

Instead of making excuses, he'd have to tell her the truth and hope for the best. That hope would go a lot better with some protection, so on the way, he picked up his bow and golden arrow. Then he returned to Cara's room with a fluctuating confidence. He raised his fist to knock again, until he heard Finn inside the room saying, "Princess Cara!"

Aidan's heart skipped a beat and froze his fist inches from the wood. Then he ripped open the door and flung himself inside, nocking the golden arrow against the bow. He searched for his brother, but only saw the back of a ginger head. The rest of him was wrapped in one of the dragon's hands.

He didn't hesitate now. He raised the arrow and fired at the dragon's chest, trusting the magic of the arrow to pierce the scales even if he couldn't find a chink in the armor.

The flight of the arrow reached a quick end as it found its mark on the right side of her chest – the only part of her chest that had been exposed to him. It slid in like he was shooting into butter, and the dragon fell back with a blood-curdling scream, releasing her grip around the young prince.

"No!" Finn said, to his brother's surprise. "Aidan, why would you do that? We were only playing!"

Aidan gaped in horror at the dragon lying there with a bleeding wound and his own arrow protruding from the center. For just that moment, it was like there were two Cara's laying there. His eyes still saw the dragon, but his mind saw a slender girl around his age with cascading brown curls and pale blue eyes just like her serpent counterpart's. A white dress flowed around her warm brown skin, though a patch of red spread outwards from where the arrow pierced her shoulder.

The moment ended when Cara whimpered, "Help me, please! Aidan!"

Only the dragon remained now, but Aidan flew to her side, banging his knees against the treasures strewn across the ground. "Finn, go get help!" he said, tearing off his jerkin and doublet and pressing them around the arrow wound. He needn't have bothered, since guards poured in at the commotion. One took charge of Finn and another sped for a physician.

"Aidan..." Cara said again, tears streaming down her cheeks, "...take it out. It burns. It burns."

Ordinarily, he wouldn't pull a weapon out of a wound without a plan to stop the bleeding, but this was a magic arrow, and if she felt it was doing more harm than good, he'd have to trust her. He owed her that much. He braced one hand against her surprisingly-smooth scales, gripped the shaft of the arrow, and pried it loose.

The dragon scales and the notched arrow head, that was

shaped like a barb to prevent this exact maneuver, trapped the arrow in place so that Aidan had to wiggle it around and yank from a few different angles. With each tug, more blood spurted over his hand. Each time, he made a little more progress, though, tearing at the flesh below the scales until the arrow eventually ripped free.

Cara struggled and writhed at first, but at the last pull, she fell back and shut her eyes. Aidan let the bloody arrow clatter to the ground and kept pressing his clothes into the wound, adding his shirt to the mix for all the good that would do. He and she were both stained scarlet. Both children had faces covered in tears, and both lay still until the physician and veterinarian both came to tend the princess's wound.

They ignored Aidan, who crawled around to Cara's head on bloody hands and knees. He couldn't tell if she was awake, but he leaned close to her ear and whispered, "I'm sorry."

It was all he could do, and not nearly enough. He would just have to wait and hope that the princess would live.

CARA LAY ON HER BED OF TREASURES FOR THE REST OF THE day. Aidan removed himself and all weapons from the room, but ordered the servants to put in more gold – coins and jewelry and whatever they could find. Maybe she needed it. Maybe it would help.

He checked on her as much as he could justify. Guilt drove him away while concern pulled him in. Each time he entered the sick room, his stomach churned with these warring emotions and threatened to overflow. He owed it to Cara to do whatever was best for her, but he couldn't say what that was while she was asleep, so he tried a little of both.

Late in the evening, he grew tired of poking his head in and asking questions about her health that the physician couldn't answer. This time when he entered, he brought a book of fables from other lands. There was one in there from Windmere, and Aidan had never paid too much attention to it. It was a cutesy tale about rabbits learning sportsmanship, that smashed its moral in the reader's face the way the story's subject smashed the prize-winning garden of his rivals.

It had no redeemable qualities, other than the fact that it was from Windmere. It was, in fact, the only story he could think of from that kingdom on such short notice, and now he sat at Cara's bedside, reading it to her.

Halfway through the story, when the town turned on the unpleasant rabbit in the middle of his crime spree, Cara's mouth parted gently and she breathed out. Aidan stopped reading until he saw her bandaged chest rise and fall a few more times, until he wasn't sure that was one last dying breath.

Far from dying, Cara finally spoke. "It's okay, Aidan," she murmured. "I don't blame you. I know…"

What she knew drifted away into the night.

"Do you want me to keep reading?" Aidan asked tentatively. He received no answer or other sign. He checked with the physician, who shrugged. Aidan kept reading.

When the story stopped, Aidan couldn't find the strength to get up, but he had nothing else to say, so he sat there until he fell into a fitful sleep. When he woke up, he found the princess much the same but was met with some encouraging news.

"She woke up once last night," the physician told the

prince softly. "She drank a little milk and then fell back asleep. That's a good sign. And don't worry. Dragons are hearty creatures. I'm sure she'll be on her feet in no time."

Aidan nodded and went for some breakfast of his own. He couldn't eat it, so he returned to Cara's room with a new, fatter book, this one offered by a cleaning woman from Windmere. This one was a story about a sphinx, and it included several confusing riddles. Aidan thanked the woman and brought it to Cara.

Halfway through, the queen entered with Finn. Aidan paused and started to rise, but the queen motioned for him to continue, so he did. She sidled up behind him, also facing the princess, and squeezed his shoulder. Finn sat at his feet but also faced Cara. This might've set off another cascade of tears, but Aidan found that he'd cried himself out by this point, and nothing more was coming. His voice stopped trembling, too, as he read. He focused on the words, doing what he could to try to help his victim.

The queen had to leave eventually, but her silent support lent Aidan some comfort even after she was gone. He kept reading until his throat grew hoarse and he had to stop for a drink.

"But it was just getting good," Cara said.

Aidan, Finn, and the physician all jumped. Aidan choked on his water and dropped the book, crushing its yellow pages and partly cracking its spine. Cara chuckled as her eyes blinked open. They didn't sparkle quite like they did before, but it was a start.

Finn hugged Cara around the neck, and she nuzzled him back. "I'm glad you're getting better. I was worried after... after..."

"After the accident," Cara filled in.

Finn's head twitched back toward his brother, a protest starting to form in his mouth. "But…"

"It was a misunderstanding," Cara insisted. "That's all."

"If you say so."

"I do. And don't worry, I feel myself getting stronger. I think the magic of the arrow is all out of my body." She'd still lost a lot of blood and would still need rest, from what everyone could tell, but hearing her say these words out loud, or even speak at all, flooded Aidan with relief. Her next words, on the other hand, were more ambiguous. "Now I need to speak with your brother alone."

He should've been filled with dread, or at least apprehension, but maybe he was too tired for those, too, or felt he deserved whatever she said or did. The other two left him alone with Cara, and he started with the obvious. "I'm sorry. I'm so sorry."

"I know. I can tell. And I really don't blame you. I know how it must've looked when I was playing with Finn. If I had a little brother, I'd want to protect him from a dragon, too." She tilted her head, and a little mischief returned to her gaze. "That said, you kind of owe me now, right?"

"Of course! I'll do anything to help you. Can I get you anything? Do anything?"

"You're doing it, mostly." She chewed her lower lip, despite the curving canines that threatened to add more holes to her skin. "There is *one* other thing, though."

"Anything! Name it." Aidan pressed in anxiously, placing his hands over part of her larger one and clutching it tight.

"Hmm. You do want to help me break the curse, right? And not *just* because you owe me for everything with the arrow?"

He shook his head emphatically. "No, you shouldn't have to be cursed like this. I mean, no one should, but you have a family and a future kingdom, too, and you..." Now he hesitated and searched for the right words. "You seem like a nice person. You forgave me. You're good with my brother. If you being a dragon changes any of that or makes you do things you don't want to..."

"Like hoarding gold?"

"Exactly. You, well, you just shouldn't have to do that. Not if I have anything to say about it."

Cara's hand had curled in response to his own, and with her face a foot from his, she said, "There's one more thing I think we could try. Something else that I heard breaks curses, but I didn't want to try it until I thought you actually wanted to help me and I hadn't just tricked you into it. Maybe this is still me tricking you, but it's hard to say for sure. It doesn't hurt to try, though."

Those pale blue eyes drew him in, and he leaned closer. "I think I know what you're talking about," he said. "The way people in stories stop magic spells."

Cara leaned her head in, too. Her eyes closed now, but Aidan didn't need to see them to feel their effect. The two young people moved nearer and nearer until they inevitably connected. Aidan planted a soft kiss on her cheek then backed away shyly.

Nothing happened.

Cara and Aidan stared at each other in dumbfounded silence. A kiss was said to break some magic curses. Or did it have to be a true love's kiss? Aidan didn't love Cara, he didn't think, at least not yet. He didn't know what would happen if they spent more time together, though, and he had to admit to a feeling of disappointment when the kiss failed to transform the dragon back into a girl. It was the first time he'd kissed someone besides his mother, so maybe there was a trick he was missing.

Aidan could've sworn he saw all of these same thoughts mirrored in Cara's face. Eventually, she raised one shoulder and said, "It was worth a try. The castle might break the enchantment, and I only have to wait for the rest of today for that."

"Sure. I am sorry, though. Is there... is there anything else?"

Cara indicated the abandoned book on the floor. "You can keep reading to me."

"Do you like this story?"

"It's better than the bunny story, at least. And I want to find out if anyone can get past the sphinx."

Aidan retrieved the book and dusted off the calfskin cover. "Me too." He settled back in his chair and began to read once more.

For the second night in a row, Aidan fell asleep in his chair, though this time, a servant brought him a plush chair to replace the wooden one that he'd hastily dragged into the room earlier. This time, though, he rubbed his eyes contentedly and felt the ghost of a smile playing at his mouth.

Then he remembered why and bolted upright, eyes snapping open to survey the room. Treasure lay scattered around the floor as it had before, but otherwise, the room lay bare before him. He broke into a full-on grin until his head swiveled around and caught sight of a giant dragon body laying against the side wall. Cara shook her head, and Aidan's smile vanished as quickly as it had come.

They didn't speak for a while, not until the queen came in to check on Cara. "I thought you might be up by now," she said. "I'm so sorry, my dear."

"That's okay," Cara replied, her voice as upbeat as possible, "it was a long shot anyway. I'll find another thing to try. Maybe I can track down a good wizard who can help me."

"You don't have to rush away. At least stay until you heal."

"I have to at least stay to hear how the story turns out." She indicated the book about the sphinx, which Aidan had been breaking into chunks and hadn't quite finished.

"We have more books here," Aidan offered. "Some of them are even better than this one. They're longer, as long as you don't mind that."

"I wouldn't mind, but..." She trailed off and ran one hand down her other forearm. "In fact, I'm feeling a lot better this morning. Maybe I should just go, before I can't go."

Aidan felt his breath hitch as he once again understood what she was feeling, because he was feeling it, too. He also remembered the human girl with the blue eyes and imagined her laughing wildly in abandon, maybe as she rode a horse too fast and pretended she was flying again. "Wait," he begged. "Stay here one more night. I think it could make a difference."

The two women regarded him curiously. "Do you think the first day didn't really count?" Cara asked. "Since you didn't want me here then?"

"No. Maybe, but that's not what I was thinking. Um, this may sound weird, but do you have brown hair, Cara?"

That gave her pause, and both she and his mother continued to screw up their faces in concentration. "Yes," Cara said slowly.

"Curly brown hair that comes almost to your waist?"

"I do."

"I think I saw that. I saw *you*. Wait here."

Aidan sprang from his chair, morning lethargy flying away as he went to his room and retrieved the golden arrow. Cara and his mother both recoiled when he ran in brandishing it. He dropped it onto the treasure pile and raised his hands against their protests. "It's a magic arrow. When Cara was shot, I saw her for just a second. I think the arrow might help her."

Cara approached and poked at the arrow, circling around it slowly. "You want to shoot me again?"

"No! I want you to keep it with you. Sleep with it. See what happens."

The queen nodded slowly. "You may be onto something. Cara, will you stay long enough to see if the arrow helps?"

The thing lay between them all now, partly crusted with red scabs but otherwise bright and shining as always. Aidan had hastily wiped it down after the incident, but he seemed to have missed some spots. "I'll try," Cara said. "Aidan, can you finish the rest of the story today so that it's done before I go?"

"I can do that."

The queen left them to it, coming in once more before bedtime to wish Cara luck, Finn clinging to her bright green surcoat. "Are you staying Aidan?" she asked.

"One more night," he confirmed. The queen kissed him on the forehead and then had to practically drag Finn outside.

Cara arranged her treasures and curled up on top of the small pile while Aidan tucked the golden and now-spotless arrow beneath her. "Good night," he told her, for lack of anything better, "and good luck."

Returning to his place in the chair, Aidan prepared for a

night of sleep. Cara faced him head-on, making that nearly impossible. "Good night, Aidan," she replied. "And whatever happens, thank you."

Aidan closed his eyes. Cara began to snore. It was the first time he'd heard this loud rumble, and it should've startled him awake at every sound, but instead, the steady rhythm soon had him sinking into his own relaxed state. "Good night," he murmured one more time before finally drifting off.

THE FIRST THING AIDAN NOTICED WHEN HIS BRAIN STARTED the brave crawl out of dreamland was the profound emptiness of the room around him. Maybe it was the temperature or the echoes, but Aidan knew that there was less in that room than there was the previous night. Cara hadn't just moved to another corner of the room this time.

When he stirred, something fell into his lap, and Aidan soon found himself examining the golden arrow.

"I believe that belongs to your mother, Prince Aidan," said a girl's voice. It was Cara's voice, but not. The slender brown hand that clasped his, that was also Cara's, but not.

Aidan's gaze made its way to his face and stared into those pale blue eyes. Those eyes, without a doubt, were all hers.

When Cara pulled him in and pressed her trembling lips to his, he realized something else. He was hers, too, and he would be happily, for ever after.

LYDIA ANNE STEVENS

Lydia Stevens is a full-time author and freelance writer having written over 75 novels for clients-with two series having become Amazon Bestsellers.

She is an active member of the Maine Romance Writers Association, The Horror Writers of Maine, The Fantasy Writers of Maine, The Maine Women Authors, The Maine Writers and Publishers Alliance, Sigma Alpha Pi's, National Society of Leadership and Success, and Sigma Tau Delta's, International English Honor Society.

Lydia graduated from the University of Southern New Hampshire with a Bachelor of Arts in Creative Writing and English on May 12th, of 2018 and she graduated with a Master of Arts in Creative Writing and English on May 11th, 2019.

She's the author of a paranormal/humor trilogy, *The Ginger Davenport Escapades* and is contracted with a six-book series, *The Hell Fire Series*, with Dragon Soul Press. Lydia worked as an internist within a literary agency and plans to pursue as a PhD in Creative Writing.

Lydia lives in Maine where she enjoys living life with an active eight-year-old and a black cat, Sirius Black, who is equally competitive for her attention.

In her spare time, Lydia loves knitting, reading, coaching soccer, completing fantasy-themed jigsaw puzzles for inspiration, traveling and having a laugh with her best friends.

FATE AND FAMILIARS

Lydia Anne Stevens

$\mathcal{F}$ragile. Handle with Care. I have never understood how these words constitute the delivery person's endeavors to smash the package they are handling into a pancake. Is there some unwritten rule of rage when it comes to the postal workers going postal on the poor packages?

I pick up the sodden box on the doorstep and cringe as I hear the tinkle of glass on the inside. Whatever was in there is smashed to smithereens now.

"Hey, thanks, man!" I yell at the back of the retreating delivery guy. He waves his hand behind his head and I consider all manner of derogatory gestures I could direct at him, but the box I am holding is leaking like a sieve. I carry it a few inches in front of me and make a mad dash for the kitchen where I plop the package into the sink. "Grandma! Your package arrived, but--"

"Oh, dear." Grandma comes clumping into the kitchen on her wooden cane. I had pointed out to her when I came to live with her last summer as her companion, that one of the newer aluminum canes might be less heavy, but we have since learned to mix the old with the new and we get on great. She tsks lightly at the gadgets and gizmos strewn around my dad's childhood bedroom that I bring to the house, and I groan whenever she needs companion time and I am forced to accompany her above stairs in the attic to help her dust off the dozens of collectable snow globes she has amassed over the years. Our happy medium is the flat screen Dad bought her for Christmas last year, and we watch the Hallmark channel together quite often.

"I think it might be one of your snow globes you sent away for, Grandma."

"Of course, it is, Phoenix. Can't you see the Magycke leaking out into the world?" Grandma reached out a shaking, withered hand and I got so caught up in watching the blue veins writhe under her papery skin that I didn't see what she was pointing to. When she touched the side of the box, the cardboard was so sodden, it collapsed under her fingers, and she snatched her hand back as if it burnt her.

"Grandma, have you been cut?" I worry over her; the blood thinners she is on means if she starts bleeding, it's almost impossible to get the flow to stop.

"No. This one is powerful. I'm afraid we've lost another good one."

"Grandma, you know I stopped believing in that stuff a long time ago. I'm in college now. I'm working on my PhD and thesis in Fantasy Literature. You can't expect me to believe in the Magycke of children's stories, can you? At least, not in reality. There is something to be said for the Magycke of a story but, come on, Grandma." I try to say it gently. Grandma has always been so adamant about the lore surrounding her precious snow globes. It had gotten me interested in Fantasy Literature to begin with. Even Harold, the ginger cat, knows better than to mess around with her gems hidden away in the attack. I look deep into her milky eyes, wishing she could still see me. She has been the light of my life, the center of my world since I was little, and Mom died. Dad did the best he could, but it was always Grandma's outlandish stories of Magycke and faraway places that tucked me in with so much love at night.

"You only say that because that school of yours down the road is filling your head with practical nonsense." Her lips quiver and I hug her. I hadn't meant to hurt her feelings, and the guilt I feel because I did, is too much to bear.

"I'm sorry, Grandma, you're right. What Magycke did this globe contain?"

"I'm afraid the Magycke of secrets."

"Don't they all have secrets? How can you tell?" I look at the box and see the glitter and little white pellets of snow begin to seep towards the drain in the sink. I'll play her game for a while. It will make her feel better that her prize has been crushed and is unsalvageable.

"I can tell by touching it there." She points to the liquid. "It's been decades since I first learned I was a Guardian. You need to open your mind, Phoenix. Because when I am gone, who do you think inherits this house and the title?"

I look around the kitchen with its cheerful sunflower wallpaper. I hadn't had the heart to tell Grandma that when she goes, Dad has already made it clear he doesn't want this place. It was the place we lost Mom. I don't have the heart to tell her that I intend to pack up and sell off all the snow globes to collectors around the world, and then sell the house.

"I know, Grandma. I need to protect the snow globes

because inside lies the secrets of the Magyckeal realms, and if any of them smash, then the Magycke is set loose on this world, and can cause madness, mayhem, and mischief. You've told me once; you've told me a thousand times. Grandma, I'm not a little girl anymore. They are just glass spheres with glittery water in them, see?"

I reach for the faucet and Grandma's hand lashes out and smacks mine so fast I jump, not realizing she can move so fast still.

"Phoenix Aurora Renault, you will not spread the Magycke into the sewers, and you will not dismiss this responsibility so casually!" Her voice shakes, like the rest of her body and I nod, despite the fact that she can't see me. I look at the worn dining room table and chairs and contemplate dragging a chair over to her, so she can sit and have a rest, but she points in the directions of the paper towels.

"Grab a roll and make sure you mop up every drop, so it doesn't go down the sink, and get the trail leading to the front door, and then bring it to the attic so we can dispose of it properly." She turns and begins clunking away, leaving me wondering if I should have called the assisted living place the next town over a long time ago. I do as she asks, mopping the mess up out of the sink before it can drip down and then stoop and mop with paper towels to the door. I plop the whole mess into a plastic trash bag, along with the box. The last thing I want is another case of hysterics if I miss any and the woman has senses like a bat, I swear. She would know if I skimped on the scourge.

When I am finished, I make my way back down the hall, glimpsing at the memories held up by plastic thumbtacks, held in frozen capsules of time in the photos. I am going to miss this house once it's gone, but I also recognize the fact that there is a time and place for change and new things. It's a wonder I've lasted here this long. If it weren't for the fact the University wasn't right down the road, I might not have come to stay at all, but I would have assisted Dad with moving Grandma to a senior home.

I trudge up the stairs to the second-floor landing, wishing Grandma would have let me change out the faded burgundy carpet years ago, but she insisted the house remain the same whilst she still resided in it. More photos adorn the walls and a flicker of comfort passes through me as I glimpse my room and my laptop waiting patiently on the bed for me to return and plug into the real world.

I continue down the hall and see the tray set across the bed in Grandma's room and make a mental note to grab it on my way down to the kitchen again. A picture of Grandpa is on the nightstand, and it is worn where Grandma has rubbed her fingers over it, wishing she could see the man in the frame she is trying to remember. It makes my heart hurt, knowing that her loved ones are leaving her faster than she is leaving them. First Grandpa, then Mom. She had adored Mom. And Dad had even moved on to bigger and better business ventures now that Mom was gone. I suppose me too, now that I'm off to college. It must be an equal kick in the gut to Grandma now that her sight has been stolen from her, and she can't see the ones she loves in her dozens of photographs. It must be so lonely.

I reach out and turn the crystal knob on the old door with the peeling white paint. Grandma wouldn't even let me scrape and repaint that either. She told me it would hurt the house's character. I climb the steps towards the attic space and see her just cresting the top ahead of me. I'm not sure which creaks worse, her bones or the old steps.

I climb the steps, sneezing from the dust as I go. Didn't I

just dust up here last week? Dust must breed more dust. Either that, or the squirrels living in the rafters have been stirring up trouble again. I wanted to call an exterminator. The look Grandma gave me when I suggested it was enough for me to know the only thing that would be exterminated around here if I did, was me.

Grandma sits in an old wooden rocking chair which echoes across the floor. Sunlight filters in through the witch's window and I catch my reflection in the glass. My red hair is falling loose out of my ponytail, and my amber eyes flicker back at me with fatigue. It had been an all-night study session last night, and I am in sore need of a nap.

"Don't look at the witch's window or your neck will get stuck that way."

"That's an old wives' tale, Grandma." I straighten my neck anyway.

"The old wives were smart to put in windows at an angle, so the witches couldn't fly in straight on their broomsticks."

"It doesn't explain the rest of the windows which aren't slanted in the house, Grandma. Are you suggesting you were a witch when this house was built? Where do you want this?" I lift the bag and the glass clinks again.

"Right up your smart alley, Missy!" She claps her hands together almost like a child and I can't help but grin. So, some tales are inexplicable like witch's windows. I know Grandma isn't nearly as old as the house, but I like to tease her about it anyway.

"Set it on the table and start to open the top, carefully."

I do as she says and move to the small round wooden table in front of her. I set the bag down and separate the ties and slowly peel the tape to the side on the top. When I open the box finally, I peer inside, expecting something to jump out at me, but sigh when all I see is broken pieces of glass, fragments of pewter figurines and the milky, glittery liquid saturating it all.

"Ok, Grandma. We didn't let any beasties out into the world. What now?"

"Have some respect, child!" She whacks my shin with her cane and I crumble to the floor. The tears stinging my eyes make me temporarily blind, but not as much as the resentment.

When I finally have my faculties back, Grandma is leaning over the box, peering inside. I look at the rows and rows of shelves that contain snow globes. I'd only managed to dust maybe a quarter of them when I had been up here last week. I want to smash all of them and then maybe Grandma would feel how much the egg sized lump on my shin feels.

"You know what, Grandma, I don't have to take this. I have a mountain of homework and midterms coming up, I'll be in my room. If you want help throwing that junk in the garbage, yell down to me. But I'm going to get some ice for my leg. Have fun with your trinkets up here, all by yourself!"

I hobble towards the stairs and I think I hear her whisper, "I'm sorry, Phoenix." But when I turn back around, she is leaning over the box again, muttering to herself. I make my way downstairs to the freezer and get some ice and notice one shining fleck of glitter in the sink. I must have missed it, but glitter breeds like parasites and that stuff gets everywhere.

I glare at the ceiling and turn the faucet on, not caring anymore if some of her precious snow globe goes down the drain. How will she ever know?

I gimp back up the stairs and want to slam my bedroom door, but the fact is, she's older than mummy dust and will probably need help getting back down the stairs, and as mad as I am for the bashed in shins, I might be a little vindictive sometimes, but I try not to be cruel.

What concerns me, when I wake up several hours later lying sideways on my bed, is how dark the house is and how quiet everything is. Had I fallen asleep? I must have. Awareness creeps into my consciousness as swiftly as concern, followed by panic. Why hadn't Grandma called down to me? Was she stuck in the attic? Oh my God, how awful of a granddaughter can I be?

I jump from the bed and race past her bedroom. She hadn't made it back downstairs, because the tray is still on her bed. I take the stairs to the attic two at a time, smashing my shins on the ledges of the steps as I go, which only adds to my previous injury, but in my haste to make sure Grandma hadn't fallen up there or suffocated in the late afternoon heat, I can feel my heart pound in my chest.

When I crest the stairs, the only thing I see is an empty rocking chair, still swaying gently on the floor, and the box inside the bag that had been delivered earlier today. I run to the box, reaching over my head in the moonlight and tugging on the string above the table. The single bulb overhead flickers on and threatens to go out. Where is Grandma?

I look down the rows of snow globes which all seem to glow eerily in the moonlight and the soft pale glow of the one bulb. Grandma's cane is lying on the floor next to the rocker, and I run to the window, checking the latches to make sure no one had come in through the window and kidnapped her. Panic is pumping through my veins.

"Grandma!" I call, again and again despite how futile

that is. I know she isn't here. I can feel it in my bones. Just as I know calling the police, or my dad or anyone on this earthly plane, can do nothing to help her. I look at the soft glow coming from the box on the table and I walk towards it. I can feel the lump in my throat where the scream is stuck inside me.

I peer down into the box and gasp, jumping backwards at the sight. Inside, a perfectly intact snow globe sits nestled at the bottom of the box. How did she fix it? There was no way she could have repaired all that damage? Where was she? I look back across the room, expecting her to come thumping out of the shadows, but in my heart of hearts, I know the answer to my question lies in the bottom of that box.

I approach the table again, and with trembling fingers, I reach down in and cup my hands around the glass sphere. I expect it to be cool to the touch, but it thrums underneath my fingers. I let it go and then flex my hands and grab it again. The thrum becomes a pulsing, which turns to a throb of pleasure as it races from the pads of my fingers through the rest of my body. It is a strange sensation, like I know exactly what I am supposed to do with this snow globe. I am meant to protect it, cherish it and keep it safe. It is my first charge. I am its Guardian. The thoughts whirl in my head, causing a dizzying sensation and I have to sit in Grandma's rocking chair. It, like the snow globe, belongs. It belongs here in this house, and so do I. I can't fathom how I have ever questioned this before. Why had I doubted Grandma so? She had set me up to be prepared for this moment, although I am still readying myself for what I know I must do.

I take a deep breath and open my eyes which I had closed when I sat down. I lift the snow globe and peer into the sphere, taking in all of the details. There is a pewter dragon, sitting high on top of a cliff, and a saber tooth cat snarling up at it. I smile at the cat, and realize, I haven't seen Harold since I woke up. The cat reminds me of him in a way. He has that ancient, all knowing look whenever he stalks the house. I'll have to endeavor to look for him once I've gathered my wits and realize this must all be a strange dream. I shake the snow globe and watch the snow swirl around the mountain and the cat. I wonder if there was a name for this world, or for this Magycke, what it would be called. I feel like this is one of the stories Grandma used to tell me when I was little. It was one of the ancient places, where Magycke meshed with reality and the beasts of old were hunted to extinction or captured and secreted away in the realms of these hidden places. I wind up the small dial on the underside of the globe and watch as a small pewter woman rounds the back side of the mountain and ends by standing next to the saber tooth cat, holding a small staff up towards the dragon in defiance.

I almost drop the globe.

Grandma is the pewter woman inside the sphere.

"Grandma," I whisper. I shake the globe again and the snow and glitter swirl faster. I wind the tab on the bottom and again Grandma races around the edge of the realm, and ends up always next to her companion, standing off against the dragon inside. Panic renewed, I flip the snow globe over, wondering how to get her out. I shake the globe and scream her name, thinking that somehow, she will hear me in the far-off world she has been sucked into and solidified into pewter. It's as useless as if she were to scream at the frozen pictures of Grandpa, or Mom.

I sit back in the chair, letting it rock me gently back and forth, and carefully, I set the globe on the table and start running down the rows of globes, picking them up and peering inside. How many creatures and people and species of lore are trapped inside the tiny spheres. I'd once asked Grandma why the globes of places on this planet weren't in her collection, and she had told me that they were designed to confuse the ones who wished to leash the power of the Magycke into our realm. Fakes, as they were, had been created and sold amongst the masses, so the real gems, the real portals wouldn't fall into the wrong hands. I see now why she collected only the Magyckeal ones. They weren't stories or fantasy at all. Dragons and sirens were caught in their respective worlds. Unicorns and fairies danced amongst the spheres. Some were cast in eternal winter, and some were in worlds of spring grass and glitter falling from the sky, but no snow as was custom was mixed in with the liquid. All manner of creatures big and small of the worlds of fantasy were housed in these delicate containers, and the most precious was sitting on the round table in the center of the room.

I walked back to it, picking it up and turning it over in my hands. What I hadn't noticed in my panic before was the inscription on the bottom written in minute handwriting.

It was the only way to show you, to make you see. There is still Magycke loose in the world Phoenix. Take your familiar, Agni, and go out and find it. It has been washed away, but as you call it glitter, it is known as Magycke. Magycke that has been lost to the world of humanity, and humanity seeks to destroy the most precious of secrets the worlds have to offer. Recover the Magycke, Phoenix, and you shall set me free.

I turn the globe over in my hands and wonder who Agni is, and what she means by my familiar. I have to wonder at what point I went crazy. I think it might be right around the midterms, but I'd have to check with a psychiatrist for the official diagnosis. I can't help but stare into the tiny fierce face that is my Grandma, stuck inside the globe. What is happening where she is? Does she win? Is she frozen like this forever if I don't find this, Magycke? I sit back down in the chair knowing that whatever is happening on the other side of the glass, is not what is being presented for the naked human eye to see.

I set the globe on the table and finally decide to reach down and pick up Grandma's cane, and it too warms in my palm. I study the cane. I had seen it before, and figured she picked it up at a crafter show. It was engraved with similar beasts from the globes. Dragons, drakes, unicorns, elves, fairies, and the like. I hadn't given it much thought until it grew so hot in my hand, I almost dropped it. Light poured from the cane and I thought it was going to splinter the wood. I did end up dropping it in the end because the light and the heat were too brilliant, and when I finally lowered my arms, my jaw hit the floor.

Floating, just above the table, swirling in a pool made from it's own light and fire, was a small golden drake. It's tiny wings flapped as the serpentine body followed, and it spewed little puffs of fire as if to light its own way. I knew what this was, but the rational part of my brain was telling me it couldn't possibly be real.

"Agni?" I whispered. The drake paused, dropping to the table, leaving a charred trail on the wood as it slithered around the table.

"Yessss." Agni said. I reached out with shaking hands when he slid past Grandma's globe and snatched it up, so he wouldn't knock it on the floor and break it. His jaws clapped together, and I knew from my own degree and from the countless hours studying what themes, morays and tropes that fantastical beasts meant to human stories, that the venom in a drake's mouth was more potent that its bite.

"You're really, real?" I whispered, and the drake chuckled and coughed on a cloud of smoke.

"Yessss. And we have Magycke to ssssave!" Before I could react, Agni leapt from the table of a flap of his tiny golden wings and shrieking, I tried to cover my face where he launched, but I felt the burn of his body as he hit my shoulder and wound his way behind my neck. Grandma's snow globe fell in my lap, and it was only by chance that it didn't roll off my lap and fall to the floor, because I had rocked away from Agni when he leapt off the table.

I felt the burning in my shoulders as I fumbled to put Grandma safely back on the table. I slapped at my shoulders and the back of my neck, feeling the warmth subside from the burning, to a warm glow as his tail dipped down my spine. I stand, ripping at my shirt to get it off, but already knowing what I am going to see in the reflection of the moonlight in the window. A golden drake is tattooed along my skin, with the head pointing up my neck, the wings and the body draped across my shoulders and the tail dipping down my spine.

"Agni! Get off me!" I holler at the tattoo.

"We have to ssssave the Magycke!" I hear Agni's voice in my head this time and I freeze. I am standing, shirtless in Grandma's attic with the voice of a drake inside my head. I pull my shirt back on and feel the itching of the material along my new ink. Although it isn't ink, not really.

"Agni--" I begin. But then my mind is racing down a sink drain into a dark and dank sewer pipe. I feel like my skull is going to split open as the rushing of water fills my ears and then I clutch my skull as a small glittering bit of Magycke zooms through pipes, processing plants, and filters through a system deemed suitable for disposal. I see the night sky then, as the glitter dumps out into the water below from an old cast iron pipe. I hadn't known dumping was still permitted as long as the wastewater had been processed, but the feeling I get from the shining piece of glitter as it twinkles up at its brethren in the sky is euphoric.

I feel so happy and elated to be free and out into the world where my Magycke can spread and grow, and I can bring back the wonders that have been quelled from this world.

And then I am in a dusty attic with a newly throbbing tattoo on my back.

"Hurry," Agni whispers in my head, and then I am running. I stumble down the steps to the old Volkswagen car, and without having to program a GPS or anything, I can feel the pull of the Magycke as I drive my way towards the lake where the glitter was dumped into it. I don't know how I am going to find one speck of glitter in a lake of thousands of specks of flickering crystalline sands, but I know the draw of the Magycke will aid me, and Agni is there, in me, a part of me, and able to help.

The lake is only half a mile from Grandma's house and when I pull under the oak tree by the water, I put the car in park and kill the engine. I get out of the car and feel Agni begin to slither on my back, and it feels like getting a warm massage, and then it feels empty and I want to cry because I feel like a piece of me is missing. Grandma had been right all along. I don't need to ask to know the saber tooth in her globe is Harold. Grandma hadn't lied about the Magycke. She hadn't lied that it needed to be protected and it needed its Guardians. I'd once asked her when I was really little, would happen if all of her globes were smashed by a bad guy and she'd openly shuddered. I had thought it was the thought of someone breaking into the house that scared her, but it was the thought of the world's breaking into and taking over ours.

"Magycke is delicate, Phoenix," she'd said to me. "Treat it with respect, and it will show you wonders you never thought possible."

I understood that now as I crouched at the lake's edge, looking for a tiny speck of glitter I'd carelessly washed down the drain. If wishes were on falling stars, it's no wonder the Magycke created the fantasies of so many wonderful things. It's a shame those wishes were sent up to the heavens so carelessly though. It had created the necessity of Guardians finding the Magycke and keeping it secreted away in the globes.

I felt rather than saw the glitter as I walked the edge of the lake. I stood with my hands on my hips as Agni swirled in his golden body ahead of me. It was one of those feelings of déjà vu, or the feeling like I was forgetting something important that I had ignored all my life, but I listened to it now as I stared down into the water at the back of a snapping turtle.

"This is how the Ninja Turtles are made, Agni," I said. My tone couldn't be any dryer.

"What'ssss that?" Agni asked.

"Never mind. It's there." I pointed at the turtle, wondering how I was going to fetch it and keep all of my fingers intact. In the end, I ended up getting wet, but I suppose it was fate and Karma's little revenge kick for my earlier temper tantrum and disrespect towards the Cosmos. When I picked up the turtle and swiped the glitter from it's back, I set the snapping, angry turtle gently back in the water and danced like a Mexican jumping bean to get back out of its way before it snapped at me and latched on to my toes. I had worn sandals and my digits were a prime target if I wasn't careful. I could have sworn the spot on the turtles back glowed a little brighter in the moonlight though.

Agni slid along beside me as I walked back to the car, drenched and he slid into my skin, this time I didn't resist the process, as I slid into the car, driving one handed back to Grandma's house. I raced up the stairs and held the glitter, Magycke as Agni and I watched, to the snow globe, and when I touched it, light burst into the room again, and when I opened my eyes, a very tired Grandma, sat in her chair again.

"Grandma!" I sank to my knees in front of her and hugged her lap. I couldn't help it. I sobbed. I cried so hard I thought my soul was leaking out. I hadn't admitted that I had needed her in my life, as much as she needed me in hers in a very long time. Losing her, even for the briefest moment, was too much. I wasn't sure how old Grandma was, maybe she was older than her driver's license said, but the one thing I was sure of, was she was going to be around for a while, and for that I was eternally grateful. I needed a mentor as I began to explore this new responsibility and part of myself. I needed a Guardian to teach me how to respect the delicacy of the Magycke contained within the small glass realms. I needed someone who had traveled them, to explain to me and stress how important it was to keep them safe, and how to find them and recognize them amongst millions in the market and bring them home where they couldn't be let loose into our world. Because it wasn't just the Magycke in the small worlds that could bring about the destruction of the human realm, I knew without asking, humanity could bring about the destruction of the Magycke if it got its greedy hands on it.

I knew this by looking into the irate eyes of Harold. They

glowed green and angry at being squished into the confines of a ginger tabby cat. I knew he was so much larger than what he appeared to be, and I felt for him that he had to be poured into a mold that wasn't meant for the magnificence of all that he was. But humans had hunted his kind to extinction long ago. Or so they thought. I wondered if Harold was one of the last living sabretooths' in existence, whether in this realm or any other. I shuddered, grateful he was Grandma's familiar and not mine. I wouldn't want to be responsible for the temperament of an overgrown cat in our world. A deadly one at that. As it was I was responsible for Drake who--

"Agni of the Seven Kingdoms, what have you done to my table?"

I mopped my eyes and looked around. The scorch marks on the table were still there, although Agni was floating in midair, twisting and writhing using his little wings to keep just out of reach of Harold whose tail was twitching and he was perched on the back of the chair, ready to pounce.

"It wasssssn't my fault, misssss. We had no time. We had to sssssave the Magycke," Agni said.

Agni didn't cringe under Grandma's withering stare, but I did. I kind of felt responsible for him, and in a way, I was because he was my familiar, making him a part of me. Familiars don't all work the same. Grandma's was an external familiar, Harold and my Drake can apparently be both. It doesn't mean either one can't get into trouble because in the next instance, Harold pounced.

"Haidar!" Grandma scolded.

"Haidar, I thought your cat's name is Harold?" I looked up at her.

"You couldn't pronounce Haidar, which is Arabic for lion, when you were younger, so he became Harold." I looked at Haidar—Harold—as he sat in the middle of the room with a hissing Agni in his paws. No wonder the brute didn't like me much.

"Haidar, you put Agni down, right now," Grandma scolded.

Haidar let Agni go who snapped at him from the air and then flew over and curled around my shoulders. He didn't sink into my skin but sat hissing at the cat on the floor whose tail was twitching again. I swear, if he instigates and I get a face full of claws from a saber tooth, that's the last time I play his protector. He can scorch in the bowels of hell in that cat's stomach.

"Grandma, don't leave me like that again."

"I'll try not to, but I had to make you see."

I nodded. I understood now. I wouldn't question again. I looked at the snow globe, which now only had a dragon in it.

"What happened in there, Grandma?" I point to the globe which sits dormant on the table.

"It's a long story, but I'll tell you, that dragon doesn't give up his secrets easily."

I look at her quizzically. She had said secrets before, but what secrets? I ask her this and she smiles.

"He's the one who came up with the original plan to pour the Magycke into the snow globes, Phoenix. That's Abraxas, the Secret Keeper. He works with the guardians, but he's been stuck on that mountain so long he's become ornery and refuses to give up the secrets on how to make more globes in case the Magycke gets out. He won't even tell me, but I am not worried."

"You aren't?" I am. I don't want a dragon half the size of a mountain roaming the streets of Maine. "Why not?" I wonder.

"Because if there is anyone who can get him to give up his secrets, it's you." I look at her open-mouthed. "You see, the heart of a dragon bursts into living flame from the inferno of love of a human man. The dragon you're staring at is also your grandfather."

NATHAN SLEMP

Nathan Slemp grew up wandering amidst the shelves at the local public library, devouring any fantasy or sci-fi book that caught his interest. The years since his first encounter with *Eragon* have been spent conversing with dragons and chronicling their tales.

When not lost within the windings of fantasy worlds, or exploring the storytelling arts of movies and video games, he spends his time as a software developer in Michigan.

A selection of his short stories can be found in the *Continuum* series of anthologies on Kindle, and he is on a path to publishing his first novel. His works and musings can be found at wordwyrm.wordpress.com.

THE CLAWS OF THE HUNT

Nathan Slemp

"*H*ail, Sir Lorant of Gelbridge."

Lorant pulled on Ash's reins until the warhorse wheeled about. The road he traveled cut through the heart of the Godslost Forest. No towns or villages stood within its bounds. None fit for a mortal, at any rate.

"Who goes there?" His hand lowered to his sword hilt.

"One who would speak to you in peace." The voice came from everywhere and nowhere, echoing from shafts of light piercing the canopy. "Will you give me your word that we might do so?"

Ash whickered, dancing from side to side. Lorant steadied him with a hand to his neck. "I don't even know who you are. And I have no time for delays."

Laughter like birdsong rippled around him. "Ah yes. You return home, do you not? But you will not find what you seek there."

"Show yourself!"

Shadows shifted in the lee of a lightning-scarred oak, and a woman emerged, clad in gossamer and crowned with a circlet of holly. Her eyes glittered gold as she smiled. "I am here. Now may I have your word?"

Drawing his sword, Lorant leveled it at the woman. Her expression didn't shift, but she leaned back. "Why would I give my word to one of your kind?"

"Ah." The woman's smile widened. "You know of us."

"The knights of our realm are educated in the ways of the fae. I know your kind all too well."

Gesturing at him, she asked, "With all your fine steel armor, Sir Lorant, do you expect me to be a threat to you? I wish only to speak."

Lorant stared at her, grinding his teeth. Every moment spent confronting this creature kept him from home and reunion with Angela, but if the legends were true, ignoring the fae could be more dangerous than humoring them.

He rammed his sword into its scabbard. "You have my word as a knight."

The faerie smiled. "How gracious. I am Seona, of the Count of the Erlking."

"And what is it you want of me?"

"Can you not guess? To invite you to come with me to the emerald paths."

"Then spare us both the bother. You will not tempt me."

Seona's eyes glittered. "Indeed. You long for your beloved. Lady Angela, yes?"

"How do you know her name?"

"Why, I've met her. In the Erlking's court. Such fine hair she has, like sunflowers on a cloudy day."

Lorant froze. "What?"

"And her dancing. Quite lovely."

Lorant leapt from Ash's back, whipping his sword free. "You lie! I should cut you down for those words!"

Seona's eyes widened. "Do you not know? My people cannot lie. I came to offer to help you free her."

"She is at Gelbridge, not in your court of devils!"

"As you say. But I make you this bargain. Go in peace to your home. See for yourself that Angela is not there. Then return, if you wish to win her back. I will await you here."

Glaring at her, Lorant mounted Ash and spurred him into a gallop.

WHEN GELBRIDGE MANOR CAME INTO VIEW, ASH WAS staggering along the road, his coat covered in froth. How long he'd been galloping before he lost his strength, Lorant didn't know. The whole ride was little more than a blur in his mind. He dropped from Ash's back and walked him to the front door, his hand tight around the reins.

There was no reason to worry. Angela would be there to greet him. The faerie witch was a liar and a temptress. Her words were worth nothing.

Except, what she had said was true. The fae could not tell an outright lie. So said the loremasters, at any rate. And Seona said she had seen Angela at the Erlking's court.

Fire Above, please, let her be well. Let her be here.

As he neared the door, a groom rushed from the stables to meet him. "Sir Lorant! We didn't expect you—"

"Where is Lady Angela?"

The groom recoiled. "I—y-you should speak to Mortant. He—"

Lorant shoved Ash's reins into the fool's hands and threw open the doors. "Mortant! Where in blazes are you?"

The antechamber was empty, but as Lorant stomped inside, Mortant crept into view. The old majordomo's face was scarred from the pox and a half-dozen other diseases, but his eyes were still keen.

Or they normally were. Today they were bloodshot.

"Oh, sir—"

"Where is Angela?"

He shook his head. Lorant grabbed him by the arms, holding back from shaking the old fool. "Where is she, Mortant?"

"She—she was out walking the garden paths one night. The sentries saw her run into the forest. Your brother Erdin pursued her, but neither has been seen since."

"When did this happen?"

"A month ago. We sent couriers, and they told us they left their messages with the royal quartermasters. Did they not—"

"No." Lorant turned aside, cursing under his breath. King Henrik must have ordered the letters withheld, lest the Butcher of Gelbridge realize he was needed at home. It was just the bastard's style.

"What about Saul? Where is he?"

Mortant sighed. "He went after her three weeks ago. No trace of him has been seen. Again, we sent missives, but—"

"Damn that bastard!"

"Your... your brother, sir?"

"Henrik." Lorant closed his eyes as Mortant gasped, forcing himself to breathe, to think. It was hard. He didn't want to think. He wanted to fight, to kill whoever stood between him and Angela, the people who had killed his brothers. Surely, they were dead. If not, they would have returned, either to seek help or with Angela beside them.

He opened his eyes. "Order the grooms to prepare a fresh horse."

"Milord, if I may—"

"You may not. I will bring her back, Mortant. You cannot persuade me otherwise."

"You do not even know where to search, milord."

"I do. Now call the grooms. Immediately."

THE STALLION'S HOOVES DUG INTO THE ROAD AS LORANT reined him in. This was the spot where Seona had stopped him before—he knew that lightning-scarred oak—but there was no sign of the witch.

"Seona!" Dismounting, he stared into the forest. "Show yourself!"

"As you wish, sir knight."

He spun around. She stood at the forest's verge, considering him with a frown.

"It is as you said. She's gone. As are my brothers."

She nodded. "They sought to rescue her. They failed."

Lorant's hands clenched. "What happened?"

"Their will faltered, and they fell to traps set for the unwary. You need not fear the same. I will guide you."

"Why would you do such a thing?"

Seona swayed towards him, bare feet whispering over the leaves. "I care little to see the Erlking dallying with mortal cows. It serves my interests to aid you."

Lorant shook his head. The idea of Angela with some unearthly scum was ridiculous, but if half the legends whispered of the fae were true, this Erlking could be more than capable of tricking or ensorcelling her. "If he has laid a hand on her, I'll slay him."

"Of course. Such is your right to attempt, under the ancient law. Assuming you are able to reach his throne."

"What must I do?"

"You will follow me into the emerald ways. I will guide you to the Court." Raising a hand, Seona said, "The Erlking's realms are unsettled at present. Factions vie for supremacy. Marauders prowl the hills, seeking foes to slay and thereby prove their prowess. You must be vigilant as we travel. All those who speak to you, you must strike down, no matter their demeanor."

"You want me to kill everyone we meet?" Lorant shook his head. "That is barbaric."

"Then it is a good thing you are barbaric, is it not? We know of your deeds, Butcher of Gelbridge. We watched from the trees as you slew the legions of Dernholm. At Siren's Bridge, we took up the men you cast into the Songwater and lulled them to their rest. In the Morrentwood, our trees sucked deep of the blood you spilled." Seona's mouth curled into a sneer. "If you could kill so many for your king, why can you not kill for your beloved? Or do you care for your Angela so little that a bit of death will dissuade you?"

"Of course not, but innocents—"

"Did I not say war is afoot? There are no innocents in the verdant realms. Especially now." Seona drifted closer, her eyes glowing like a cat's. "If you fail in this, you will become ensnared by the web of the emerald paths, and never again return to your home of stone and glass. As befell your brothers."

Grimacing, Lorant nodded. "Very well."

Seona's lip curled. "I can taste your hesitation. But we will see what passes. I care little. It is not my life that is endangered here. Leave your horse—where we go, it cannot follow."

Tying his horse to a tree, Lorant followed Seona into the

forest. The stallion whickered as he disappeared amidst the trees.

SEONA FOLLOWED NO PATH HE COULD SEE, NOT EVEN GAME trails. She wove amongst gaps in the underbrush, and thorns scraped his armor as he struggled to follow. Sap and mud coated him with slime, but her dress remained immaculate.

"How much farther?"

Seona laughed, her voice colored with alien timbres that sent shivers through his scalp. "We pass from waking into dream, and you ask of time or distance? It is an eternity, and yet a single step. One might spend years searching for the ways and never find them, only to lose themselves as they walk home from the market."

Lorant ground his teeth. "You waste my time with these riddles."

"Only because you are too foolish to see." Brushing aside a branch, Seona waved him onward. "Behold."

Lorant stumbled to the opening and gasped. A plain lay beyond that stretched to the horizon, interrupted by intricate gardens and houses sculpted from living trees. Beings visible as nothing more than ripples in the grass stalked across the vista. As Lorant watched, a trio converged around a pod of five, crimson splashing the grass as they fought.

One figure escaped the melee, fleeing towards a river that bisected the plain. Far downstream the river coursed around a tree the size of a fortress-city, its roots stretching away from the trunk like siege walls. Its branches rose through the clouds, casting weird shadows over uncounted acres.

Lorant stared beyond the canopy. There was not one, but three suns gleaming through the leaves. His knees turned weak, but he couldn't look away.

"Do not let them ensnare you." The words brought him back to himself, and he ducked his head. "Come," Seona added, gliding past him. "We dare not tarry here. Warbands prowl nearby, and your right to challenge the Erlking means nothing to them."

He stumbled after her, staring at the beauty all around. An arch stood before them, made of a pair of trees that bent towards one another, weaving together overhead. As they passed through the arch, movement caught his eye, and he put his hand to his sword. Something was emerging from one of the trunks—a human head, with hair the color of autumn leaves and skin like hazelnut. A body followed the head, wrapped in a dress of vines and leaves.

As the fae-woman stepped from the tree, Lorant shifted his grip on his sword. His armor clinked, and the woman whirled towards him, her hands flying to her mouth. "A mortal? How did you come here?" Her eyes twitched to Seona. "You! You brought a Bane-wielder here? Why—"

"Sir Lorant." Seona's voice sliced through the air. "Remember what I told you."

Lorant stared at the tree-woman. She looked like a girl of sixteen. He couldn't—

"It is your life and your beloved's if you weaken now, sir!"

Lorant drew his sword. The tree-woman screamed. He swung, but she dove aside and his blade bit into the tree. At its touch, the wood blackened, burning and decaying at once. The tree groaned, its leaves falling as its bark bleached and crumbled, revealing slimy patches of wood.

The tree-woman screamed, louder this time, scrabbling away without taking her eyes from Lorant. "Please, no more, mortal sir, no more use the Bane, please, I will do anything for you, but do not harm the trees!"

"Slay her, Lorant." Seona rounded the dead tree, staring at him. "She will tell the Erlking of your coming. She is his creature. She helped him lure your Angela here. She guided her through the emerald paths."

"I swear—"

"Slay her!"

Lorant raised his sword, and the tree-woman wailed. He stared into wide, emerald eyes, the rage within him shuddering.

A blade of stone appeared in her hand. She lunged and stabbed, but the flint shattered against Lorant's breastplate. His arm moved on reflex, ramming his sword through her.

The tree-woman didn't scream as her body burned. She collapsed, curling onto itself, a wheeze escaping from her chest. Lorant yanked his sword free and stumbled away from the body as it disintegrated, blackening the grass around it.

"Incredible."

He flinched and stared at Seona.

"Incredible." Her lip curled. "And I thought you had backbone." She walked towards the tree filling the horizon. Lorant staggered after her.

"Did you forget why you are here?"

Lorant glared at Seona's back. They had walked in silence for hours, and the great tree was no closer than it had been. Bands of marauders had passed by near them, but none had dared to attack. Perhaps they were as scared of him as the tree-woman had been, of him and the steel he carried.

"You insult me. How could I?"

"Then why did you hesitate?"

"There was no need for her to—"

Seona whirled to face him, her face contorted in rage. "Did I not tell you what to do? Did I not warn you of the consequences of failure? Did I not speak of your brothers and their failures?" She spat on the earth between them and stalked away. "I don't know why your weakness surprises me. I should have expected as much."

"What is that supposed to mean?" Lorant stomped after her, his hand falling to his sword. "To kill when unnecessary is not strength, it is evil."

"I instructed you in what you must do. You must kill all who speak to you, lest you be ensnared by the magics of this place. And yet, when the moment came, you weakened. Perhaps you do not wish to find your Angela? Perhaps you already suspect the truth and fear to have it proven to you?"

"What truth?"

"Why would Angela choose to remain with some weakling mortal when she has the eye of the Erlking, Lord of the Emerald Ways?"

Lorant growled. "I will hear no more of your slander."

"Ask yourself this." Seona pivoted on one foot, staring at him from the side of a hill. "Why did she leave Gelbridge?"

"She was bewitched, surely."

Scoffing, Seona turned away. "If that is what you wish to believe."

Lorant followed her with a scowl. As they neared the hilltop, a patch of sod swung outward, an invisible door opening into the bowels of the earth. A squat, bearded dwarf emerged and goggled at Lorant. "A human, here?" He pulled a crossbow from within his tunnel. "By the—"

Roaring, Lorant slashed his sword through the dwarf's throat. The corpse tumbled backwards, the door dropping closed as it fell. As fresh blood sizzled on his armor, he glared at Seona. "Now are you satisfied?"

She stared at him, her face alien and emotionless. "More than before," she said, and passed over the crest of the hill.

THEY WALKED FOR AN HOUR, OR A YEAR, OR FIVE DAYS. THE great tree grew no closer. For all Lorant knew, they weren't even moving, but instead trapped in place by some unearthly power. Then, in the blink of an eye, he was walking through a lattice of shadow, following Seona through the fringes of the tree's canopy. The light around him dimmed as cobwebs of branches reached across the sky. They thickened slowly at first, then all at once, submerging him in twilight.

A darker shadow whipped overhead, and Lorant dropped into a crouch. A winged shape was darting between the lower branches, fleeing towards the trunk, with a trio of great eagles in pursuit. As Lorant watched, it wheeled about and spat a jet of fire at the nearest eagle, casting it towards the ground. The others peeled away, and the creature escaped into the heart of the canopy.

"There are dragons in this realm?"

Seona followed his gaze and nodded. "There are. Beings of great fury and rage, servants of an illustrious noble. You should hope that you do not cross one."

"I've fought such beasts before."

"That means little. The dragons of your realm are but whelps compared to those found here."

Lorant shuddered, keeping one eye on the sky as they continued on. They passed into a clearing at the edge of the river, opposite the trunk of the great tree. A bridge of vines crossed over the divide. They writhed against one another, but somehow, they seemed to maintain a solid path, wide enough for a dozen mounted knights to cross side by side.

As Lorant approached the bridge, Seona raised a hand. "Wait."

"Wait? We have come all this way, dragons prowl above us, and now you tell me to wait?"

"The dragon is not interested in us. Catch your breath, sir knight. The moment you step upon the Heartweb Bridge, the Heart-Tree's guardians will come for you."

"What sort of guardians?"

"Agents of the Wild Hunt, chosen by the Erlking's whim."

Lorant dropped to one knee, breathing in through his nose and out through his mouth as old Sir Gwyn had taught him. He rested his sword point against the ground. Its blade was crusted with charred blood, some of it still wet. Where had it all come from? Had he killed even more of the fae-folk?

He couldn't remember. Everything in this place was strange. Time itself was diseased here, winding in ways it ought not to.

Angela. He had to find Angela. Groaning, he struggled to his feet. "Very well."

Seona nodded, and he stepped onto the bridge. A ripple coursed across its surface. A howl rent the air. Lorant's neck crawled.

A creature like a giant wolf bounded onto the far side of

the bridge. It stood on all fours, its shoulders level with Lorant's own, but it didn't carry itself in the way of a wolf. Despite the fur and fangs, its limbs were jointed like a man's.

Slaver pouring from its jaws, it arched its back and howled.

"Ah," Seona said. "I should have guessed."

Lorant took his sword in both hands, putting the fae-witch from his mind as he stared the beast down. It snarled, creeping forward a step. Then another.

It charged, almost faster than Lorant could follow. As it lunged at him, he sprang aside and slashed. The beast howled, skidding to a halt. Blood coated its side and sizzled on Lorant's sword, but the beast wasn't burning or decaying. With another howl, it leapt towards Lorant, claws and fangs reaching towards him.

Roaring, Lorant threw himself forward, bracing his sword. The beast's claws raked across his armor before its chest fell on the blade, driving it between the ribs.

The beast screamed. Blood gushed from the hole in its heart. Lorant scrambled away as it thrashed and convulsed, ripping clods of dirt from the ground. Its writhing slowed, and it choked up a mouthful of blood.

Lorant approached the thing. It met his gaze, and something about its eyes was familiar. It coughed, growling out sounds almost like speech. "Brr... thrr... Err—dnn."

Lorant hissed through his teeth. "Erdin?"

The beast blinked. "Srr... ry."

"By the Fire, Erdin, what did they do to you?"

With a groan, the beast went limp. Lorant stared at it, his hands clenching and unclenching at his sides.

"He failed in his quest."

Lorant turned and stared at Seona. "This was my brother Erdin?"

Seona nodded. "He made it this far, pursuing Angela. When the Wild Hunt confronted him, he fought valiantly. But the Erlking spoke with him, and he lost his way." Her lip curled as she considered the body. "In the Erlking's honeyed words, your brother heard the song of the wilds, the call to abandon the ways of men and take glory in the hunt. He abandoned your love to her fate. He chose to join the Hunt."

Lorant shuddered, staring at the twisted monstrosity that had been his brother. Ever since childhood Erdin had been brash and wild, more at home in the wilderness than in any village or city, but never had he abandoned his duty. Not until it really mattered, when Angela's freedom was at risk.

"Such is the Erlking's way. He twists mortals into his creatures. His slaves."

Lorant ripped his sword from Erdin's chest. "Are we free to cross now?"

The corner of Seona's mouth twitched. "Yes."

"We continue, then."

Nodding, she led the way across the bridge. Lorant kept his sword high as he traversed the writhing vines, relaxing only once solid stone lay underfoot once more.

The Heart-Tree's roots ran by them on either side, knotted walls that stretched as high as a castle's walls. Where the roots joined, steps of marble led to a vast doorway, twenty feet by seventy. Pictograms decorated its edges, but Lorant kept his gaze on Seona's back, rather than allowing the alien artwork to snare him.

"Will there be more guardians?"

"Nay. There are rules to these things. Traditions to uphold." Seona passed through the archway, into an antechamber lit by luminescent fungi sprouting from the walls. Three passages led out of the chamber. The middle one was wider than the others, its walls covered in more carvings.

"The throne room," she said with a gesture.

"Then let's go."

"Your beloved is not there." Waving at the left-hand passage, Seona said, "She is up there."

Lorant broke into a run, the wood of the Heart-Tree groaning around him as he ascended a spiraling path. The ramp opened onto a balcony bulging from the side of the tree. A shadow flickered overhead with a sound like sails snapping in the wind.

Somewhere out of sight, a woman screamed.

"Angela! Angela!"

Lorant raced around the balcony and onto a bridge that arched away from the trunk, towards a platform the size of a castle yard. At its center crouched a dragon, thirty feet tall at its shoulder and fifty long. Hellfire simmered through cracks in the scales covering its belly.

Beneath its claws lay a body, torn and bleeding.

Lorant screamed, the platform quaking underfoot as he charged. The dragon reared its head, backing away a step, but it failed to dodge his first strike. His blade caught a gap in the scales on its legs. Blood steamed as it spattered across the body beneath the dragon.

Roaring, Lorant struck again, stabbing into the softer skin at the dragon's armpit. The dragon bellowed and lashed out with its tail, knocking him from his feet. It loomed over him, smoke boiling from its mouth, but it didn't strike.

Before it could, Lorant stabbed at its chest. His sword caught on a scale, which cracked as it turned the blow aside. The dragon reared, howling, and slashed a claw at his head.

He rolled out of its path. Its talons drove into the wood of the platform. Before the dragon could tug them loose,

Lorant spun around its leg and drove his sword into the broken scale. Blood and fire erupted from the wound, burning Lorant's skin like hot oil. The dragon howled and fell.

Lorant ripped his sword free, gasping as his burned fingers screamed with pain. The flames gushing from the dragon's chest faded, but blood still pulsed forth, pooling around his boots. Gripping his sword with both hands, he advanced on its head. "You... you killed..." He held the blade's point over the dragon's eye. It stared at him, its pupil dilating. "You killed her."

One of the dragon's claws scraped against the platform. He ignored it. The monster's neck was long, and where he stood, he was well beyond its grasp.

"All this way, all this blood, and you killed her." Lorant's hands twitched. The dragon's eye flickered closed, and the point of his sword drew a line of blood across the lid. "Know this, you hellspawn. Know that Lorant of Gelbridge has slain you."

The dragon's claw tapped the ground. Lorant glanced at it and froze. There were lines etched into the wood, jagged and messy, but forming letters. A word.

<u>Angela.</u>

He stared at the carving, then at the dragon's blood-stained eye. It stared back, still but for its gasping breaths. Edging towards the body at the center of the platform, he brushed the flat of his sword against a bare foot.

The skin charred and blistered at its touch.

Gasping, he turned back to the dragon. "You... it's not possible. It's not.... I couldn't..."

The dragon—Angela—coughed again, dragging a foot under herself. She tried to rise, but fell with a gasp. Lorant dropped his sword and staggered towards her, ripping his helm free.

"He caused this, you know," Seona said from behind him. She hadn't been there a moment before. "The Erlking caused this to occur to your beloved."

Lorant stared at her. "Why did you not tell me this was her?"

"You gave me no opportunity to do so before you attacked." Seona knelt and ran a finger through a pool of Angela's blood. "The changeling was meant to kill you. Your beloved was removed from the field to allow this. She must have realized what was planned, and came to stop matters from progressing."

Lorant knelt by Angela's head. He reached towards the exposed eye, then hesitated. "Will she... survive?"

Seona shrugged. "Dragons are tenacious, but her wounds are grave. I cannot say for certain. I will do all I can to heal her, that I promise."

He bowed his head and shuddered. "How can we make her human once more?"

"The magics that bound her are most potent. But if you slay the Erlking, you will be rejoined."

Thunder cracked across the platform, and in the thunder was a word.

"Deceiver."

A figure emerged from the shadows at the far end of the platform—a giant of a man, clad in furs and a helm of stone, antlers arching from his temples. Scars from a legion of blades, arrows, and claws scrawled over his chest. The sight of him woke something within Lorant, something primal and ancient that filled his muscles with fire, howling with the need to hunt, to eat, to mate, to live.

To give his life and soul to the Erlking, and join his pack.

He took a step forward.

A gasp like a bellows bubbled from Angela's chest, breaking through the haze filling his mind. Before he could take another step, Lorant wrenched his eyes away, gasping for breath. Now he understood how Erdin had fallen. If not for Angela, he would have done the same. But her presence gave him something to hold onto, an anchor against the Erlking's lures.

This creature had turned her into a monster. He was not about to swear fealty to him.

Yellow light flared from Seona's eyes. Her face twisted into a snarl as she stared at the Erlking. "That is rich coming from you, oh king of honeyed words."

The Erlking crossed his arms, his eyes glowing with emerald fire. "Enough of this charade, woman. You deceive your champion."

"We cannot lie."

"Did I say that you lied?"

Tension filled the air, a prickling on Lorant's skin as if lightning was about to strike. He eased away from the space between Seona and the Erlking. Neither reacted as he crept towards Angela's head, retrieving his sword as he did.

"I will give you credit, mine queen." The Erlking advanced, and shadows shifted amidst the branches behind him. Wolf-beasts, like the creature Erdin had become, eyes flashing as they watched the conflict unfold. "Your gambit was a clever one. Find one who might lay claim on my blood over the matter of Angela, and arrange to become his guide. An inspired way to defeat the exile I placed upon you."

"Now it is you who seeks to manipulate the mortal." Seona stepped forward to match the Erlking. "I brought him here so that he might avenge the insult done to him by your wanton lusts. It was your desires that brought the woman here, not mine. I have not wronged the knight in any way."

The Erlking laughed, once, a booming sound that recalled memories of bears Lorant had hunted in his youth. "Perhaps you might ask the lady Angela if she believes you have wronged her knight."

"She is as she is by your own doing, you wretch."

"Ah, but it was not my hand that worked the flesh-change upon her."

Angela tilted her head until she could meet Lorant's gaze. Her eyes dipped towards his sword, then Seona.

He nodded and stepped towards Seona. Neither she nor the Erlking reacted. For all he knew, they hadn't even noticed. They glared at each other across Angela's body, the air before their faces trembling with power.

"Erlking," Lorant said. "We have a score to settle."

The Erlking didn't react, not even to glance at Lorant.

"He challenges you, great king," Seona said, her snarl relaxing into a smile. "Will you not respond?"

Again, the Erlking remained silent and still. Lorant moved to stand beside Seona, a dozen growls rising from the wolf-beasts in the shadows.

"Slay him, sir knight," Seona said, her grin stretching wider than any human face could manage. "Claim the justice that is rightfully yours. Face him with your full wrath and fury, and be reunited with your beloved once more."

Shaking his head, the Erlking said, "I trust that, as your champion's elected guide, you have instructed him in the ways of his path, to slay all who spoke to him."

Seona froze.

"I wonder that he has not fulfilled your instructions." The Erlking blinked, his eyes not straying from Seona.

"Surely there is one left whom he must slay. And it is not I. I have not spoken to him, have I?"

Seona whirled on Lorant, whipping a stone dagger from some hidden place beneath her dress, but his sword was already driving towards her belly. He ran her through as she stabbed him in the side. She screamed, clutching at the sword, but the touch of steel set her hands ablaze.

With a roar, Lorant ripped his sword to the side and out. As Seona fell, he staggered towards Angela's head and dropped to his knees, almost falling on top of her as the pain in his side spiked. "Erlking. They say—they say the fae make bargains. I offer you a bargain. Three boons, and in exchange, I will abandon any suit against you."

The Erlking waved a hand, and the growling of the wolf-beasts stilled. He approached Angela, the platform trembling beneath his feet, and crouched at her side. "I am truly sorry for your pain," he said. "I did not expect such venom from the queen, else I would have been more circumspect." He rested a hand on her leg, and her breathing steadied. Lorant stared, gritting his teeth against the fire in his side, as all the wounds he had given her closed. After only a few heartbeats, it was as though they had never been.

"Your bargain, I accept." The Erlking moved to Lorant's side, taking the knife in one hand and resting the other on his shoulder. "And another boon I give to you—a gift of healing, to balance the wounds dealt by my traitor queen's hand."

Lorant howled as the Erlking ripped the knife free, but the pain died in a second. Warmth coursed through his body, soothing away aches and weariness. When the Erlking stepped away, Lorant felt as though he'd spent the past days resting at home, rather than marching through half of Faerie.

With a grunt, Angela rose to her feet, towering over Lorant. Some part of her mind screamed at him to run, but he held still as she brought her head close, staring at him, her breath washing over him like the fumes within a smokehouse.

"I'm sorry," he said. "For everything."

She nodded, crooning deep in her throat.

"She cannot speak your tongue," the Erlking said. "Not as she is. Now, name your boons. A bargain we have, and it shall be honored, but I care not to have you remain overlong in my realm, clad as you are in the Bane and covered in the blood of my subjects."

Lorant nodded. "First, I ask for safe passage to the mortal world."

"Done. But I warn you, if you return to my realm, my Hounds will rend you asunder. A puppet you may have been, but I will not forgive the blood you spilled."

"Second. Allow Angela to return with me. Her and my brother Saul, if he is still alive."

The Erlking chuckled. "Under the circumstances, it would be churlish of me to deny you this. You beloved I return to you willingly. Your brother, however, has chosen his path. He remains among the Hunt."

Lorant turned to the shadows surrounding them, and the glints of amber watching them. He shuddered. "Very well. I will accept that."

"Then done and done."

"Third, let Angela be human again."

The Erlking rumbled. "A hard asking. The Traitor Queen's curses are not easily broken. But I understand your desire, and again, it would be unworthy of me to do nothing." Nodding, he said, "Kiss your beloved once you return to the mortal world, and you will be together once more. Now take your Bane and leave in peace. And remember, do not dare return again."

AS THEY VENTURED INTO THE GRASSLANDS SURROUNDING THE Heart-Tree, Lorant asked, "Are you in any pain?"

With a rumble, Angela shook her head. Her body trailed out behind him; her head held low so their eyes were level with one another.

"Good." Lorant shuddered. "Good. I'm sorry. I had no idea... I saw the body of that faerie and thought it was you. Exactly what they wanted me to think, I suppose. All the same, I'm sorry for hurting you."

Angela blinked, silent but for the thumping of her footsteps and the scraping of scales over grass.

"And for leaving you alone for so long. War or not. I should have made time for the wedding. Then you could have come with me." Lorant scraped a trail through the gore coating his armor. "There's no joy or glory in war. It's all the same as this. But you wouldn't have been alone."

He grimaced, staring at the hills as they warped around them in time with their footfalls. "I couldn't disobey the king when he ordered me to kill, but when Seona did it, I just let her twist me into doing the same for her. Maybe you're better off without me. Maybe we should go—"

Angela growled.

"Very well, then." He reached towards her, but she shied away, staring at his hand. "Oh, of course." He pulled off his gauntlet. She blinked, and he touched his fingers to her cheek. Her scales felt like paving stones on a summer day, hard and hot. She blinked again, water pooling in the corner of her eye.

"I have to know... Seona told me you came to this place willingly. Is that true?"

Her head twitched in a nod.

"And, about what you've become. I know what happened to Erdin. He attacked me at the bridge. Seona said that he chose what happened to him. He chose to become a Hound of the Hunt." Lorant's fingers curled against Angela's scales. "Did you choose this too?"

Angela hesitated, nodded, then shook her head.

"You made a choice, but you didn't know what the consequences would be?"

This time she nodded, leaning into his touch.

"Was it all because of me?"

She nodded once more. Her tears rolled down her scales and scalded Lorant's skin. With a shudder, he shook them from his hand. "I am truly sorry. I beg your forgiveness, and I offer you my own. For all of it."

She nodded, fresh tears flooding her eyes.

WHEN THEY REACHED THE ARCH OF INTERWOVEN TREES—ONE living, the other a withered husk—a path lay open through the forest. It brought them back to the road, to the place where Seona had led Lorant into Faerie. His horse was gone. Its hoofprints led into the forest, disappearing amidst the mulch of fallen leaves. Hopefully the lands of Faerie would be more hospitable to the steed than to the rider.

Lorant dropped his helm and gauntlets by the roadside. Angela watched in silence as he removed his armor, offering a claw to cut through straps he couldn't unbuckle on his own. When he was stripped to his arming coat, he hung his sword from a branch above the pile.

So much blood spilled, for so many different causes. None of them seemed worth it anymore. None but the cause that brought him here, in its own twisted way.

Angela rumbled behind him. He turned and smiled. "There's still one thing yet to do. Come here."

With a snort, she shook her head.

"You're thinking of what the Erlking said. That we would be together. Not that you would be human. Possibly, if I kiss you, I would become a dragon also."

Angela's pupils widened. She didn't look away.

"I don't care." Lorant shook his head. "I don't care how this ends. So long as we're together."

With a strange, choked sound, Angela lowered her head to the earth. Lorant smiled and kissed her.

GINGERBREAD AND ASH

Nathan Slemp

*T*he deer carcass twitched as Marita sliced into its shoulder, its eye glazed with a sheen like oil on water. Some residual magic, perhaps. After three years of famine, magic was the only explanation for how the witch could provide this much meat every day. It was how she snared Marita and her brother, after all.

"Don't you look at me," Marita said, rolling the deer over to get at the other shoulder. "She treated you gently, far as I'm concerned."

The cabin door creaked open on rusted hinges. Footsteps shuffled inside, but Marita didn't turn away from the carcass. If the witch wanted something, she'd say so. Otherwise, best not to draw her attention.

"Are you not done with your chores yet, child?" The witch's voice was like a shovel scraping through mud and gravel. "The sun climbs high, and here you are still."

"I already cleaned the outhouse and swept the floor. I'm almost done." The chores were pointless—every day the filth returned as if it were never gone—but the witch didn't seem to care. It was probably her doing that brought it all back each night.

"See that you are faster tomorrow, child." The rocking chair by the fireplace creaked as the witch settled into it. "Your sweet brother is hungry, I'm sure. I don't know why you seem so set on starving him."

Scowling, Marita finished the butchering and rinsed her hands in the basin beside the oven. It lurked against the cabin wall, cold and dark, an iron beast large enough to swallow a whole deer. Or a whole person.

Shuddering, she said, "There isn't enough wood left to heat the oven."

"You will not need it today."

"The meat is still raw."

The witch cackled. "I think you will find that your brother no longer minds, sweet child. And you will not be eating today."

"What? Why?"

"Because you stole from your darling brother last night, and I will not have that. You must not starve him."

Marita's jaw dropped. "I'm not—you're giving him two buckets of meat a day, and you say I'm starving him because I take one piece? You're starving *me*, that's the problem!"

"One more insolent word," the witch said, "and I'll take that wicked tongue of yours. I don't see a reason for you to keep it if you can't be responsible with the privilege."

Marita clenched her jaw, her left thumb throbbing with remembered pain. The witch had torn off its nail in the first week of Marita and Jan's captivity. A demonstration, she'd called it. An effective one.

"Why—" She stopped herself and took a breath. "If I may, why will Jan not care if the meat is raw?"

The witch cackled. "Ah, so she can learn. It's quite

simple, child. Your brother is very special, unbeknownst to him. But blood does not lie, and I mean to draw forth his wonders. I fear you share none of his gifts. Nor any of his heritage. Adopted, are you?"

"I—yes."

"Well, it matters not, so long as you continue to mind your chores. And your place." Holding out an object wrapped in cloth, the witch said, "Do bring your brother this sweet. Very important, it is. Helps him grow good and strong."

Marita snatched the bundle from the witch's hand and retreated. Whatever was inside was fever-hot. She shivered, pinching it between finger and thumb as she hefted the pail of meat.

It didn't make sense. More food went into Jan's stall in a day than their father could provide in an entire fortnight. But somehow, he was eating it all. And now it was being served raw. Whatever lurked within that bundle couldn't be good for him, but she didn't dare throw it away or look inside. The witch would know. She always knew when Marita resisted.

Grimacing, she hauled the pail outside. When she and Jan first arrived... however many weeks ago that had been, they'd found a cabin alone in the forest, surrounded by grass and flowers, a tray of pies cooling in the window. Instead of a witch, they'd been greeted by a woman who could have been their grandmother.

As soon as they bit into the pies, the illusion died. The clearing turned to bare earth, devoid even of weeds. The cabin sagged into ruin. Creepers and thorns choked off the paths back to the forest. And the witch...

Marita shuddered as she hauled the stable door open. It was as lifeless as the barn back home, no animals within other than flies. All but one of the stalls had collapsed. All but the one Jan was trapped in.

The door was solid wood. A box on rails sat before a slot at its base, leaving no room for Marita to peek around the edges. She set the pail in the box and shoved it through. "Wake up, slugabed."

Weight shifted within the stall. "Did she notice?" Jan asked.

Marita slumped against the door. "Of course she noticed."

"I told you she would."

"Yes, thank you. She didn't let me cook—"

Chewing sounds whispered through the wood, and Marita's stomach roiled. "Jan?"

"Mm?"

"That's raw venison you're eating."

After a moment, he grunted. "So it is."

"And you're going to eat it anyway?"

"It's good. And I'm hungry."

"Oh, you're hungry?" Marita scowled. "Can you count your ribs anymore, or have you put on too much weight? I still can, if you're curious."

"Come on, Marita. That's not fair."

"So, you can't. Wonderful. Do you have a plan for getting us out of here, or are you just going to keep gorging yourself like a hog?"

Jan's weight shifted, bumping into the wall. "I've tried to break out, but there must be some spell protecting the wood. Or else I don't have the strength."

"Then what's your next plan?"

"Wait until I do have the strength."

"Jan, what is she doing to you? She said something about you being special, and that I wasn't."

Renewed chewing echoed from within the stall. Sighing, Marita retrieved the box and sent the witch's bundle through. "She told me to—"

Jan slammed into the door. Cloth tore, and the chewing turned frantic, ending with a gulp and a sigh. Marita stared at the slot. "What was that?"

"Nothing."

"Jan, if you lie to me again, I will come in there and beat you senseless."

His sigh reverberated through the door. "It's dangerous. Addictive. The only reason she made you bring it to me was to try and snare you. Don't eat any of them, Mare. Don't even open them."

Marita clutched the hems of her sleeves, loose threads coming free in her fingers. "What is she doing to you?"

The box slid out to her, holding the empty pail. Its inside bore scratches that hadn't been there before. "You should go, before she takes notice."

"Jan—"

"Go. Please."

Marita grabbed the pail and left. As she closed the door, she glanced back at the stall. Whatever was happening to Jan, he seemed unable to act against the witch. Unable, or unwilling.

Whatever was in that bundle, the witch said it was making Jan stronger. That strength did them no good locked inside a cage. But what did it cost? What were those bundles doing to Jan, and what would they do to her?

It didn't matter. Anything was better than waiting for the witch to carve out her heart.

A GUST OF WIND RIPPED THE CABIN DOOR OPEN AND SLAMMED it against the wall. Marita caught it as it rebounded, staggering as a fresh gale snatched at her. As she regained her footing, a great oak on the clearing's edge keeled over and slammed to earth, throwing up sheets of mud that splattered the stable walls. She hauled the door closed and slapped the latch home, gasping for breath.

"Out you go, my lovely," the witch said from beside the oven, stirring a cauldron full of things Marita didn't want to name. "Your brother is hungry. Such a healthy young thing."

"That's madness! A giant tree just fell out there!"

"Ah, yes. Such lovely decay it will bring." Without turning, the witch gestured towards the table, where another bundle rested. "Don't forget his sweet. Must keep him strong and growing."

Gritting her teeth, Marita dropped the thing into the pail of venison. The smell of fresh meat was torture. It had been two weeks since she stole any food.

That changed today.

As she pushed through the cabin door, Marita hunched her shoulders against the waves of rain. Mud sucked at her feet as she staggered towards the stable, fighting through the wind's grasp.

When she reached the stable, she stopped fighting.

The next gust kicked her in the back. Marita fell on her face, Jan's pail upending in the mud. She scrambled to her feet and put the meat back, shaking off as much of the muck as she could.

She hid the witch's bundle in the woodpile beside the stable and scrambled around a little to cover her tracks, then struggled back to the cabin. As she opened the door, the witch turned to frown at her. "Back so soon, dearie? No chatting with your... ah, you fell, did you?"

"I... I lost the... the thing."

The witch lunged across the cabin to loom over her, her hands inches from Marita's face. "What? You lost your brother's treat? You didn't eat it, did you, dearie?"

Marita twitched her head, staring at the claws hanging before her eyes. "The storm—I fell and the pail spilled, and I can't find—"

"You lost it?"

"I'm sorry—"

"You are sorry. A sorry excuse for a sister." Without her legs seeming to move, the witch slid back a pace. She closed a hand, and when she opened it, another bundle rested in her palm. "Very well, but see that you don't lose this one. I would hate to think you were putting such lovely eyes to no good use."

Snatching the bundle, Marita fled the cabin.

SHE BROUGHT BOTH BUNDLES INTO THE STABLE. AS JAN TORE into one of them, she teased the other open. Inside lay a lump of gingerbread, marbled with streaks of black and white. It smelled of woodsmoke and strange spices she couldn't name.

Before she could reconsider, Marita gulped it down. It sank through her throat like a ball of acid, driving needles of corruption into her. She groaned, falling to her hands and knees as her guts caught on fire.

"Marita?"

She emptied her stomach onto the floor. The foulness disappeared, but it left burning heat in its wake. As she gasped for breath, tremors coursed through her muscles. Patches of skin ached as if sunburned.

"Marita!"

Wiping her mouth, she pushed against a barrel sitting beside her. Rather than taking her weight, the barrel tipped over and rolled across the stable, thumping against the far wall. She stared at her hands and curled them into fists.

"Mare, answer me! What's going on out there?"

"Relax, Jan. I'm fine."

"What—"

"I said I'm fine." Marita retrieved the pail and left before he could prod her further. The storm had given way to fitful sunlight, but even so she hunched her shoulders as she slogged back to the cabin. If the witch was watching, she couldn't give her any clue that anything had changed.

Best to kill her soon. Today. End the nightmare and burn her to ash.

Hot air washed over her as she shuffled into the cabin. While she was out, the witch had stoked the oven. Light blazed from within as she withdrew a tray of the enchanted gingerbreads. "I trust you managed to feed your sweet brother this time, child," she said, scooping dough onto another tray.

"Yes." Marita edged around the table, staring at the fires in the oven's heart. "I'm sorry."

"See you don't make the same mistake again. I hate to see good food wasted."

"I won't."

Turning to the oven, the witch slid the tray inside. "Very good, child."

Marita crept up behind her. All she had to do was push and—

The witch spun. A taloned hand lashed out and seized Marita's throat. "You little imbecile."

Marita choked out a scream, slamming her fists into the

witch's arms. For all their spindliness, they were as strong as fence rails.

"You think to steal my power without my knowing it? And you couldn't even keep it down, could you?" The witch cackled. "Pathetic. Pathetic! Perhaps your ashes will add a certain piquant tang to this next batch. I'll be fascinated to see if your brother is too far gone to notice."

With a heave, she threw Marita into the coals at the bottom of the oven.

She shrieked as her skin burned. Fire soaked into her flesh and bones, melding with the heat awoken by the stolen magic. The stench of burning hair filled her throat. She tried to push her body away from the coals and screamed. Her arms were skinless, bloody muscle glistening in the hell-light.

But the raw flesh wasn't burning.

Within her the roar of power deepened. Her arms buckled, and she fell into the coals with a howl. Itching ravaged the places where her skin had been. Bones stretched and flesh unfolded, flooding her mind with sensation. Gasping for breath, she struggled through the coals to face the oven door. Some part of her body dislodged the tray of gingerbreads above. They tumbled into the coals and burned with green smoke that burned her eyes.

She slammed the door open with her head and dragged herself through. Someone screamed as she flopped onto the cabin floor. She blinked her eyes clear and found the witch staring back at her, her claws tangled in her hair. "What—what madness—"

The inferno within Marita howled for release. She opened her mouth to scream, and fire erupted from her throat.

The witch threw out a hand, parting the flames before

they could burn her. With her other hand, she threw a spiral of yellow light at Marita. It struck her chest, slamming her back into the oven. Pain flooded through parts of her she couldn't name.

She shook the stars from her eyes and screamed. The body sprawled before her wasn't hers. It was a dragon's body, coal-colored scales blending to orange over the chest and belly, cracked where the blast of magic had struck.

The witch waved a hand, and Marita rolled out of the path of her next curse. It blasted the oven apart, coals and shrapnel flying everywhere. Marita yelped as a chunk of iron struck her shoulder, but it bounced off her scales without drawing blood.

"What did you do to me?" Marita scrambled behind the table, knocking it onto its side as another bolt of curse-light blew a hole in the floor. "What did you do?"

"You worm in sheep's clothing!" The table exploded, and the witch advanced on Marita, power oozing over her hands. "I should have sensed it! How did you hide your true nature from me, you wretch?"

Marita lunged, but the witch knocked her down with another blast to the chest. On reflex, her tail lashed out and struck the witch's knees. Bone shattered. The witch screamed and tumbled to the ground.

Without thinking, Marita lunged across the cabin, caught the witch's head in her jaws, and bit down. Blood exploded into her mouth, crackling with power that spiked into her gums. She spat the head out, but the pollution remained, turning her blood to acid.

She retched. What came up her throat wasn't vomit, but a torrent of fire that burned the foulness from her mouth and ripped into the wall. She staggered back, staring at the smoking rent in the bricks.

"What... Oh, Almighty help—"

With a shriek, the ceiling beams tore free of the wall, and the whole roof tipped inwards. A chunk of wood slammed into her, pinning her to the ground. Marita curled into a ball and screamed as the cabin disintegrated around her.

WHEN IT WAS OVER, SHE OPENED HER EYES. BRUISES ACHED all over her body, but nothing was broken. Maybe the Almighty had finally decided to show some pity for her.

She eased the rubble off her back, coughing as dust and ash billowed into the air. Part of the roof was pinned between the ground and the chimney, enclosing her in a sort of cave. Sunlight glowed through an opening at one end. Flaming debris lay all around her, spreading fire into the floorboards. A black, snakelike thing lay beside one pile, shifting as Marita stirred.

Her tail. Right. She had a tail now. And it was—

With a yelp, she yanked it away from the fire. In the next heartbeat, the enormity of what she'd done stunned her. She'd just moved it, without even thinking, the same way she'd move a hand. She shouldn't know how to use a tail. She was a woman, not a lizard.

She glanced at her chest and shuddered. No, she wasn't a woman. Not anymore.

Pain flickered across her ribs from the bruises left by the witch's curses. It grew sharper as she sucked in air, breath after breath after breath after—and she was panicking, she shouldn't be breathing so fast, but it was hard to think, hard to believe this was her body when it was all so wrong and the world was going dark around the edges and Almighty help her she was a <u>dragon</u>—

She writhed through the wreckage, scrambling towards the patch of sunlight, but a tide of warmth poured into her tail and stopped her in her tracks. It had slid into a fire, but it wasn't burning. The heat felt... <u>good.</u> Like a mug of mulled cider after a long day in the fields.

Marita closed her eyes and let it mingle with the fire in her heart, easing away her panic. It was weird, and sort of terrifying, but she couldn't afford to lose control.

"You're alive," she told herself. Her voice was too deep, but at least it was still hers. "You're a... a dragon, but you're alive, and the witch isn't. That's what's important. Worry about everything else once you're back home with Jan."

And she could worry about that after a nap. It was so comfortable here, with the flames crackling around her...

She yanked her tail from the fire and shook her head clear. Even for a dragon, falling asleep inside a burning building couldn't be wise. She had to get out.

Bracing herself, she crawled into the fire between her and the wedge of sunlight. As the flames licked over her chest, they filled her with contented exhaustion, as if she'd just slipped into a hot bath after a day spent mucking out the barn. Power tingled through her bones, the energy from the witch's blood somehow made pure, lulling her towards sleep.

She forced her foot forward, but the ground swept up and carried her into darkness.

SHE WOKE WITH A ROAR AS THE ROOF FELL ONTO HER. Writhing to her feet, she tore through the wreckage, splinters and ash bursting into the air. Most of the roof must have had burned away, because it didn't weigh much.

Sneezing, she staggered away from the cabin. All that was left was the chimney and scraps of the frame, but they seemed smaller than before. Marita frowned, putting a hand on the chimney.

Her thumb was as long as the bricks were wide. Her heart—no, her hearts lurched. She'd grown while she was asleep. She'd grown a lot.

Stumbling away from the wreckage, she struggled to recall one of the old prayers, some plea for salvation, but all she could think about was the play of wind and sunlight on her wings. "Please, Almighty, please—"

Someone shouted behind her, the words too muffled to understand. She whipped her head around and cursed. The shout was coming from inside the stable. It was Jan. She'd gone and taken a nap and left Jan alone in his cell.

Marita ran across the clearing, snarling at her own weakness. She yanked one of the sliding doors open, but instead of sliding across its rail, the whole thing tore loose in her grasp. She threw it aside. "Jan!"

"Mare!" Jan rattled the stall door, but it was still locked tight. "Are you all right?"

"I..." Marita stared at herself, shivering. "I don't know."

"Is the witch dead? Everything she did to me went back to normal."

"She's dead. Stand back. I'll get the door open."

"Mare, are you—"

"Just stand back."

She tore the lock off the door and eased it open. Jan stood within, dressed only in ragged pants. His chest and arms bore more muscle than they had since the famine began. Mouth agape, he edged away from her. "Mare? How... I don't... How many gingerbreads did you steal?"

"Only one. She threw me into the oven, and—Jan, why am I still like this? Why did you go back to normal when I didn't?"

Jan shook his head. "Mare, I must have eaten a hundred of those things. If you only had one, she must have done something different to you than she was doing to me."

"But she didn't do anything to me! I tried to push her into the oven, but she threw me in instead, and then this happened, and when I got out of the oven she started screaming. She wasn't expecting this to happen. She was trying to kill me." Smoke trickled from her mouth as the bonfire within her surged. "Why did this happen? How are we going to fix it?"

Jan began to reply, then shook his head. "I don't know. I just don't know. Maybe Father or Mother will have an idea."

Marita shuddered. "I can't imagine what they're going to..."

"Me neither."

"We still don't know how to find home."

Waving at her wings, Jan asked, "Maybe, uh, maybe if we were in the air, that could help? Can you use those?"

"I... I don't know." Marita flexed her wings and shivered. "Let's find out."

SOMEHOW, SHE DID KNOW HOW TO FLY. REFLEXES SHE HAD NO reason to possess guided her aloft, showing her how to use the updraft from the burning cabin to climb over the forest. As wind coursed over her wings, Marita found herself smiling. There was something here she'd been missing her whole life, something she hadn't even known was absent. She tilted out of her spiral, gliding north, flapping her wings every so often to maintain altitude. The world stretched out below her like a courier's map, but with infinite detail. Acres of forest sprawled across the earth, a river winding through them like silver thread.

Something tapped against the base of her wing. Marita flinched, glancing over her shoulder at Jan. "What?"

"What's wrong?"

"Nothing. Nothing new, anyway. Why?"

"You were making a sort of rumbling noise."

"Oh. I was just noticing the Erdin River."

"Where?"

"Right in front of us. Can't you see it?"

Jan shifted forward on her back. "Your eyes must be better than mine. All I can see are trees. But at least we know how to get home."

"True." Marita frowned to herself. "Remember all the times we talked about climbing those mountains, seeing what the world looked like that high up?"

"I guess we know now."

"I suppose. But I still want to climb them. See what's up there. Maybe other dragons. Maybe they could help me become human again."

And if there was no reversing what had been done to her, she would need their help even more. She couldn't stay with her family like this, or live anywhere people might find her. She'd have to make a home of her own, or find one amongst other dragons, out in the wilds.

"Mare?"

"What?"

"You're turning towards the mountains."

"And?"

"We're supposed to be going home. Remember?"

Marita's stomach writhed. She angled back towards the river, shaking her head. "I don't know what—I was just thinking about them, Jan. I didn't mean to."

His hand twitched along the side of her neck. "It'll be all right, Mare. We'll... we'll figure out something."

"Like what?"

"I don't know. Something to make this right."

A growl trembled in Marita's chest. There was nothing to make right. The only thing that wasn't right about the situation was the direction she was flying.

And the fact that she was a dragon. Or was it?

Shuddering, she turned her eyes downwards, away from the lure of the mountains. As she followed the river, the forest gave way to fields, starved and empty. The farm came into sight, the charcoal kilns sitting in a row beside the stream, the stable and fields empty. Only one of the kilns was burning. All five should have been. Charcoal was the only thing they had to sell these days.

Jan tapped her shoulder. "Maybe you should land out of sight, so you don't scare them."

Nodding, Marita tipped into a spiral. As she landed, Jan slid off her back and landed in a sprawl.

"Are you all right?"

"Yeah." He scrambled upright, rubbing his back. "Just—just a little stiff. I'll go explain things to them."

"Be quick. I can see the road from here."

Jan nodded and broke into a run. As he rounded the barn, Marita curled her wings and surveyed what she could see of the property. The farm was much as it had been when they'd last been home. More decayed and faded, but little else was different. How long had they been gone? A month? Two?

She wandered around the side of the barn. There was something different behind the house, a standing stone, all but its crown hidden behind the henhouse. Marita rose onto her hindlegs—she was so much taller now!—and squinted. Even from so far away, she could make out carven words.

It was a gravestone.

The house's door slammed open, and Father lurched onto the porch, clutching an axe. "Into the barn! You want any fool riding by to see you?"

"Father, I—"

"Go!"

With a glance at the stone that bore Mother's name, Marita fled into the barn.

"Marita," Jan said, "calm down."

She growled, pacing across the barn, her claws tearing into the earth. "This is how he welcomes us? We're gone for months! Months! And he can't even be bothered to speak to us?"

"He needs time to adjust, that's all."

"He's not the only one!" Marita reached the wall and twisted around. "And Mother! Not a word! Did she starve, was it disease—why didn't he tell us?"

Jan slipped past her neck and hugged her. She froze, smoke trickling from her jaws.

"Why doesn't he care?"

"He does, Mare. But he must have resigned himself to never seeing us again. And now here we are, alive but... not what we were." He massaged the knots of muscle at the base of her wings. "Give him time."

"How are you so calm?"

He shook his head, his forehead rubbing against her scales. "I'm not. But I'd given myself up for lost too. At this point, I'm happy just to be alive."

The hasp on the side door slid back. Marita and Jan disentangled as Father entered, shutting the door behind him. When he met Marita's eyes, he flinched.

"Papa." She stepped forward, her wings trembling. "It's me. It's Mare."

He gulped. His hands fidgeted at his sides. "Jan told me. I never expected—certainly not like this." Swallowing, he said, "You've been gone for seven weeks. Your mother passed five weeks ago. She couldn't... she gave up."

"You gave up on us after two weeks?" Jan asked, moving between Father and Marita.

"No. It wasn't like that. How do I say this..."

The fires within Marita's chest guttered. "Say what, Papa?"

He met her eyes for half a second. "You remember, when we told you that you were adopted, we said Father Karl brought you to us before he left for the cathedral?"

"Of course."

"It wasn't like that. In truth, I was gathering wood in the forest and I found you hanging from a branch. I touched you with my axe and it didn't hurt you, so I knew you were no faerie, and there was nobody else around. So, I took you home. When I found you, you were swaddled in... well, dragon skin."

Marita flinched. "Dragon skin?"

"Father Karl said it was part of a wing. He thought a dragon had wrapped you in part of itself and left you for me to find. When the food ran out... we thought, perhaps if the dragon were still nearby, and they found you in need, they might help you." Tears dripped down Father's cheeks, disappearing into his beard. "So, we... ahh..."

Marita's hearts lurched. She tried to interrupt him, to drown out whatever was coming, but she couldn't move, couldn't even breathe.

"We were running out of food. We didn't tell you, but we all would have starved by now. So, we—we abandoned you, out there." Father's voice broke, and he wiped his eyes. "Your mother and I thought, if the dragon found you, you would be saved. And if not—if not, any fate you met out there would be easier than ours."

"Easier?" The fires in Marita's chest exploded. She shoved Jan aside and stalked towards her father, smoke boiling between her fangs. "Easier? We were kidnapped and tortured! That witch would have killed me, she did horrible things to Jan, and you call that easier?"

Father backed into the wall, trembling, reeking of terror. "I'm sorry. I'm sorry, Mare."

"If you hadn't—I'd still be a woman if you hadn't—"

A hand pressed against her leg. "Mare," Jan said, "he's telling the truth."

"You can't seriously—"

"I saw the larders before I came out here. I don't like it either, but... he's right. We'd all be dead."

The inferno within clawed at her throat, howling for blood. Marita wheeled away from her family and hauled the barn doors open.

"Marita, wait!"

She ran from the barn and took flight, smoke and tears streaming in her wake. The mountains loomed before her, shadows in the fading light, and she fled towards them with all the speed she could muster.

They never should have come home. They should have just fled into the forest and made a new life for themselves. Better to have never seen home again, never learned that their parents had left them to die. Maybe she could have endured their betrayal if Jan supported her, but for him to side with Father... how could he forgive him? How could he ask her to?

Snarling, she shook the tears from her eyes. Below her sprawled a farm she recognized—not the one neighboring her father's, but the one beyond that, the Lindens' place. Its fields were just as barren and wasted as those back home.

No, not home. Not anymore.

As she passed over the Lindens' barn, she sucked in a breath. Crows were piled atop something behind the building, feasting and squabbling with each other. Marita dove towards them, and they fled screeching into the sky as she landed.

There wasn't enough left to tell who it had been, the husband or the wife. Marita whispered a prayer and, with her breath, set the body aflame. The Lindens hadn't been friends, but they'd been good people. They deserved better than to be eaten by scavengers.

So did Jan. So did Father, no matter what he'd done. If she fled to the mountains, if she abandoned her family, how many nights would she lie awake wondering if they were all right?

With a sigh, she flew into the forest. The mountains lingered in the corner of her vision, calling, begging, demanding.

But they would have to wait.

Marita stumbled as she hit the ground, losing her grip on the deer clutched in her fore claws. Its ribs shattered as she tripped over the carcass. She winced, then cursed under her breath as the door to the house shook.

"Mare! Mare, wait!"

She leapt into the air before Jan could get the latch open, wings laboring to lift her aloft. The past few hours had taught her a valuable lesson: never gorge yourself before flying.

She circled over the house as Father and Jan emerged, examining the deer. They scanned the sky for her, but there wasn't enough light for human eyes to see by. To them, she would be nothing more than a patch of darkness against the stars.

For her, though, starlight was almost as good as sunlight. She lingered overhead as Father and Jan cleaned the deer and packed the meat in the smokehouse. Father returned to the house, but Jan stayed, carrying a bucket to the charcoal kilns.

"I know you're up there!" He set the bucket next to the kiln that was burning. "These are for you! Liver, kidneys, heart!"

Marita tipped her wings and spiraled towards him. He flinched as she landed, but held his ground. "Lonely up there?

"A little. I'm sorry. To both of you."

"Yeah... I'm sorry too. Are you going to eat?"

"Keep it. I can catch more deer if I need to."

The corner of Jan's mouth quirked. "You brought down more than one, didn't you? What happened to the other?"

"I, uh..." Marita rubbed her bulging belly. "I lost control a little."

"Well, you always did have a dragon-sized appetite."

"Oh, do shut up." She curled around the kiln with a sigh. "How's Father?"

"Not good, but he blames himself, not you. When he saw that deer, it really helped." Laughing, he added, "You could have brought something else, though. I'm tired of venison."

Marita grinned. "Well, I didn't care to start off hunting wild boar. I might want to work up to that."

"Probably." Jan shook his head, his smile fading. "What happens now? If anyone sees you here, it won't end well."

"I know. I need to find somewhere to live. But I'll stay close, help with the hunting when I can."

"Good. I'll need all the help you can give me."

"Why's that?"

"He's not well, Mare. The last two months all but killed him. Even if we do everything we can, I don't think—I don't think he has long left."

Marita shuddered. "I need to talk to him. Make this right."

"Tomorrow. He needs sleep." Jan grimaced. "After... you know. What will you do?"

Her eyes crept to the horizon, the outline of the mountains beyond the forest, and her wings trembled. "Go looking for other dragons."

"For your, uh, your mother?"

"My mother is buried over there. But the one who... birthed me? Hatched me? I don't even know which. I might try to find her. I'm not sure."

"Will you take me with you?"

"Why? Not that I mind your company, but I'm pretty sure you're going to have trouble living in a cave in the mountains."

"I know, but... what the witch did to me, it went away

when she died, but it's..." Jan pulled his shirt open. Scales speckled the skin over his chest. "It's coming back."

Marita stared at him. "She was turning you into a dragon?"

"Something like that. I don't know how long it will take, but last time it messed with my head. I wasn't thinking right."

"I know the feeling."

Jan shuddered. "If something goes wrong... it'll be safer if I'm with you. For me and everyone else."

"All right, then. I won't leave without you." She hesitated. "If it helps, being a dragon's not that bad. Once you get used to it."

Chuckling, Jan returned to the house. Marita rested her head atop the kiln and stared at the shadows of the mountains, the corner of her mouth twitching into a smile.

ABOUT THE PUBLISHER

Visit our website to learn more about how to submit your manuscript for publication.

www.dragonsoulpress.com

facebook.com/dragonsoulpress

twitter.com/dragonsoulpress

instagram.com/dragon_soul_press

pinterest.com/dragonsoulpress

youtube.com/DragonSoul_Press

Made in the USA
Middletown, DE
26 April 2021

38423138R00189